# HEAR ME

## JULIA NORTH

First Published in 2017
Re-published in 2023 by Bloodhound Books.

www.bloodhoundbooks.com

Print ISBN: 978-1-5040-8963-0

*Dedicated to the memory of my youngest sister, Lady, one of the most special and generous souls I've ever known. What a privilege to have shared my life with yours.*

*'Hide nothing, for Time which sees all, exposes all.'*
*— Sophocles*

# PROLOGUE

My death comes as a surprise. Not because I find myself in the afterlife - I knew there would be one - but the problem is I've always expected my passing to be a kind of '*Aha*' moment where everything finally makes sense... Instead nothing does.

I don't look any different, nor do I have any fear. I'm still Melissa Windsor, my twenty-eight-year-old self, even wearing my favourite white lace top and dark Levi jeans, yet I know with certainty that I'm dead. This is no vivid dream, no astral-travel experience; it's too real for that.

I don't know why, when or how I've died. There's no spinning tunnel, no angel voices, no welcoming light like the near-death stories we hear about – nothing but a mountain of mist, ebbing and flowing.

The jigsaw of life, with its misty memories, does flash past. I suppose it has to because we live so fast, so superficially. *'It goes so fast we don't have time to look at one another,'* Thornton Wilder wrote, and he was right; most of us pass each other by while trapped in self-obsession, indifference and mediocrity. That is until Time snatches us away and throws us to the stars. But where are these stars? I close my eyes and will the mist to give me the answers that I crave...

# CHAPTER ONE

The oppressive heat fuels the growling storm. The sky is a curious mix of light and dark with tufts of low-lying cumulus reflecting the rays of the late afternoon sun, while a smudge of heavy cloud drowns out the blue above. Thunder rolls ominously overhead, followed by a sudden crack of earth-to-sky forked lightning. As a child I loved to listen to the undulating rumble of the thunder. I imagined it came from the giants who lived up there behind the black clouds, rolling out their barrels to have a party. It sounds like they have a pub full today as another crash of thunder, accompanied by a sharp vein of lightning, claps out across the sky. Large drops of warm rain break free and hammer against the lounge window. I get up and rest my face against the burglar bars to gulp down their earthy wetness and let it wash through my mind.

'The rain's coming in.'

I turn to Nat as she sits frowning at the open window. 'I know. It'll be over in a few minutes.'

Nat swallows. She tucks a strand of fly-away blonde hair behind her ear and fiddles with the end of it. 'Liss, please think about...'

'Leave it.'

I turn back to the window and press my forehead against the iron bars. I should've known that's all this visit was about.

'You need it.'

I jolt around and slap the rain from my face. 'No, I don't.' The air grows hot between us as we lock eyes. I blink away and click my tongue. 'I'm going to make coffee. Want some?'

She nods and I lurch towards the kitchen. I switch on the kettle and snatch open the cupboard.

'What're you doing?'

I turn to see Nat standing behind me. 'Making coffee... what the hell do you think I'm doing?' I jerk my hand forward and hook my fingers around the handles of two of the mugs.

Judgement clouds Nat's eyes. 'What kind?'

'For goodness' sake, Nat.' I slam the cupboard door shut and twist open the coffee jar.

'I just want to help...' Nat's voice cracks and she places a hand on my shoulder. I shrug her off with one angry movement.

'I'm twenty-eight... not fucking twelve.' The kettle whistles and I snatch it up and slosh the water into the mugs. 'Get the milk if you want,' I say as I pick up my mug and stomp back into the lounge. No wonder we've got this chasm between us. How can we be sisters if there's no trust?

I bury myself in the rising coffee steam and clutch my mug with white knuckles. Nat perches on the armrest of the chair opposite. She blows on her coffee and drinks it down in slurps which echo through the stiff silence. Her small, hunched frame and pained blue eyes just make me feel worse. Why does she even bother coming?

'The storm's over... I guess I should go.' Nat waits for me to say something. 'Please, think about what I've said,' she implores as she gets up.

'I'm fine... but thanks anyway.' I keep my head down as I utter the words, and lift it only when I hear my security gate clang closed. My whole body feels like a coiled spring. I wish she hadn't come. I love my sisters but I'm so sick of their never-ending judgement. They also drink. They're just deluding themselves like half the people out there. At least I'm honest, and anyway they're married; their lives are so different from mine. How can they understand, let alone judge?

My jaw clenches and I tramp back into the kitchen and throw some of the coffee into the sink before opening the cupboard and finding the Johnny Walker hidden behind the muesli. I splash in a double helping and take a large swig. I breathe out a long, shaky sigh and lean back against the counter as it burns straight through me. I glance down. My hand's trembling, creating small ripples across the surface of the brown liquid. I frown. I can't deny that the comedowns are getting worse and I need a drink to ease them. I shake my head and gulp down some more. No, it's just Nat upsetting me that's made me tremble a little. I've been through a lot. Who wouldn't break under the kind of strain I've had? She's way off. I don't have a problem. I don't drink every day. In fact I can go days without drinking. No, actually I can go for weeks.

My back straightens. I go into the lounge and flick on the TV. The sportscaster is rattling on about the India versus South Africa cricket match. I click him off mid-speech with a scowl. Sure, it's great that we're no longer the sports pariah of the world, but we lost the series, and anyway there're far more important things going on than cricket. People in the townships are still burning each other like human torches, for fuck's sake. Maybe that's what they should be talking about and trying to stop. The image of the writhing, burning body jumps back into my mind. Water fills my mouth and my stomach jolts. I retch. The acrid stench of molten rubber is back in my nostrils. My throat tightens. I jerk my head from side to side and glug down the rest of my whiskey coffee. I push the memory back as the alcohol eases its way through my veins.

A slow smile slides across my face. Nat doesn't understand. She wasn't there. All I'm doing is blurring the edges. It's no bloody big deal, and anyway alcohol's much better than going on Prozac or Valium.

My armpits grow damp. The afternoon sun is still hot and streaming in through the window. Humidity smothers the room. Perhaps what I need is some sea air and crashing waves to drown out the fire-fuelled memories. I find my bag and fumble around for my car keys. I've only had one. I'm still okay to drive.

---

I speed over the rushing Umgeni River, its brown waters swollen from the summer rains. I've got both front windows open so the sea breeze blows wildly through my hair. The sound of the whooshing water fills my ears. I turn and look down at the river as it roars under the viaduct to join forces with the crashing Indian Ocean. I jerk back as someone hoots behind me and give them the finger, but swerve away from the fast-approaching concrete balustrade. I put my foot down as soon as I'm straight on the road again and smile to myself as the engine purrs out its power like a panther. Minutes later I reach the crowded beachfront. I slow to a crawl and scan the wide promenade of North Beach. My hands grow sweaty. It's five o'clock and it's still so busy? I don't want crowds of people around me. I just want a parking space and a little bit of beach to myself. Is that too much to ask?

At last I spy a gap, squeal towards it, and swing half-in, cutting off a Kombi coming from the opposite direction. The blonde surfer behind the wheel lifts his hands into the air and shakes his head. I grin at him and yank my steering wheel to the left. The arsehole Mercedes next to me is so badly parked I can't get in. I wrench my gear lever into reverse and grip the steering wheel as I squeal backwards, and then in again, missing it by inches. I climb over the seat and get out the passenger door. I'm at quite an angle, but who cares. I march onto the crowded boulevard and push past one fat, lobster-tinged couple who're waddling, gawking at the waves with their puffy tongues glued to white mounds of a soft-serve ice-cream cone. What the hell's the matter with them; haven't they ever seen the sea before? Why don't they just go back to the Transvaal instead of taking over our beach?

My cheeks grow hot as the anger prickles through me. Deep inside I know I'm behaving badly, but I can't help it. I just want some peace and quiet. Don't they realise I need it? A beaming curio seller holds out strings of bright Zulu beads and calls, '*Sawubona*, nice necklace for you, Madam.' I ignore her, and her eyes harden. I rub my fingers across my forehead. Shit, why did I do that; now she probably thinks I'm just another white, racist bitch and hates me, but she should realise I'm not a tourist.

I pace down the concrete steps towards the beach and rip off my sandals. I roll up my Levis. The swimming area is packed with people, but the far side, away from the shark-net area has only a few stragglers lolling about. I run on tiptoes towards it, stopping only when I hit the cool, wet band at the water's edge. I sink down onto the damp sand and draw in a long, slow breath of the sweet sea air. I stare out at the rhythmic coming and going of the swelling waves with their white sea-horses as they crash and recede onto the sand. Weird to think they've been coming and going like that forever, and will carry on long after I'm gone, never feeling the pain of what it means to be alive. I shake my head as the emptiness suddenly consumes me. My eyes blur. I just want to dive into their crashing power until they pummel me into nothingness. I don't want to live any more. I really don't.

Mike's face rears up like a rancid boil in my mind. You'd think by now I'd be mature and in control. All he did was use me. I remember his smug words of greeting when we first met. '*Welcome, Mike Mathews, senior microbiologist.*' He'd savoured the power behind each word while he watched me squirm blushingly before him. Why was I so transparent, so weak, just because he was good-looking? The more I'd tried to wish my blush away, the hotter I'd become. I was like some silly little schoolgirl and he'd wallowed in my unease, using it no doubt to feed his ego and loving the power. He'd even given a low victory laugh at my flinch when he touched my arm to guide me to the back of the lab.

'*I'll introduce you to Mia*,' he'd said, bending down towards me and squeezing my arm a little tighter. '*She's in charge of the poo bench which, I'm afraid to say, is going to be your first port of call.*'

I guess the shit bench should've been a warning of what was to come, but I was too blind to see it. I can't believe how gullible I was. I think I'd even felt grateful he wanted sex with me that first time because I thought it must mean he found me attractive. I let out a wry laugh. I also thought that for the first time I had one up on Nat and Els when he'd raved about my chestnut hair and said he hated blondes. I really thought he loved me. What an idiot I was. Bastard! This is all his fault. I hate him. My hands begin to shake and a hot panic smothers me. It's no good. I need a drink.

I push myself up and pace back across the soft sand to the promenade. I slap on my sandals and dust the wet grains of sand from my jeans. I shove past the strolling holidaymakers in the direction of the Maharani Hotel which stands tall and white, saluting the sky. I climb the tiled steps with jelly legs and stride through the revolving door into the white marble foyer with its smart reception area. My eyes dart around until they find a blue neon sign proclaiming *Ladies Bar*. 'Thank God,' I mutter as I head towards it with quick steps.

The interior is cool and darkened with a classy tourist feel. Good, this is just what I need. Semi-circular, plush velvet kiosks with low-slung blue glass shades are nestled up against the walls like cosy pods. My shoulders relax. Only a few are occupied. You never know if a bar will be crowded at this time of day.

I head towards the oak bar with its high silver stools. A few patrons are perched at the far end. Their heads turn as I approach but I keep my eyes fixed to the front and ease myself onto the first stool. The bow-tied Indian barman gives me a wide, welcoming smile.

'A red label Johnny Walker and coke, please,' I murmur. 'Make it a double.'

'Yes, ma'am. Ice?' he asks, before giving me another of his practised smiles.

I nod, fearing my voice will break and betray me. I clasp my hands in my lap to stop them trembling. The barman shows his professionalism by pretending not to notice, and in no time he's placed a paper lace doily in front of me, followed by a crystal glass a third full of whiskey.

'Say when.' He clicks off the bottle cap and pours the coke in.

'Okay,' I say, as the darkness reaches the halfway mark. I hold my hand tense around the glass and take a big sip. The warmth of the whiskey sinks instantly to my legs and I let them dangle deliciously against the bar stool as I gulp down some more. I sigh deeply as it burns straight through me, melting away my anxiety. I'm sure the barman hears my sigh, but he keeps his eyes fixed forward and continues stacking the ice bucket. I guess he's had enough experience of hearing the liquored relief, and the Johnny Walker wisdom. I wonder how many sob stories he's heard from drunks once their numbness has blotted out their inhibitions and their pain comes tumbling out. There should be counselling awards for barmen like him.

'Hard day?' asks a low, masculine voice behind me.

I jerk my head around to glare at a middle-aged arsehole with a lustful sneer slashed across his face. His eyes are bulbous and he's clearly drunk. I look him up and down. His tight chinos show an ugly bulge almost hidden by his beer paunch. The three open buttons of his black shirt expose a thick gold neck chain. My top lip moves instinctively upwards. What a prize prick. He even has that awful long strand of hair combed back across his bald head as if it's fooling anyone. I give him my best 'Get lost!' glare and turn back to the bar. Cold shoulder's the best treatment for his type. I've no interest in being chatted up. I'm here for the drink and nothing else. I hear him huff behind me for a second and then mutter 'Bitch' under his breath. I suppress the urge to turn around and smack him one.

The barman moves over to me. 'Let me know if anyone bothers you and I'll deal with it,' he whispers, motioning with his eyebrows at the arsehole.

I nod and smile. 'I'll have the same again, please.'

'Yes, ma'am.' He rustles up another one and fills it up with the right amount of coke. He's a nice guy and I have to bite back the temptation to start talking and let all my angst flow out. I must finish this one and go, otherwise I'll end up staying here for hours and have to get a taxi home.

I down my second double and order a third. I smile broadly at my friendly barman. He really is a one of the best and has lovely, honey-coloured eyes. They'd go well with my green ones. We'd have beautiful children. My mind jumps to an image of the two of us lying, wrapped sweetly together under satin sheets. I bet he'd be a really attentive lover, a decent gentleman who'd care and not just use and abuse. I grimace. I guess one tiny slither of light in this dark, racial mess of a country is that we won't be invaded by crashing doors and judgement police snatching our sheets for evidence under the Immorality Act. I lift my glass in a mock salute. Cheers to the new South Africa. Mandela is free and petty apartheid is dead. I won't be arrested for sleeping with my barman any longer, that's if he'll even have me.

I wake with a pounding head and cotton wool tongue. I open blurry eyes. My mind's a dark cave. I blink up at the ceiling while my breath lodges in my throat. Where the hell am I? A painting of a lion nestled in the long veld beneath a crimson sunset adorns the wall opposite. To the side stands a mahogany counter with a large mirror and a stool in front. A tray with tea and coffee and cups and saucers sits on it. I push myself up onto shaky elbows with my heart thudding in my ears. I clutch the sheet against me. Why am I naked? An A4 leather-bound book sits next to bed. Maharani Hotel is etched in gold across the top. What the hell am I still doing in the Maharani?

Someone's in the shower. Is it the barman? Did my fantasy come true? I swallow back my shame and reach out quivering hands towards the pile of crumpled clothes lying strewn in the middle of the room. I must've been completely out of it to not even be able to remember. I pull on my knickers and yank on my jeans. They're stiff against my crotch. I collapse on the bed and bend my head towards my legs. I gag as the stink of urine assaults my nose. Did I wet myself? Was I really that drunk? Oh Lord – the barman must have known I wet myself, maybe even seen me do it? I retch and grab my bra and top as I hear the water stop. I put them on as fast as I can with shaking hands before grabbing my sandals and slapping them on. I don't want him seeing me like this. I push myself up and take a dizzy step forward to pick up my handbag from the floor. The bathroom door opens behind me. I turn. My eyes freeze on a pasty roll of white fat bulging over the top of a hotel towel. I move my eyes up and gag at the thick gold chain. Chino-man leers at me from the open doorway, his bald head shining and his long strand of hair stuck damply against the side of one fat cheek. He half-opens his mouth and shows me a bloated tongue.

'You were good,' he says, ripping away his towel. His flaccid trophy hardens as he grabs it. 'Fancy some more?'

Bile spews from my mouth as I rush to the door and stagger, crying, to the lift. 'Oh God! How could I? How could I?'

I stumble into the shower as soon as I reach home. I need to cleanse, wash away the indignity and the stink. Never again, I promise myself, but even as I scrub my skin raw the fear that there will be another time stands strong in my mind. I shudder. I still can't believe I actually slept with that repulsive man; how much lower can I go? The barman must think I'm a whore, and maybe he's right. It's not the first time I've woken in a strange bed and not known how I got there. I did it a few weeks ago with that bristly, moustached guy I met at the Keg and Thistle bar, whose name I don't even remember. What the hell's wrong with me? Dad would be so ashamed. God must hate me. Tears well in my eyes and I bend over and clutch myself as the truth of my disgrace sobs out. I can't even be proud of my job any more. I've made three mistakes with test results in as many weeks and that's three too many in the medical profession. Dr Pillay knows there's something wrong. I could kill someone next time. I'll probably get fired and be left with nothing but an STD. I'm nothing more than a drunken slut. I hate myself. I hate who I've become. I freeze. My thigh is mottled with ugly, purple bruising. When did I bump myself? I turn my hands over. My palms are also bruised. My heart jumps to my ears. Oh God. That's not a good sign. Maybe Nat and Elsa are right. Maybe I really do need help?

# CHAPTER TWO

My head's as light as air and my whole body feels numb, as if it belongs to someone else. I stare at the back of Elsa's head as the phrase 'I can't believe I've agreed to this' plays through my mind again and again like a stuck record. Elsa's knuckles are white around the steering wheel as she whizzes in and out between the rush of pulsating African taxis belting out their rap music. As she squeals through the amber traffic light up Goble Road and ignores the angry hooting and shouting of the taxis, she reminds me of that cartoon coyote with road rage I used to watch as a child.

We blur past the tall, white-walled mansions on Musgrove Road, all gated and electrified from the lurking black danger outside. I know this road so well and yet it feels so strangely unfamiliar. I shiver from the air-con inside the car. Why did I let them talk me into this? Why? My hand grips the door handle. Maybe I should just fling myself out, smear myself across the hot tarmac and end this farce called life?

Nat turns around and gives me a half-smile. She glances at my hand and reaches over to give it a squeeze. I shrug her away and seconds later we're winding our way up a long, leafy driveway with a large sign: *Welcome to Shaloma.* I'm surprised they don't have their slogan, *'Place of hope and new beginnings'* and their status as Durban's premier rehab printed below. I should've jumped while I had the chance.

'This looks nice, Liss,' says Nat, as we pass under the dappled shade of tall wattles lining the driveway. I stare up at the thin, white-streaked trunks with their high clumps of rich green leaves. They look so serene, so strong and timeless. I wish I could just hide away in that greenness so that no-one could ever find me again.

Chino-man with his fat, naked body vomits back into my mind. I clench my jaw and give my head a shake in an effort to get rid of him, but it's no good; he remains squatting centre stage like some perverted toad. I'll have to stick this out. I can't let something like that happen again. I've got to get myself out the gutter.

The long tarmac drive ends in front of a sprawling, whitewashed building. A wide wooden veranda draped with honeysuckle surrounds it, while a rolling lawn, dotted with clumps of purple hydrangea, stretches out in front. The green corrugated-iron roof gives it a farmhouse look and reminds me of those hazy childhood days on Aunty Yvonne's Karoo farm. A buxom, fifty-something woman with a bun of blonde hair and a nurse's uniform comes bustling down the wide front steps towards us. Her fat, round face and big blue eyes remind me of a cabbage-patch doll. She smiles broadly as she reaches the car.

'One of you must be Melissa. Welcome, I'm Helen.'

The air grows hot and I stifle the urge to run, screaming madly, back down the long driveway like some fleeing character in a horror film.

Elsa climbs out of the car. 'I'm Elsa, this is Natalie; we're Lissa's sisters.'

I clench my jaw as my cheeks grow hot. Fuck Elsa and her

lawyer façade, always pretending to be in control. I glare at her and get out of the car to mumble, 'Hello.'

Helen shakes my hand and smiles before turning to Nat and Elsa. 'You two are welcome to come in and see Melissa into her room, but then I'm afraid you'll have to leave and only see her after the treatment is over.' She pauses and lowers her voice to a maternal tone. 'That might seem a bit harsh, but it's important for recovery.'

I yank my suitcase from the boot without looking at either of my sisters and follow Helen, stiff-backed, into the building. A bright, lime-green wall greets me as we enter the tiled foyer. My breath sticks in my throat as a childhood memory of sitting at the Aquarium Wimpy Bar happily slurping up a lime milkshake with Dad comes flooding back. Lime was my favourite childhood colour.

'Your room is down here in our female quarter.' Helen's voice breaks into my thoughts. I jerk my eyes away from the wall and follow as she pads down a long corridor. 'The men's bedrooms are on the other side of the building and the communal lounge and dining room are at the end of this corridor.'

Nat comes up at the side of me and squeezes my arm. Pressure constricts my chest. I increase my pace. Helen stops halfway down the corridor and opens a door to reveal a room swathed in pink with a candy pink duvet covering the bed like a giant marshmallow, while rose-coloured curtains frame the large, paned window and its ingrained iron bars. A mottled pink, shaggy rug in the middle of the wooden floor completes the room's rosy hue. I know pink is the stereotypical girlie colour, but it feels a bit over the top. I let out a wry laugh. I wonder if it's blue for the boys in their segregated rooms. The childhood rhyme of *'Pink and blue will never do cause all the boys will wink at you'* reverberates in my mind. This is ridiculous; it's like being back at school.

'There's a wardrobe and dressing-table for your things and

your en suite is through here.' Helen pushes open a door to reveal a white tiled bathroom with bleached towels and a white bathmat. It's bland and a bit clinical, but at least it's a pink-free spot.

'You've got your own tea and coffee facilities and we'll bring fresh milk every day if you wish. I'll leave you girls alone in a minute; the rules and regs are in that book on the dressing-table, but I'm afraid first I need to have a quick search.'

I step back and stare at her. 'Pardon?'

'I know it's not nice, but it's the rules, I'm afraid. You'll be amazed at what some people try and smuggle in.' She gives a maternal smile.

My mouth drops open and I don't know whether to laugh or cry.

'It's standard procedure, don't worry,' says Elsa. She picks up my suitcase and flings it open. The red lid clashes like a wound with the candy pink duvet. 'Have a look through, Helen.'

A cocktail of disbelief and anger washes through me. Since when is she an authority on rehabs? She stands smug and blonde in her pinstriped power, suit and heels, and purposefully avoids my burning eyes. Nat moves towards me and pulls her *you-know-what-Elsa's-like* face, as Helen has a quick fumble through my things.

'That's fine, Melissa. Now just a quick pat down, dear.'

I close my eyes as dark clouds of anger swirl and Helen's hands pat up and down my body.

'That seems fine,' says Helen. 'Right, I'll leave you girls alone for a bit.' She turns to me. 'Don't worry, the six weeks will fly by.' She pads out and closes the door while an awkward hush consumes the room.

'It's certainly uber-pink,' says Elsa. She stands tense, with her legs a little apart. Her face is set in a smile but a sad shadow flits across her eyes. I look away.

'Can I help you unpack?' Nat's voice cracks and she hastily

clears her throat and tries to look helpful by closing my case and smoothing the duvet around it.

'It's okay,' I mumble.

Nat bites her lip. 'Sorry, Liss. I know it's hard…'

'You don't know the half of it actually…'

'It'll be a turning point.' Elsa comes towards me and tries to take my hand. I jerk away.

'Leave it… I'm not a chronic alcoholic. I'm not.'

Nat and Elsa say nothing, but I can read the disbelief in their eyes. 'Oh, just go. Give my love to Mom and Yvonne. Have a fucking G & T together, why don't you.' But instead of leaving, my sisters remain staring at me with wide blue eyes like those girls in a Margaret Keane painting.

'There's a difference between having a drink and being dependant,' says Elsa in a measured tone.

'And how the hell do you know I'm dependant? Don't you think I'm the one who should make that decision?' My chest tightens as I spit out the words.

Elsa takes a step back. 'You agreed to come, Liss, and ultimately it's the right decis—'

'Why don't you both go back to your cosy little lives with Dave and Greg? I've had enough. I just want to be alone.' I stomp over to the window and turn my back, waiting for the clip-clop of their heels. Instead a heavy silence shrouds the room.

'We'll be back to get you at the end of the treatment. We all just want you well again.' Nat comes over and puts her arm around my shoulder.

I drop my head down and hold it in my hands. The reality of being left here alone for the next six weeks hits me. Oh God, it's going to be so lonely. My heart pounds into my ears.

'Remember we love you,' whispers Elsa and, uncharacteristically, I hear her voice falter.

I turn towards my sisters and give them a small nod accompanied by a tight smile. They both give me an awkward wave and make for the door. It clicks closed. God, I wish I could have a drink. If I'm going to get through this, I need to shut them and everything else out of my mind. This is going to be far worse than I thought. Heaviness creeps over me like a darkening sky. I'm going to crack. I shouldn't have come. I collapse onto the edge of the bed and bury my head in my hands.

When I look up the sun has begun its downward journey across the sky. I go over to the dressing-table and page through the 'Rules and regs', as Helen called them. Bold letters along the top announce: *All programme activities are designed to introduce structure, self-discipline and other qualities essential to ongoing recovery.* What fun. Welcome to addict boot camp. This is going from bad to worse. *Wake-up is at six-thirty, a 'tidy room' at six-forty five, followed by an inspection and then breakfast at seven.* What the hell do I need a room inspection for? I'm not in boarding school, for shit's sake.

My shoulders hunch over as I skim-read the daily timetable. This isn't some spa break where I can relax and be pampered; it's an institution with therapies, doctor visits and medication. Four medication slots are listed. No way are they going to drug me with anti-depressant shit. I know what Valium can do.

I flinch at a soft knock at the door. It opens and Helen stands in the doorway, a black bag in her hand. 'Have you managed to unpack?'

'No.'

My chest tightens as she comes into the room and sets the bag down on the dressing-table. 'It's okay, my dear. The first day's always the worst.'

'What's this…?'

'I have to check your vital signs.'

'What for?'

'Detoxing can be dangerous,' says Helen.

I roll my eyes at her patronising tone and feel like I've regressed twenty years.

Helen carries on as if she's oblivious to my resentment. She takes out a blood pressure monitor and stethoscope from the bag before pulling forward the dressing-table stool. 'Please sit over here, Melissa,' she says. 'This won't take long.'

I remain on the bed for a few seconds before clicking my tongue and plonking myself on the stool. Helen tightens a pressure bandage around my bare arm and then records my blood pressure reading on a sheet. I sit tense and hunched as she takes out a stethoscope. 'If you'd like to just lift your shirt, I'll listen to your heartbeat. If needs be we'll do an ECG.'

I snatch up my satin shirt and flinch as the cold steel touches my chest. 'Is this really necess—?'

'We've quite a number of clients who need admission to hospital, I'm afraid,' interjects Helen sharply. 'I do need to do a basic check for you to stay.'

I pull down the sides of my mouth. A part of me hopes there will be something wrong just so I can get the hell out.

'Not too bad,' says Helen, filling in her sheet. 'I'll just take your pulse. When did you last have a drink?'

'The day before yesterday,' I mumble as my cheeks grow hot.

Helen places her fingers on my wrist and records my pulse.

'Please hold your arms out in front.'

I grimace and thrust out my arms. My hands tremble. I tense, trying to still them, but the quivering increases.

'The shaking will ease with time,' says Helen, scribbling more on my sheet. 'Any bruising?'

I keep my palms down and shake my head. Helen snaps the bag closed. 'You're one of the lucky ones. Some patients are in a very bad way when they arrive. Hopefully you've…'

'I shouldn't be here.'

'Really?'

My head jerks back at her sarcastic tone.

'Acceptance of your problem is the vital first step. You know that, and so do your sisters.'

'What the hell have they got to do with anything?'

Helen studies me in silence for a few seconds. 'You're right. At the end of the day your recovery will be your decision and no-one else's, but what you need to remember is that alcoholism is a fatal disease.'

'Of course I know it's a fatal disease,' I snap, 'but I'm not that type of drunk.'

Helen ignores my outburst and points to a red button on the wall near my bed. 'That's a *help* button. There's someone at the desk 24/7 so please press it if you need anything. There's another in your bathroom, and if you need a sick pan, it's under the bed.'

I remain stony-faced while she pulls open the drawer of the bedside cabinet. 'There's a *Gideon's Bible* in here with some highlighted passages that might help, and also some AA magazines to look through.'

I let out a wry laugh. 'Wonderful.'

Helen moves to the door, then stops and turns. 'It'll get better. Remember we're here to help.' She gives me a smile. 'Let me know if you need a sleeping pill later and try and drink as much water as possible.'

'I'm not taking any medication.'

'You don't need to. You can have a chat to Dr Brink. Don't worry, he's lovely. We won't force you to do anything you don't want to, but my hope is that you'll stick it out. This is rough, but it's a turning point. You're turning away from the nowhere road to one that will lead to victory. Keep that in your mind.'

For some ridiculous reason her words make me want to cry and I rapidly blink my eyes.

'There's a cream tea at four-thirty in the lounge.'

'I'm not hungry.'

'You do need to meet the others. We have three patients who are doing a further six weeks to really conquer their addiction. So I promise it won't be as bad as you think. The lounge is straight down the end of the passage. You can't miss it.'

My chest tightens. 'I don't want to.'

'I'm sure you don't, but it'll be better if you do. Withdrawing from everything will make it worse.' Helen's tone is firm and measured.

'So much for free choice,' I snap.

'I promise you'll feel better tomorrow.'

'What are you, a bloody psychic?' I mutter.

'Four-thirty in the lounge... just down the corridor.' Helen's voice does not rise to meet my anger. 'You do need to go.'

The door closes. I throw my clothes into a pile on the floor. Oh God, I hate this. I really do.

# CHAPTER THREE

---

I push open the door at the end of the corridor marked *The Lounge*. It's large and L-shaped, with magnolia walls and a bare pine floor. It smells strongly of polish and stale smoke. A woman stands with her back to me, gazing out of a floral-curtained bay window. She's small with an explosion of pink punk hair and a fluorescent pink tracksuit with Doc Marten boots. Perhaps this place and its rose-tinted perspective colours you pink after a while?

She turns, and I see she's much older than I expect, probably late-thirties, with sunken cheeks and dark rings etched around her eyes. She gives me a smoke-filled smile, showing a row of small, bad teeth. I return a tight smile, but remain standing just inside the entrance.

'I'm Hattie...' Her voice has an ugly, rasping tone.

'Melissa.' I dig my nails into my palms and flinch. The bruising's still surprisingly tender.

'Used to be called Heroin Hattie,' she speaks through another long exhalation of smoke. 'What you here for?'

I swallow. 'Uh... not heroin.'

A scornful smile slides across her face. She raises her eyebrows. 'What then?'

'I just drink a bit, that's all.' I clench my jaw at the admission. Damn Nat and Elsa. I should never have listened to them.

'Sit,' says Hattie as she plonks herself in one of the armchairs and gestures to the one opposite.

I frown at her demanding tone, but move towards the window and sit down. Hattie leans back and stretches out her legs. She takes a deep drag of her cigarette, leaving a fragile tower of ash tottering in its wake. She looks down her nose at it for a second and then flicks it expertly into a glass ashtray on the floor. It's overflowing with a mound of ugly, unfiltered stubs, most of them stained with fuchsia lipstick.

'Don't they mind smoking?' I ask, as the air grows thick between us.

Hattie sniffs. She bends forward to stump her cigarette out. 'No, it's the one drug we're allowed.' She fishes in the pocket of her tracksuit pants and pulls out a crumpled packet of plain *Lucky Strikes* and holds it out towards me. 'Want one?'

I twist a strand of hair between my fingers and shake my head. 'I don't smoke.'

She looks at me with weathered eyes and leans back in the chair. 'So… alcohol your only vice?'

My chest constricts at her derisive tone. I nod. 'Only alcohol.'

Hattie sniffs again while I shift uncomfortably on the squeaking leather.

'Dr Brink says I need a second round,' she says, pulling out another cigarette and lighting up. 'He says Karlos and Alison must do the same.' She utters the names and takes a deep drag, tilting her head against the back of her chair, waiting no doubt for me to ask about them. I give a small nod. She forms her mouth into a wide 'O' and puffs rings of smoke out towards the ceiling. 'Neither of them is as fucked as me though. Had to go cold turkey in the first week. *Yslike*, it was hell.' Her face distorts in a repulsive snarl.

I feel sorry for her, but it's obvious she's looking for sympathy. A cool 'Shame' is all I offer, as I watch the rings drift up and dissolve one by one into the sullied ceiling.

'Alcohol's nothing compared to that fucker.' Hattie pauses and leans forward. 'You should've seen me – fuck, I was shaking, screaming, itching all over like a million red ants were eating me. It lasted three fucking days – I never want to go through that again – never.' Her pink chest heaves up and down like a dying flamingo. 'That's why I'm still here. I'm going to defeat the fucker. I am.' Seconds later her face contorts into an ugly cry and she lets out a loud wail.

I sink back into my armchair, wishing the soft leather would swallow me up. 'I'm sorry,' I murmur.

The wail transforms into crude laughter. Hattie takes one last drag from the burning cigarette before stubbing it out with a sharp jab of her hand. She sits back against the chair. 'There're three other okes who arrived on Friday night: Nic, Wolf and George – none of them done heroin.' Her eyes wash over me. 'How come you didn't come the same time as them?'

I shrug. 'I only made the arrangements yesterday.'

Hattie lets out an ugly laugh. 'You have a crisis?'

My chest tightens and my cheeks grow hot. 'Something like that.'

Hattie takes another drag and looks at me with narrow eyes. '*Agh*, you can let it all out in the group meetings. We all have to wash our dirty panties for each other.' She gives a self-satisfied smirk. 'But no-one else's have been as dirty as mine.'

My head grows light and begins to spin. I grab the arms of the chair and move to get up just as the lounge door creaks open. I sink back down and turn. Two men enter. I draw in a sharp breath to try and chase the lightness from my head. The first guy looks like a male model with a touch of Michael Douglas about him. He's dressed well in Wrangler jeans and a crisp white shirt with the first two buttons undone; obviously one of Durban's surfer boys with that tan and sun-bleached hair just touching his collar. I was expecting ravaged addicts with dug-out crater cheeks and vacant eyes. What's he doing here? I swallow what spit I've got left in my mouth and try to ease the dryness which is constricting my throat. I don't want to let him know my dirty secrets. That's the last thing I want.

My cheeks warm as he watches me, watching him.

The other one is big and blonde with thick unbrushed hair. I feel a shiver of distaste as I take in the dull blue eyes, straight nose and square jaw. He's far too German looking for me and has those shapeless hippo legs I hate. I'm conscious that Model-man is still watching me with the type of pose you put on when you want to look like you're in control. I turn unsmiling to the window to stare intently at the hydrangeas as his footsteps echo over the pine floor towards me. My chest mottles. Why do I have to suddenly feel so self-conscious just because a good-looking guy's come in?

'Howzit, Hattie.'

'Howzit, Nic. Meet Melissa, she's just arrived.'

I turn my head and give him a small nod of acknowledgement. He's got a faded bruise just below his hairline and a network of broken capillaries under the surface of his cheeks near his nose. Must be a drinker. Probably fell over?

A smile edges across his mouth. 'Good to have you here, Melissa. I'm also a newbie.' My name slips in syllables from his tongue. He offers me a smooth, tanned hand with no ring.

I push my body back into the chair and hold out my hand for a cursory shake. 'Thank you,' I mutter. Good, my voice sounded cool and confident. He's obviously a player; I'm not going to let him read into my soul like Mike.

'This is Wolf,' says Hattie. 'Luckily he doesn't bite.'

I cringe as Wolf throws back his head in a fake howl, revealing teeth like blackened corn. He strides over on his hippo legs. He's even more repulsive close up with a bloated stomach and dry red patches under his eyes.

'Place is full of wackos, I'm afraid,' says Nic.

I ignore him and turn with a fixed expression to Wolf as he offers me his hand. My nose wrinkles. He stinks of sweat.

'Volfgang, but you can call me Volf.' He grins as if I should be grateful.

The accent is German. Damn, I'm good. I limply shake the offered paw and wipe my hand against my jeans as soon as he lets it go. Stereotypical Aryan. Hitler would have loved him. I can just see him in an SS uniform. He moves to the side of Hattie's chair and scratches his forearm. Bile rises in my throat. He's got at least four open sores dotted across his arm. He really is vile.

'Wolf's from South West,' Hattie offers in a loud voice.

'It's Namibia now,' says Wolf, and his face contorts into a snarl.

Hattie snorts. 'Ja, sorry, I forgot. I suppose we'll be Azania soon, thanks to fucking De Klerk.' Her top lip curls. 'I don't trust that fucking Mandela.'

Wolf mirrors her sneer. 'Another fooking terrorist just like Njuoma. They'll fook zis place up just like South Vest.'

I turn on Wolf. 'Mandela's not a terrorist.'

'He let off bombs,' snaps Hattie. 'That makes him a terrorist.'

I lean towards her with my heart pounding in my ears. 'Only because our bastard racist government wasn't prepared to give an inch...'

'She's right,' interjects Nic, 'Mandela's our only hope.'

'You're fooking *mal* if you think that,' says Wolf scornfully.

'Ja, hope for the kaffirs...'

'Please don't use that word,' I snap at Hattie.

Hattie's head jerks back at my angry tone. 'I'll use...'

'Leave it, Hattie.' Nic takes a step towards her. 'You know it's offensive...'

'Ja, and I suppose they're going to throw us in jail now if we call them kaffirs?' She lets out an ugly laugh and leans back into her chair. 'I'm going to get the fuck out of this place...'

'Who's for a drink?' says Nic. His tone is falsely jovial. 'Believe it or not, Melissa, I discovered we've got a bar here, except its stock is, wait for it: cream soda, ginger beer, Coca-Cola, lemonade and Fanta. What more could you ask for, hey?' He pauses, waiting for a reaction from me. 'I'm having the green fizz. Can I get you one?'

He stands waiting.

'Ginger beer, please,' I mutter. My heart is still hammering in my ears and I turn to the window and stare at the hydrangeas until they merge into a purple haze. Tension like this is the last thing I need.

'Good choice.'

'I'll have a coke,' shouts Hattie, as Nic makes his way to the far end of the room. She pulls out the packet of *Lucky Strikes* and offers it to Wolf. He takes the squashed pack and helps himself. He places the cigarette between his ugly teeth and bends down with his jeans halfway down his arse as Hattie flicks a cheap pink Bic lighter over the dangling end. Wolf inhales with a grunt. The cigarette trembles in his fingers. He blows out a long line of grey smoke and makes his way over to the bar. He examines a large poster plastered on the wall behind the bar and turns back to Hattie. 'Hey, this is a take-off of the *Mainstay* advert. You seen it?'

Hattie leans over the side of her chair to look in the direction of the bar. 'Ja,' she says and laughs. 'They put it up this morning; it's good, hey? Karlos says that's what happened to him except it was brandy, not *Mainstay*.'

Wolf laughs. 'Ja, Afrikaners like their brandy, was probably the Klippies brand. I've had a few Klippies and coke in my time.' He takes another long, shaky drag of his cigarette.

The poster shows a down-and-out drunk, holding a bottle of *Mainstay* cane spirit. Under him is written the usual slogan: *You can stay as you are for the rest of your life, or you can Mainstay*. I can hear the tune as I read it. It brings back memories of the beautiful people on their luxury yachts, sipping their *Mainstay* and sailing away to freedom in exotic places. A memory of me stumbling down a hotel corridor to bed and hardly being able to open my hotel door during a holiday in Mauritius creeps into my mind, igniting the shame deep inside. There's nothing glamorous about being drunk and don't I know it.

Nic comes back with my ginger beer. 'No *Mainstay* in it, I promise.'

'Thanks,' I mumble as I take the glass with my thumb and forefinger poised, making sure I avoid touching his hand. He lingers next to me and takes a loud slurp of his cream soda before saluting me.

'I'm going to sit in the "business class" area. Why don't you guys come over there?'

Hattie stubs out her cigarette in the overflowing ashtray. She looks up at Nic and nods. 'Ja, okay. We can put on some sounds.'

I stay seated.

'It's over this side,' says Nic, waiting for me to follow. I supress a sigh of irritation and follow him around the corner of the room. A thin girl, who looks about nineteen, is slouched at the end of one of the couches. She's immersed in reading a *Cosmo* magazine and keeps her eyes firmly fixed to the glossy pages as we come near.

'Alison, this is Melissa.' Hattie flops down on the couch next to her. The leather squeaks. Alison's jaw jerks, but she says nothing.

'Hello,' I murmur as I settle on the couch opposite.

She glances up with hooded eyes. Her face is pale with a long, thin nose. She reminds me of an Indian Mynah bird. She flicks a strand of straggly black hair away from her face and mumbles an almost inaudible, 'Hi.'

28

'Alison likes to keep to herself,' says Hattie. 'She's on her second round, but still not better.'

'I'm sure Alison can speak for herself,' I say, shaking my head at her lack of tact.

'She doesn't like talking,' snaps Hattie.

'Scones,' says Wolf, snatching up one from the piled plate. He ladles large dollops of cream and strawberry jam onto it and, as he stuffs it in his mouth, jam runs down the side of his chin. I turn away as he chews loudly with the masticated mess clearly evident.

'Let them eat cake,' says Nic, helping himself to a scone. His hand shakes as he picks it up. 'The more we stuff our faces with the sweet stuff, the less we'll cry for booze.'

'Or heroin,' puts in Hattie.

'Yes, or heroin,' says Nic, in a patronising tone.

Hattie's eyes harden. She takes another drag of her cigarette before picking up a saucer from under one of the teacups and stubbing it viciously onto it.

'Scone?' Nic places his on a side plate and picks up another one. He holds it out to me.

I shake my head. 'No thanks.'

'*Agh*, such a charmer,' says Hattie with a sneer. 'You better take what he says with a pinch of salt.'

'A dose of salts maybe,' says Wolf. He throws his head back in an ugly laugh.

'What's this, pull Nic apart day?' Nic's jaw tightens.

No-one speaks. Hattie smirks. She lights up another cigarette and sucks deeply on it with twitching fingers. She crosses her legs and jerks her dangling boot up and down. A slow smile slides across my face. She might appear strong, but the constant chain smoking and this jerking speak volumes.

'So, Melissa, tell for us your story,' says Wolf, licking his lips but leaving smudges of jam down the side of his chin.

'Don't answer,' says Nic, picking up a cup and sloshing in

29

some tea. 'Leave the shit for group therapy tomorrow.' He gives me a sideways smile. 'So much to look forward to, hey?'

I shake my head as Hattie's dirty linen comment slinks back into my mind. I'm not saying anything about Chino-man or anything else for that matter. Fuck the group therapy. They can't force me to talk.

Hattie laughs. 'Ja, you need to talk if the H-man's...'

'We've all got the T-shirts,' says Nic. His shoulders stiffen.

Hattie sniffs and gets up. 'I'll play some Crash Test Dummies, that should suit us, hey?'

'Ja, make it *Afternoons and Coffee spoons.*'

'Ah, just the thing for a car crash afternoon,' says Nic sardonically. He wipes a shaky hand across his forehead, his fingers lingering on the bruise.

Dark laughter rumbles across my mind as I can't help but agree.

# CHAPTER FOUR

I leave the dining room after breakfast having only managed a coffee. My head's groggy from lack of sleep. Anticipation of the dreaded group therapy went round and round in my brain all night. And when I did finally get to sleep, the ridiculous six-thirty alarm woke me. I'm sure I've only had about three hours. My cheeks grow hot at the memory of the sharp knock on my door for the humiliating room inspection. Do they really think any of us could smuggle booze into this ridiculous prison during the night, when we can't even leave?

My stomach cramps and acid shoots into my gullet. I gag as I try to swallow it back. I draw in a long, shaky breath. I probably should've eaten something, and I'm sure I would've if Hattie hadn't turned up like an unwanted stench and put me off. Why the hell did she have to come and sit with me? Can't she see we've got nothing in common?

I push open a door to a terra-cotta courtyard with flowerbeds of aloes and yellow gardenias on each side. The morning air's already hot and humid.

Hattie is loitering outside. 'That's the medical block.' She points towards a red-brick building on the far side. 'We have all our sessions there.'

*'Fuck the sessions!'* I feel like screaming, as she marches towards the building. She stops and waits until I'm nearly at the door before striding through it like a troop leader. My hands grow sweaty. This crap is the last thing I need. I'm not going to talk. I'm not.

'We're in here.' Hattie pushes open a door at the end of the corridor. I wipe my damp hands against my jeans and follow her in to a conference room with a circle of blue armchairs. The lighting's dim and the air smells strongly of lavender. A low wooden coffee table holds a tray of water glasses, a bowl of mint imperials and pamphlets. A granite, egg-shaped water-feature tinkles away in the corner. Every detail suggests a pseudo meditation retreat.

Nic and Wolf are sitting in two of the armchairs, both with their legs crossed. Nic is giving me the *I'm interested in you; are you interested in me look?* As if we're in some sleazy nightclub instead of a bloody rehab. I blink away from him and look straight at another guy seated near the door. He gives me a smile, while I stand tense, feeling like the awkward new kid on her first day at school.

'This is Melissa. She arrived yesterday,' says Hattie, pointing at me as if she owns me. 'This is Karlos.'

Karlos gets up and strides over before I even have time to answer. His smile widens and he offers me his hand. 'Nice to meet you, Melissa.' He has a thick Afrikaans accent. 'I'm one of the oldies like Hattie.'

His hand grips mine and I flinch as he presses into my bruised palm. He lets go and I feel his fingers glance over the small of my back as he ushers me further into the room. I pace towards an empty chair near Hattie and sit down. I push my knees together and stiffen my body. My cheeks are on fire. Why the hell am I blushing? I draw in a deep breath. *For shit's sake, Melissa. Get a grip.*

Alison appears in the doorway. She stands pale and stooped for a few seconds before shuffling in my direction with her head down. She stops and slinks back two steps. Her eyes flick around the room like a frightened deer.

I half-lift myself from the chair. 'Do you normally sit here, Alison?' She shakes her head and moves back like a sliding shadow to a vacant chair and hunches down.

Karlos shakes his head as he looks at her. He's sitting comfortably with his khaki-clad legs sprawled out in front. His hands rest in his lap with his fingers linked. He's either very confident or very good at hiding things. I envy him whichever. He's not the type I usually go for, and he looks like he could be about forty, but for some reason I find those khaki pants and suede veldskoen shoes comforting. He's got a down-to-earth look, and I think he must be an outdoor type from his tan; maybe even a game-ranger with that short brown beard. I can see him sitting tall behind the wheel of a Land Rover, bumping through the hot yellow veld with a shotgun over his shoulder. He's not as good-looking as Nic, but he's at least six feet two and has that Camel cigarette advert look about him. I bet Elsa would like him; she always went for the rugged types rather than the pretty boys. His arms are lined with fine, dark brown hairs and a few are visible from the open top button of his shirt, but he's not a gorilla type; not like those hairy-backed Afrikaners you see frolicking in the waves on the Durban beachfront like they've never seen the sea before.

Wolf is watching him with snake eyes, while Nic leans back into his chair, trying to look relaxed with his one leg still crossed over the other and his arm sprawled across the back of the chair. His jerking foot and clenched fist say otherwise. I look over at Karlos and wonder why he's making Nic and Wolf so uncomfortable?

'So, Melissa, welcome to the funny farm,' says Karlos. He pulls his legs in and leans towards me. 'It's not a patch on my old mealie farm, but what can you do? If a man makes a mess of things, he must change and put things right. That's what I'm here to do.'

What is it with these people and their open confessions? 'You look like a farmer,' I say, cringing at the high pitch of my voice and stupid comment.

'They're killing white farmers in Namibia like fooking flies. They'll kill them here too now,' says Wolf in a tone of authority.

Karlos ignores the comment as Helen bustles in followed by a casually dressed, fifty-something man with salt-and-pepper hair. He must be the doctor, although his large glasses make him look more like a friendly owl. He gives me a wide smile and comes over with his hand outstretched.

'Welcome, Melissa. I'm Gareth Brink. I'm really pleased you've joined us.'

I suppress a smile. His name reminds me of the game *Happy Families* I used to play with Nat and Elsa. What could be better than *Dr Brink* for the doctor who brings people back from their self-created disaster?

The room falls silent as Dr Brink rustles through some papers. 'Right, I think we're all here. George is not feeling too well this morning so he won't be joining us in the sessions until tomorrow. Helen, please set up the video for me.'

Hattie turns to me. 'Time to share,' she says with a smug smile. 'Alison doesn't like to talk,' she whispers. 'You can only do so much, you know.'

My palms grow damp. I just want to go home! But, of course, I can't. '*Group therapy is a very important part of recovery*', Helen had admonished this morning when I voiced my opposition. I don't see why. This is my problem, not theirs. Why can't I just have therapy on my own? My head grows light and I don't think I can do this. I'm going to have to leave.

'I'd like to welcome Melissa to our group.' Dr Brink's voice has a professionally honed, calming quality. His eyes shine at me through the owl glasses and all eyes turn to me. I push myself back into my chair and clench my jaw and fists. 'We're only starting the programme proper this morning, although some of our patients are repeating it,' he says, flicking his eyes across the chairs. 'But first we'll start with some pseudonyms for our names for a bit of fun.' Dr Brink pauses while I bite back dark laughter. I don't know which is worse - the typical alcoholic introduction or this so-called 'fun'. How the hell can any of us have 'fun' in a place like this? Maybe what we should rather do is crack open a bottle.

'You need to choose the same letter as your name to convey how you feel now, and then choose one you'd like to aim for by the end of the course. Nic, you start.'

Nic thinks for a few seconds with pursed lips. 'Nasty Nic, I'm afraid, when I let the beast enter my brain, but now I'm sober for a few days I'll be Nice Nic.' He follows his revelation with a wink in my direction.

'Was Heroin Hattie, now I'm getting to be Heroic Hattie. Not many okes can keep fighting to defeat the H-man,' says Hattie, puffing out her chest like some ridiculous bantam cock.

I tense my face to stop the scorn parading over it. I don't even know what the hell I'm even doing in the same room as someone like her? All I do is drink a bit too much sometimes.

Karlos' deep voice breaks into my thoughts. '*Agh*, I was "Kicked Karlos",' he says, 'but now, hopefully, with round two, I'm getting to be King Karlos.'

'Ja, like King Kong,' says Hattie, following with an attention-seeking laugh which Karlos ignores.

'I'm fooking Vashed-up Volf, but I vill be Vonderful Volf,' says Wolf, clenching his fists. 'This fooking detoxing is bad man. I don't fooking want to do it again.' He scratches his septic arm with dirty nails and stares at the carpet.

I wrinkle my nose and look away from the weeping sores.

The room falls silent. It's Alison's turn but she continues to stare forward, fear etched deep into her eyes. She's as fragile as a butterfly's wing, poor girl.

'Alison?' Dr Brink coaxes her as if he's talking to a two-year-old.

Alison stays silent, her eyes fixed on Karlos.

'Still Anxious Alison then perhaps,' says Dr Brink. 'Not to worry, we'll move on.'

Dr Brink turns to me. 'Melissa?'

Shit, I haven't been thinking of anything. What should I be? Malicious, Mocking? 'Uh… Miserable, I guess.' I recoil inwardly, surprised at my own honesty.

'That will change,' says Dr Brink.

My chest mottles. I can feel them all watching me. I give a wry smile. 'I guess I'll aim for Merry Melissa sans the alcohol.' Nic guffaws while Hattie sneers. They're all looking at me now. I draw in a deep breath and slowly exhale to calm the sudden panic inside.

Dr Brink clears his throat. 'Right, we're going to look at the *Twelve Steps*. Do you know anything about them, Melissa?'

I give a curt nod and swallow hard. I've got some vague recollection of them when someone visited Mom years ago and left a booklet. I remember Dad telling her they were proven to work, but I don't think she ever read it. Whatever, they certainly didn't stop her drinking. This is all going to be a complete waste of time. I know it is.

'Good. We start each session reminding ourselves of the steps by reading them aloud. You don't have to accept them all, but I ask that you keep an open mind. They have helped millions of people worldwide, so perhaps they can help you too.' He turns to Helen. 'Please hand them out.'

Helen hands me a leaflet, and I scan down the numbered steps while the paper trembles in my hands. Why the hell am I still shaking? I push my legs together and lay it on my lap. I wipe my hands against the sides of my jeans and press against the sides of the paper to hide the traitorous tremor. I keep my palms hidden.

'Karlos, could you start, please,' says Dr Brink.

Karlos recites the first step of, '*We admit we are powerless over alcohol – that our lives have become unmanageable.*'

As I listen to the words, the memory of repulsive Chinoman and the stink of my own urine regurgitates back into my mind. That was probably my worst low, but if I'm really honest with myself, there were so many others. I think back to that night at Antonia's when I fell drunkenly back in my chair with my feet stuck out in front like some dead chicken, and then catapulted face forward straight into my spaghetti. We were supposed to be celebrating Elsa winning her case against that racist bastard landlord, and instead I was asked to leave and had to stagger out looking like some drunken Rastafarian puppet with spaghetti stuck all over my hair. They must've been so ashamed of me. There were other nights, more than I can count, when I'd toddled to my bedroom and collapsed into bed fully clothed, or stayed sitting double-eyed and slack in front of the television until I fell asleep in the chair. I remember falling over on the dance floor and flashing my knickers to everyone at Nat's party and rolling out of countless pubs at closing time. I close my eyes and shudder. They were all embarrassing, but none of them top the shame or revulsion of that night in the Maharani. Do all these add up to an unmanageable life? Do the sodding maths, Melissa, of course they do!

The room is silent. They're all looking at me and waiting. Hattie's eyebrows are raised. She points down at the paper. 'You need to read step two.'

I stare down with an irritated frown. 'Sorry... *We have come to believe that a Power greater than ourselves could restore us to sanity.*' My voice echoes back to me. I've never thought of it as a form of insanity before but I guess that's exactly what it is. I hold my head in my hands. I can't deny I've done this to myself. Why didn't I stop?

Alison refuses to read so Wolf reads steps three and four in his ugly, guttural accent, promising to, '*Made a decision to turn our vill and our lives over to the care of God, as ve understand him.*' Scorn parades across my face, although I'm sure he means every word.

The emphasis on the next steps of the '*fearless moral inventory*' and the '*admitting to others and God the nature of our wrongs*' brings more guilt. I probably won't even be able to count all the wrongs I have to admit to. So much for the steps helping. Surely there must be something better we can do? A heaviness lodges in my chest, eased only by irritation as Hattie dramatically recites her request of '*Humbly we asked Him to remove our shortcomings*' and settles back smugly in her chair. It's obvious to anyone with brains that she doesn't mean a word of what she's just read. Stupid bitch probably thinks she doesn't have any shortcomings other than heroin addiction.

But, as Nic reads the promise to '*Make a list of all persons we had harmed, and become willing to make amends to them all*', my irritation turns to despair. I hear my nine-year-old self screaming, '*I hate you, you horrible drunk... I hate you!*' at Mom as she lay in her sour and stinking bedroom one night. '*Get out of my room... you bloody brat,*' she'd spat back. '*It's okay,*' Nat had said as she placed her arms around me. '*She doesn't mean it.*' But I'd screamed back, '*Yes, she does... she hates me and I hate her.*' My shoulders sag as the angry words replay in my mind. I really don't want to end up like Mom.

'Try and read step eleven now, Alison, you can do it.' Dr Brink's coaxing voice breaks into my thoughts. Alison sits frozen, staring at the paper clutched between her trembling hands. My heart goes out to her. Poor child. She's worse than all of us. She swallows and attempts to stutter through the penultimate step, '*Sss... ought th... through p...prayer and m...mm..m..editation to*

*improve our c...conscious contact with God as we understood Him...'*
She stops and glows red as if she's about to burst into tears.

'Yes, *"praying only for knowledge of His will for us and the power to carry that out"*,' completes Dr Brink. 'Well done, Alison. That was a really good effort.'

I smile wryly to myself. It's going to take a lot of prayer and meditation and knowledge of His will on my part. My conscious contact with God feels like a lifetime ago. I don't know whether I can ever get back to that.

Hattie takes over and recites the last step of *'Having had a spiritual awakening as the result of these steps, we tried to carry this message to alcoholics and to practice these principles in all our affairs'* in her loud, abrasive tone, while I flick my eyes around the group. I wonder if any of us really means any of what we've just read? This recitation all just feels so ridiculous. I certainly can't see Hattie or Wolf believing in any Higher Power, and anyway the phrase irritates me. The Higher Power is called God. We don't need the *'as we understand him'* bit added. I rub my hand across my forehead. I'm starting to feel dizzy. I'm sure they must all have seen my guilt and pain parade across my face. Why didn't I control myself more?

'We're going to watch something now which might be a bit uncomfortable, but it's necessary.' Dr Brink's tone is low. 'It's a video of patients from the liver clinic at Addington.' He pauses and looks at us one by one. 'Most of them were in the last stages of the disease I'm afraid.'

Helen switches on the video. A young man with blond hair appears on the screen. He's wearing a hospital gown and has a drip in his arm. The narrator tells us he's on day four of his detox, but he still looks drunk. His eyes are glazed with an empty look and his spindly legs and arms are covered with blotchy, multi-coloured bruises. A monotone voice tells us that his cerebellum has been damaged from the alcohol abuse and he's suffering from ataxia and he'll never have full control of his limbs again. He looks about my age.

I shift uncomfortably in my chair. The second patient is worse, with a belly more swollen than a child with kwashiorkor. A transparent pipe drains litres of yellow fluid from his stomach into a transparent bag. His liver function score we're told is twenty-two. He'll have only three months more to live if he's lucky. '*I should've listened to my wife,*' he sobs. '*I should've listened.*' His sobs grow louder until they become a wail of raw pain and self-pity.

'I'm afraid both these patients are no longer with us,' says Dr Brink. He pauses and looks at each of us. 'With addiction, everyone has their rock-bottom and sometimes, sadly, it's death.'

I place a hand on my stomach and close my eyes in silent thanks for its flatness. Shit! I've done plenty of liver scores on patients in my time and know the type of damage alcohol can do. That could so easily be me in a few years' time. Why didn't I think about what I was doing to my body? I look around the group and for the first time I have to acknowledge that, maybe, in some unbelievably surreal way, I'm not a misfit here. I guess we've all fallen off the merry-go-round of life and are crawling our way back on, hanging onto the rail despite being dragged through the dirt. What a farce my life has turned out to be. I don't know whether to laugh or cry.

'I'm sorry, we don't mean to upset any of you, but it's important that we face the reality of where addiction will take you,' says Helen as she clicks off the video.

Dr Brink clears his throat. 'We want you to realise it's not too late,' he says, his voice thick with sincerity.

I stifle back the sob which wants to break free from my belly like the dead patient's did.

'Any thoughts on the *Twelve Steps*?' says Dr Brink, breaking into the smothering silence which has covered the room.

'It's dangerous stuff,' says Nic. He rubs a shaky hand across his forehead. 'So fucking dangerous...'

'Heroin is worse. It'll tear your liver to shreds. I think maybe you need this Higher Power to help,' says Hattie. She throws back her head in a loud, ugly laugh. 'Ja, the H-man is like a demon that just climbs inside your head...'

'Yes, heroin is a powerful and very destructive drug,' says Dr Brink, as Hattie rises from her chair in a grotesque demon imitation. 'But so, I'm afraid, is alcohol.'

'He burns into you. *Yslike*, once he's got you, you're fucked, man.' She turns to Wolf and karate chops her leg. 'I've even seen okes say the doctor must take off their infected legs rather than stop injecting.' She leans forward in her chair and grips the armrests. 'Ja, they'd rather crawl on their fucking arse than give up the H-man.' Her face contorts as she spits out the words. I withdraw from the spraying saliva.

'I was like a fooking rat in a cage,' says Wolf. 'In the morning I had to have drink or I would go fooking *mal*.' He turns pale and clenches his jerking hands. Sweat dots his brow. 'It tasted like fooking petrol, but I had to have it.' His blatant agitation and the pain in his voice take me by surprise. He drops his head down and shakes it from side to side. 'I thought I was fooking dying,' he whispers. 'I really thought I was fooking dying... even my arse was bleeding.'

'Ja, I know what you mean. It takes you down like a spiral all the way to hell,' says Hattie.

Nic laughs. 'A demonic roller-coaster from which you never escape. Well, until you die, I guess.'

Wolf joins in with a crude laugh. 'Maybe ven you die and go to hell it carries on,' he says, spinning his shaking hands in front of his face.

'I think we're going off a little at a tangent,' says Dr Brink. 'Just remember, fighting addiction is like eating an elephant,' says

Dr Brink. 'You need to take it one day at a time. Don't let the thought of eternal sobriety overwhelm you.'

I smile at his metaphor. I guess the only time we'll manage eternal sobriety with no effort is when we're all in heaven. That is, if any of us are lucky enough to make it there. All I know now is that I want to get better. I don't want to end up like those patients on the video.

# CHAPTER FIVE

That afternoon I rap on Dr Brink's office door for my three o'clock appointment. I'm not going to beat this regimented system so I might as well embrace it. The last thing I need is someone telling me off and, in some strange way, the rigid timetable helps.

Dr Brink gives me a broad smile. 'Please come in, Melissa. Take a seat.'

Waves of nausea wash over me as I wipe my clammy hands against my jeans. He's a nice enough guy. Why do I feel so anxious?

'I'm just going to do a few routine medical tests and then we can have a chat.'

I sit in silence while he takes my blood pressure. He gives me a thumbs up then places the cold stethoscope on my chest. My heart beats in my ears.

'Sounds okay. I'm just going to take some blood so we can test your liver enzymes and potassium. Alcohol's not good with those two. I want to test your spleen and pancreas and I think it's best we do a MELD test. It's a liver function test. Would you like me to explain it in more detail?'

I shake my head. 'I'm a medical technologist… I know what it is.'

Dr Brink pauses and looks at me for a few seconds. 'Alcohol's no respecter of persons, Melissa. We've had all types of professionals come through here. It really is everyman's drug.'

My shoulders sag. Shame sits on me like a toad as I watch my blood rise through the test tube. The video of the man's swollen stomach being drained comes back into my mind. Thank God I never got to that stage.

'Right, time for the comfy seats,' Dr Brink says. 'Let's go next door.'

I follow him into a carpeted room with two armchairs. A ceiling fan wafts a cool breeze to ease the humid atmosphere.

'Have a seat, Melissa. Can I get you a glass of water?'

I shake my head and grip the sides of the armchair.

'I'm going to ask you to fill this in. You don't have to share your answers if you don't want to, but there may be some things that you'd like to talk about.'

I take the clipboard and pen from him.

'I'll wait in the other office for a few minutes. Try and be as honest as you can.'

The door clicks closed. I look down at the form with the pen lodged between my lips. The first question asks how I thought my drinking affected me - mentally, physically, spiritually and emotionally. I take out the pen and give a wry laugh. *'Not very well thank you'* would be the answer. Flashes of self-loathing flit through me. Those drinks at the lab when we won the St Augustine hospital contract when I got so loud and made a complete tit of myself. Dr Bachelor definitely knew I was drunk. I could see the pity in his eyes, and if he saw, then Dr Pillay must've too. I'm surprised he didn't fire me then and there. Chino-man and my myriad of drunken episodes are back loud and clear in my mind and so are the judgement stares from the people around me. I give my head a shake. Who said *'Thanks for the memories'*? At this moment I don't want to remember anything; in fact, I'd rather have sodding amnesia. But if I'm really honest, the alcohol demon had crept up without me even realising it. It deadened me inside, deadened me from God, but at the same time it numbed the pain. I didn't do it for fun: I did it because I needed help. This exercise isn't helping. It's making me feel worse and I've only read question one.

My hands tremble as I fill in the answers as honestly as I can. Questions two to five deal with my childhood and family. Are there drinking problems in your family? The bloodline of our generational curse rises up at me through the veins of time. I give a wry laugh as I remember Dad telling my nine-year-old self, *'Good news, Lissa. Mommy's given up drinking.'* He was so happy about it and I still can remember the mixture of joy and relief that flooded through me at that moment. I'd burst into a torrent of happy tears and hugged him so hard it hurt. I'd thought it must've been the visit to that revival tent that did it, that all our lives had suddenly been cleansed, that from then on our family would be new and different, and just like Pastor Jorge's happy one. What a joke. All it meant was that Mom started drinking a different brand of wine instead of her usual Zonheimer, but I guess at least its chemical reaction on her brain was of a far milder variety. What the hell was in that Zonheimer that it could turn her into such a bitch? I think Dad also thought it meant she was stopping, and I remember his smile fading as quickly as it came when he saw Mom pull the two-litre bottle of Lieberstein out of the Spar shopping packet. But if he'd been honest with himself, he'd have seen he had a drinking problem himself, albeit just a weekend one.

I hold my head in my hands and give a low laugh. My whole long, ancestral line probably had a problem. I never met my granddad, but who the hell gets hit by a train unless they're pie-eyed crossing the tracks? That's probably why granny was teetotal and hated alcohol. Well, good for her; at least there was one person in our family who saw the light - shame we didn't all follow her example. I let the rest of my family parade one by one through my mind. Aunty Yvonne, and even Nat and Elsa have drunk too much at times, despite their self-righteous attitude. They're not immune; none of us are. Perhaps the whole lot of them should've joined me in rehab - we could have added a new name to the pack of *Happy Families*: Mr and Mrs On-the-Waggon and their three daughters, Teetotal, Sobriety and Abstinence, all being happily treated by Dr Brink. Except, of course, our pack is broken and shredded, the chief card blown apart in a stinking fountain of blood.

My chest constricts and tears fill my eyes. I wipe them away and shake my head from side to side to chase away the dark thoughts which are crawling like cockroaches through my brain. Dr Brink will be back soon. I have to finish this without ending up a crying wreck. I look down at the final question. It asks me how I feel about being here. I place the pen back in my mouth and stare down at the letters until they blur. I guess if I were to answer that honestly, I do have a sense of relief. There is a part of me that's actually glad I've come. Yes, shame still eats into me, but I don't need to let it smother me anymore. I count back the days. I've been sober for two days now – that's something – a glimmer of self-respect, the start of my own resurrection perhaps? I haven't suffered any of the DTs like some drunks; in fact I haven't even taken a tranquiliser, an anti-depressant – nothing. I've done it on my own. I'm not one of the million Valium and Prozac junkies who've needed a new crutch to help them get rid of the old one. No, I've done it in my own strength, drawn deeply from my own spirit of self-control. I lift up my head and look out towards the window and mouth a *'Well done, Melissa'* to myself before leaning back into the soft armchair and taking in a long, deep breath right down to my belly. A smile creeps across my face. That's the first time for I don't know how long that I've been kind about myself.

A tap on the inter-leading door makes me jump. Dr Brink enters. 'You done?' he asks in a warm voice.

'Yes, I think so,' I mumble.

'Good.' He settles into the armchair opposite me and for a second we stare at each other without speaking. The clickety-click of the whirring fan fills the room.

Dr Brink clears his throat. 'I'm hoping we can have some sessions in which we really explore the roots of your drinking, Melissa. It'll be a bit like peeling an onion. We'll have to take off layer after layer until we get to the bitter core. Once we've exposed it; we can heal it. Is that okay with you?'

I give a wry smile and nod. Yes, I guess being an onion is a good metaphor for me. I've burnt myself with my own juices; stung my own eyes so that they're red and running and full of pain. It'll be good to shed the layers, expose the rotten core, but somehow, I doubt if it's really possible.

'Shall we go through the questions, or would you rather just talk?'

I look down in silence at my family history splattered across the clipboard. 'Perhaps just talk.'

'Okay.' Dr Brink leans back into his chair and holds his hands together like I'm about to give confession. 'What do you think the roots of your drinking are?'

47

# CHAPTER SIX

'Look... there're some dust devils playing in our wake,' says Daddy, glancing into the rear-view mirror as we speed along through the wide desert spaces of the Karoo. I turn and look out of the back window of the Zephyr. Five spinning circles of red dust are dancing behind us as we zoom over the dry sand plains.

'They're chasing us.'

Daddy laughs and puts his foot down. 'We're too fast for them.'

Mommy clicks her tongue. 'Slow down, Jon.'

I look out at the desert with its dots of dark green thorn bushes. 'How come the plants don't die here, Daddy?'

Daddy catches my eye in the rear-view mirror. 'They've got waxy leaves to keep in water, but I think even they're a bit thirsty today.'

Daddy's right, their leaves are hanging. I know just how they feel. I haven't even got any spit left to swallow. I push my head out of the passenger window and peer up at the wide blue sky. There's not even one cloud up there and the air outside feels like the inside of our stove.

'See those hills,' Daddy says. 'They're called the "Three Sisters", just like you three.'

I squint my eyes at three humped hills far in front of us. They look like rondavels with their flattened tops. Two are huddled close together while one sits further apart. I grit my teeth and look at my sisters with narrow eyes before asking impatiently, 'When will we get there, Daddy?'

'Not too long, Lissakins.' Daddy gives me a wink.

'*Agh*, this old Karoo goes on forever.' Mommy sighs and turns her head to look out at the desert. 'I don't know how Yvonne and Piet live here. It would drive me mad.'

Daddy looks at Mommy and shrugs his shoulders. 'Sheep need space.'

'It's high time people moved on from the bloody great trek,' says Mommy, pushing her lips together.

The land rolls out forever and ever in front of us, until it melts into the blue sky like it's been swallowed up by the sea. There must be dinosaur ghosts living here, it's so big.

'If you aren't careful with those ANC friends of yours we'll also end up having to run away and live in the middle of nowhere,' says Mommy, still staring out the window.

Daddy frowns. 'Oh for goodness' sake, Maria!'

'You have to be more careful, Jon. You know it's dangerous. Thabo and Isaac are visiting too often.'

'Let's just enjoy the beauty of the Karoo, shall we?' Daddy says, but Mommy's face just grows more angry.

My chest tightens. 'Why can't Thabo and Isaac visit?'

'See what you've started,' says Daddy.

Mommy turns and glares at me. 'Just look at the Karoo, Melissa.'

I push out by bottom lip and stick my head out of the window again.

'Look girls, there's a good view of the Three Sisters now,' says Daddy, as the three rondavel hills come up by the side of us.

Nat and Elsa look up from the *Jackie* magazine they're reading and roll their eyes at each other. 'Turn up the radio, Dad,' says Nat, flicking back her Barbie hair as she leans forward onto the back of Daddy's seat.

Daddy turns up the volume as the stupid Moody Blues sing *Knights in White Satin*. They look at each other and smile and then sing the words of the song. All they ever do now is talk about love and boys. I stare hard at them but they don't even notice.

At last we reach the high iron gates at the entrance to Aunty Yvonne's farm. Daddy stops the Zephyr and gets out and squeaks open the gates, pushing them hard against the high barbed wire fence. He drives us through and then gets out again to close them.

He drives up the long dirt drive lined with umbrella trees on each side. I squint up through the green-laddered leaves and thorns and smile at their round yellow pom-poms of flowers and then push my head out some more to look back and count the red dust devils which are still dancing along behind us. There's a small wind blowing and the red dust tickles my nose. It smells like my paint set.

A big field of mealies whizzes by on the side of us. It looks like a golden sea with all the hundreds of yellow stalks of corn reaching up to the sky like they're praising it. I just want to run and run forever and hide in their arms and stare at them until my eyes turn to gold. The farmhouse appears: it's white with green window shutters and a green roof. It grows bigger and bigger as we get closer.

Daddy parks near the double garage as the door of the house flies open. 'Jonnie, Maria... *Agh*, how good to see you guys!' A fat woman with long black hair piled high on her head like a coil pot runs towards us, waving her hands in the air. Her top's a bright red satin and bounces up and down like a giant strawberry jelly as she runs.

Daddy smiles and gives her a hug. 'Hello there, cuz. Long time, no see.'

She hugs him back and then smacks her lips on both his cheeks. 'It's been far too long, Jonnie. Now where's that Maria?'

Mommy climbs out of the Zephyr. They hug each other and Aunty Yvonne kisses Mommy hard on both cheeks. Mommy smiles and then pats her favourite orange and green dress which is very creased from the car. She frowns and wipes away some of the dust on it and then strokes down some hair that's sticking up from the hug.

'*Agh*, and you, little one, you must be Melissa. *Agh*, no Jonnie, she is too sweet. Come and give Aunty Yvonne a big hug.'

I try not to pull a face as she puts her fat arms around me. As soon as she lets me go, I pull away and move over to Daddy.

'She's much better than a son, hey, Jonnie.'

'Of course.' Daddy laughs and puts his hand on my shoulder.

'Three girls are just fine for me,' says Mommy, giving me a small smile.

Aunty Yvonne turns to Nat and Elsa. '*Agh*, and these two! What beautiful teenagers they are! So petite, just like little dolls, and they've got your lovely, long blonde hair, Maria. Come over here and also give Aunty Yvonne a big hug, girls.'

Elsa and Nat stand stiff like two wattle trees while she hugs them. She strokes Elsa's Barbie hair and then Nat's.

'You look like twins.'

Nat and Elsa say nothing. I frown at them. Why are they so rude? Mommy will be cross. Elsa whispers something to Nat and she giggles.

'Right, folks, in you come. Piet's got some nice cold gin and tonics waiting. We're going to have a braai later with some lovely fresh lamb chops on the fire. This is so exciting. I can't believe you're all here. It's been far too long. That Elsa was only four when I saw you last and Natalie was just three, and you, little

Melissa, was still just a twinkle in your Daddy's eye. Now you're nine years old already. *Agh*, but she's precious, Maria.'

'Yes,' says Mommy, with a faraway look in her eyes.

'Right, folks, let me show you the way to the bedrooms. I've put the three girls in the one room with a camp-bed in the corner for Melissa, and you two are in the guest suite.'

'Sounds lovely, thank you,' says Mommy.

Nat and Elsa walk towards the house. I glare at their backs. They're even wearing the same mini dress, except Nat's is bright green and Elsa's is pink. Why do they have to always have everything the same and look like Barbie dolls, while I have to have the camp bed? Why do they always have the best just because they're bigger? But as we walk deep into the big house, I feel better. It smells of polish and roses. The floor has black tiles and lots of cosy armchairs with roses on the cushions. It feels like a happy house and I'm glad I can stay in it for a week, even if I'm going to be by myself.

'Oh Maria, I can't tell you how good it is to see new faces. I can't believe it's ten years since we saw each other.'

'Yes,' says Mommy, still with that faraway look still in her eyes. 'In the blink of an eye the time's gone.'

Aunty Yvonne gives Mommy a strange look. 'You're quite a deep one on the quiet, hey?'

Mommy blushes and gives a shy laugh. 'It's probably the creeping menopause, I guess. It makes you wonder where it all goes.'

'I know just what you mean, my girl,' says Aunty Yvonne. 'But at least you've had three lovely children.'

Aunty Yvonne gets a sad look in her eyes and Mommy gives a small smile and nods.

# CHAPTER SEVEN

The next day I'm on my own with no-one to play with. I wish we'd brought Eunice, but Daddy said she needed to have a holiday back in the Transkei with her own children. I wander into the lounge and plonk myself down on the soft armchair by the window. I can see Mommy and Aunty Yvonne who are sitting on the porch. I peer at them through the burglar bars and hear them talk.

'I'm scared just now the bloody police are going arrest Jon,' Mommy says. 'He's too involved with that ANC.' Her voice sounds cross.

'*Agh*, you know how he feels about apartheid.' Aunty Yvonne leans across and pats Mommy's arm.

Mommy's face stays pouty, while my throat grows tight. I don't want the police to take Daddy away. Maybe I should talk to him. I wish he would come back now instead of being with Uncle Piet and the stupid sheep again.

'We've got children to think of,' says Mommy. 'He can't risk everything. Things are getting worse in the townships.'

Aunty Yvonne goes quiet for a bit. 'He's an ex-Royal Marine, Maria. It's in his blood. But you're right, I'll try and speak to him.

*Agh*, it's a horrible old world we live in, hey? Give me your glass, I'll pour us another G & T.'

Aunty Yvonne gets up and comes inside. I hide behind the chair as she goes to the trolley and pours some drinks from the big gin bottle. I grin. She hasn't even seen me. I wait until she closes the door before I creep out from behind the chair and sink back into its big rose cushion. I can hear Nat and Elsa giggling from the bedroom. I push my lips together and narrow my eyes. I hate them! Why do I always have to be by myself? Why do they always have to think they're such big deals just because they're older? I grind my teeth together as thoughts stomp like angry buffalos through my head. I wish everything was different. I wish I was a boy; then maybe Mommy would be happy with me? Maybe Nat and Elsa would like a little brother better; maybe they would play more with him?

I hate being the baby and having short hair the colour of a chestnut. It isn't fair. It just isn't fair! I look around the room for something to throw. I get up and pick up the glass ashtray. It feels heavy in my hand. I want to throw it at the window and smash it so that the glass shoots out like the ANC bomb Mommy shouted at Daddy about before we left. Why do I have to be by myself? Even Auntie Yvonne's Great Dane, Tiggy, doesn't want to play with me. She's gone with Dad and that stupid Uncle Piet who doesn't even talk to me.

I drop the ashtray back on the table. The loud thud makes me feel better. I kick the side table and then the trolley. I look at the bottle on the trolley. It seems to make Mommy and Auntie Yvonne happy. I can hear them laughing now. Mommy's not cross any more. Why shouldn't I have some too?

I twist the red lid with fierce fingers. I put my nose on the open top. Ugh, it smells horrible. Maybe it tastes better. It must do if grown-ups like it so much. I pour some into the bottom of a glass. It looks like water. I lift the crystal glass and taste it with the tip of my tongue and pull a face. It's bitter and burns my lips.

I pick up a bottle of coke from the trolley and fizz it in before taking another small sip. That's better. It slides down my throat and makes a small fire in my tummy. I smile as a funny feeling falls to my legs. They feel so heavy. I take a big sip and then another. This is nice; it makes my mind stop thinking. My whole body feels happy now. I grin to myself. It'll be okay. Everything will be okay. This must be why the grownups drink this. It's happy juice. I take another big sip and then fill up my glass with some more. The warm fuzziness fills my whole body and I give a little hiccup. I pour a bit more with some coke. I don't care about anything anymore. I don't care if Nat and Elsa don't want me. I don't care if Mommy wants a boy instead of me. I just feel happy, happy, happy. I start to sing, *Nkosi Sikilele iAfrika*, the song Daddy taught me but that I must only sing in secret at the top of my voice, but I stop after the first line as Nat walks in.

'Lissa, you okay?' She gives me a strange look.

'Yesh, I was jusch singing. I'm fine.'

'What've you had?' Nat comes closer, sniffing the air around me. 'You look sheepish.'

I frown. What's she talking about sheep for?

'Come on… tell me.'

'Noshthing.'

'Yes you have. Don't lie to me. What've you had?' Nat's face scrunches up like an angry toad as she glares down at me.

I turn my eyes towards the trolley and hiccup. Nat goes over and picks up the bottle from the trolley.

'How much have you had? Tell me, it's not funny.'

My head feels light. The room is going round and round like I'm on a merry-go-round. Nat's voice is making my tummy feel funny. 'I'm shorry,' I dribble, 'I'm sho shorry.'

'It's okay,' whispers Nat, putting her arms around me and giving me a hug. It makes me feel warm inside and I hug her back hard. 'You need to sick this up, Liss, before they come in, and then I'll give you lots of water. Come on, get up.'

She helps me out of the armchair and down the passage towards the toilet where she makes me put my fingers down my throat. The horrid gin shoots out of my tummy. It spills onto the toilet and the floor. More and more comes up. It burns. Big sobs come up from my tummy and the tears run down my cheeks.

'I want Daddy,' I wail. 'I want Daddy!'

'What's going on?' Elsa pushes open the toilet door.

'Liss pinched some of Yvonne's gin!'

'What?' Elsa laughs. 'Liss, you little scallywag. Why did you do that?'

'I don'tsh know,' I sob, 'I don'tsh know.'

'I think she was bored,' says Nat.

'Oh, poor Liss. Come here.' Elsa put her arms around my shivering body and gives me a hug. 'You pong. We'd better clean you up.'

Nat and Els help me down the passage, but we stop as Mommy comes towards us. 'What the hell's going on?' Her voice sounds like a snake's.

'Liss is sick,' says Nat, standing in front of me.

'She's just puked,' says Elsa. 'Don't worry, we'll take care of it.'

Mommy's nostrils are moving like a police sniffer dog. 'This child's been drinking. What the hell has she had?'

'I don't know.' Nat shrugs. 'I think she found some gin in the lounge.'

'Well, whose fault is that? Why haven't you and Elsa looked after her?'

'She's not a baby,' says Elsa with a firm jaw. 'We thought she was okay. We've also got our own things to do.'

'You shouldn't be always leaving her out,' says Mommy. 'It's not that much to ask. Take her to the bedroom. I don't want Yvonne seeing her like this. What the hell will she think?'

Mommy's blue eyes feel like knives as she looks at me.

'I want my Daddy. I want my Daddy.'

'Shush, you stupid child! Clean her up and take her to the

room. Give her some black coffee. Oh God, that my life has come to this,' says Mommy. 'My nine-year-old child, drunk. Drunk! What next! Your bloody father! This is all his fault!'

'What's Dad got to do with Lissa getting drunk?' says Elsa, frowning at Mommy. But Mommy just glares and then stomps back down the passage. Nat helps me to the bedroom.

'I'll wipe your face with a warm cloth and then change your clothes. It'll make you feel better,' says Nat. 'Get the cloth and some water for her, Els. I'll close the curtains and then you must try and sleep.'

Elsa comes back with a warm face cloth and some water. 'Do you want me to read a bit of *Wind in the Willows*?' I nod weakly as she wipes my face and makes me glug down a tumbler of water.

She pulls my stinking clothes up over my head and Nat helps me into my shorty pyjamas with the strawberries on. I feel clean as I snuggle down under the cool sheets. Elsa takes the *Wind in the Willows* out of my case. She sits with her legs crossed on the end of my camp bed and opens it. Nat sits next to me, her back resting against the wall. I close my eyes, the nearness of my sisters makes me feel better. My head's not going round so much anymore. I listen as Elsa starts to read the part about Toad and the washerwomen. A laugh bubbles up from my belly. I like the posh way she says Toad's voice.

'You mustn't do that again, little Liss,' says Nat. She strokes my hair. 'Just ask and we'll do something with you.'

I smile and push myself down deeper under the cool covers. The horrible sick feeling in my tummy is getting better. I feel Nat give my hand a squeeze. I take a deep breath. I can smell Nat and Elsa's *Charlie* perfume. I'm going to wear it too when I become a teenager. My body grows heavy.

'It's a bloody generational curse,' says Nat. 'It really is.'

'Maybe,' says Elsa. 'But whatever, the last thing we need in this family is another alcoholic.'

# CHAPTER EIGHT

'So it's always been a self-medication?' Dr Brink peers at me through his glasses.

My mind flashes through my life from the farm to now. I guess I'd still pinched Mom's gin at home because I was lonely and it made me feel better. Perhaps I was also scared deep inside about Dad and the ANC? Everything got so tense after the Soweto riots. Burning petrol and rubber jumps back to my mind. I rub shaky fingers across my forehead. I can't deal with that yet. I swallow and force my mind back to the Karoo farm. 'In my childhood, yes, I guess so.'

'And your adulthood? Has your loneliness remained?'

I shake my head. 'No, I'm close to my sisters now.'

The air in the room grows thick and hot. I blink rapidly and clench my jaw.

'I know it's painful, but if you don't face things, you'll still want to numb yourself with alcohol. It's really important that we peel off the layers.'

The iron stench of blood rises back into my mind. The memory's so strong it clogs my nostrils. Oh God. I retch. I gulp at the hot air and place my head between my trembling hands.

'I don't feel too well, Dr Brink,' I mutter. 'I think I need some air.'

'Here, have some water.' He offers me a glass from the side table. I swallow down a small sip. He clears his throat and stares intently at me. 'We'll stop there for now. It'll get better... just persevere.'

I give a small nod and take another shaky sip of the water. My stomach's alive with caterpillars and my hands feel like water. I don't know if I can deal with this. I don't want to relive that time again. I don't think I can.

Dr Brink's calm tone breaks into my panic. 'You've got an art class next, which should be fun and then there's some free time to relax and chat. I'll see you out.'

I get up in silence and move on shaky legs to the door. It clicks closed and I lean against it, gulping down some air. I've got to keep to the childhood part. The roots must be there. I can't deal with what came later.

I force my mind away from the dark past and walk with a stiff back into the art class. Dad always said I had guts. I mustn't let myself break down in front of everyone. I have to keep a grip.

Helen has gathered the other patients in a semi-circle. She's dressed in a white T-shirt, jeans and a calico apron instead of her nurse's uniform. I pull down the sides of my mouth as my eyes walk over her. She looks at least ten years younger and quite pretty despite her cabbage-patch face. I didn't realise her hair was that long or that blonde.

She looks up and gives me a broad smile. I flick my hair from my face and return the favour with a half-smile. Karlos moves to the side to make room for me to join the circle.

'Thanks,' I whisper as I stand next to him. I set my face and focus on Helen. Alison looks at me with hooded eyes from across the circle. I smile at her but her face remains frozen in intense anxiety. She twists her hands in front of her and jerks her head. There's another patient standing next to her. He's thin with grey-tinged black hair and looks like he's about forty. He's got a peaked face, thin nose and round eyes which dart around the room and flicker up and down in short starts making him look like a rook. We make eye contact. His head jerks back. An adrenalin surge prickles through me. Does he know me? Is he from the medical world? I look away as my cheeks grow hot. My eyes blur. I'm an educated person. How did I let myself get to this?

'Melissa, this is George,' says Helen, pointing to the man. 'He arrived with Nic and Wolf, but wasn't well yesterday, however I'm pleased he's feeling better today.' She beams at him while he looks down and shuffles his feet.

I still feel queasy as I take in the pockmarked face and ravaged addict look. 'Hello, George,' I mumble. He's really quite repulsive. I don't know why I thought he could be a doctor; must've been the grey-tinged hair.

George shuffles his feet and looks down. 'Howzit?' he croaks in a thin, rasping voice.

'We're doing some pottery today,' says Helen, looking at each of us in turn. 'I'll demonstrate and then you can all have a go. Put on your aprons; we're about to get deliciously messy.' She rubs her hands together in glee.

I tie my apron around my waist and glance up at Karlos. He catches my eye and smiles. For some strange reason his presence calms me. It must be his earthiness.

'Okay. You can all come and help yourselves to clay and find a wheel.'

Karlos is the first to grab a wad of the red sticky clay. He squashes it between his palms and then smells it. 'Just like my farm,' he says, before breaking into a wide grin.

I take a wad and press my fingers into it. I hold it up to my nose and sniff. He's right. It smells just like damp earth. If I close my eyes I could be right back in the Karoo.

Karlos breaks some off his clay. 'That's too little... here,' he says, handing me a blob. His hand rests for a second on mine. He moves closer so that our thighs almost touch. I can feel the heat from his body, smell his aftershave, which I think is *Old Spice*, and hear the faint rasp of his breath flowing in and out. A flicker of excitement rises deep in my belly and tingles down my thighs. I keep my face firm as I press my fingers into the clay. I must watch myself. The last thing I need is to start down that road again, but I guess at least it's a distraction from exploring my raw onion layers. I squish my fingers deeper and roll the clay between my palms before breaking some off to form a small ball.

Karlos watches with an amused smile as I pinch it underneath so that four little legs emerge. I push and prod until I've got a head, two small ears and a cotton-wool tail. Karlos lifts his eyebrows appreciatively. I look up and smile. 'I used to make plasticine sheep when I was little; my aunt's got a sheep farm in the Karoo.'

Karlos takes the sheep from me and examines it. 'The Karoo's *boere's* land and this is a very good sheep; you must be a farmer at heart, like me.'

He emphasises the last two words and looks me straight in the eyes. My thighs grow hot. I bite down on my lower lip. Shit, his masculine energy is strong. Karlos is looking down on me with a cheeky expression as if waiting for my answer.

'I had a good holiday there.' I cringe as I say the words. My voice sounds husky; I hope he doesn't read anything into it.

'Nice,' says Karlos. 'All that space... a man can breathe.'

I nod. 'It's got a rugged beauty.' I turn away as my cheeks grow hot. Shit, I mustn't let him see me blushing. What the hell's wrong with me? He's not my usual type. I don't even know why I'm feeling like this.

'If you could all just watch me for a second, please,' says Helen. 'I'll show you how to mould the neck of your pots.'

I purse my lips together and feel a twinge of envy deep in my belly as I watch her whirling hands. She looks like she's completely in control as she spins it around, wetting it periodically and easing it expertly upwards, shaping it only seconds later into a perfect pear. She strokes the clay with wet hands and then picks up a reed and draws a zig-zag pattern around the base and top. 'You might want to look at some of the Ndebele artwork over there.' She points towards some framed photographs of African huts painted in geometrical shapes of bright primary red, yellow and blue. 'There are some paints and brushes as well as stencils over here and afterwards we will glaze them.' She completes her pattern and picks up a finished pot from a side shelf. 'This is what they'll look like when we've painted them. Very bright and cheerful.'

Hattie sneers and begins anxiously rubbing her wad of clay between her hands as if we're in some kind of race.

'Right, now place the clay around your wheel and then hold and shape it as it spins. I'll come around and help.'

'It's okay, I know how to make a pot,' says Hattie, throwing clay on her wheel and starting to spin it. Her hands pat up and down in short slaps and I have to admit, she does look like she knows what she's doing.

I pick up the rest of my clay and squash it around my sheep. I pat the clay around the wheel and begin spinning. Some of the clay splatters off and I have to stop it and start again. I notice Hattie eyeballing me. *Stupid bitch. Why does she always have to be so competitive?* I concentrate with narrow eyes and wrap my hands around the whirling wheel, patting and dabbing it like Helen had done. A surprised smile slides across my face as the long neck of my pot stretches up from its bulbous base. It's taking shape and it's actually looking quite good. I dab my hands with more water and hold them gently around the spinning wheel. Amazingly, I'm making a decent pot and it's the first time I've ever done pottery. Maybe I have a hidden talent I didn't know about, and it's fun.

'Good job,' says Helen. 'Keep your hands where they are and then gently slide some more of the clay up.'

I do as she says and watch my pot settle into a firm pear shape, albeit the long neck's a little phallic looking. Helen pats me on the shoulder and moves over to help Alison who's just standing in front of her wheel with her head down with her knuckles white around the unused wad of clay.

'Let me help you,' says Helen gently, taking the clay from her and rolling it into a ball.

Hattie looks away from her pot for a second and calls to Karlos in a sneering tone. 'You not helping Alison today? I thought you were so pally with her before.'

Karlos tenses and glares from behind his rather lopsided pot. 'I was being kind,' he snaps. 'Helen is helping her this time.'

Hattie snorts. 'Ja, I'm sure you were.' She pauses and narrows her eyes at Karlos. 'You going to help Melissa now?'

'Go fuck yourself,' says Karlos, screwing up his face in a snarl. 'Melissa doesn't need my help.'

'You go fuck yourself,' says Hattie, throwing her nose in the air and turning back to her wheel. 'Your pot's wonky anyways.'

'Just ignore the bitch,' mutters Karlos, throwing some more clay onto his wheel in one angry spurt. His jawline jitters as he clenches his hand around the clay and begins spinning.

'Right, I think let's all just concentrate on our pots and if you need help, call me. I'm going to stay with Alison.' Helen motions to Hattie who has finished spinning. 'That looks great, Hattie. Why don't you do some patterns now and then you can paint and glaze later.'

'Ja, okay, but I want to do some circles, not those black people shapes.'

Helen says nothing in reply, while Hattie stands with a smirk on her face surveying her pot which is perfectly round with a short, fat neck.

'Hey, good pot,' says Wolf, leaving his wheel and sidling up to her. 'I think you must come help me before you do your patterns. Mine keeps falling over.'

Hattie grins. '*Agh*, maybe you should start again. Come, let me show you.' She takes the clay off the wheel and rolls it between her hands. 'Now, you must throw like this.' She slaps the clay onto the spinning wheel and begins to mould it.

'Hey, you're good. Where did you learn to make pots like this?'

'*Agh*, I did a pottery class when I was younger. Me and my friend made much better pots than the kaffir pots.'

Wolf splutters out an ugly laugh, sending saliva spraying out around him. 'Ja, anything will be better than those.'

They both turn and give me a sideways glance. I clench my teeth and concentrate on my spinning wheel. They can both go fuck themselves. I'm not rising to the bait.

'*Agh*, ignore them,' whispers Karlos.

'I am. No point even giving people like that the time of day. They really are the scum of the earth,' I whisper.

'Well said,' says Karlos. He looks back at his wheel. 'I think mine is looking a bit better now.'

I look over at his pot. It's still leaning to the side but has certainly improved. 'Much better,' I say and he puffs up with pride at my praise.

Hattie stands back from Wolf's pot. 'There, you see. Now it looks strong.' She gives him a sideways smile with a glint in her eyes, while Wolf straightens his shoulders and sticks out his bloated stomach. He gives her a blackened smile. 'Ja, much better. Good job, Hattie. I owe you one.'

He gives her a wink. I turn away. He makes me want to vomit, but obviously not Hattie. What a pair!

'*Agh*, no!' Karlos steps back and shakes his head as he looks at his pot which has suddenly fallen over on one the side. 'What's happened?' I move to look at it from the back.

'Don't worry, it looks okay from this angle.' We look at each other and laugh.

'You're too kind.'

'How about mine?' asks Nic, giving me a wink and looking

back at his pot, which he's been working on in silence, although I've caught him twice giving me sideways glances and scowling when I was with Karlos. His effort's not bad with a tall, slim pot and a narrow opening. It's much straighter than Karlos' one.

'Very professional,' I say. 'I'm impressed.'

Nic flicks back his blond fringe and his face breaks out in a wide smile. He looks down at his pot with his hands on his hips like a proud two-year-old who's just been praised by his teacher. 'Thanks. I think I'll attempt a Ndebele pattern now.'

'Good idea,' I say, turning away with a smile. Nic and Karlos look like they've eaten a pot of cream. Both little boys yearning for some positive attention.

Helen has given up on Alison and is now helping George who looks uncomfortable and anxious as she helps him hold the spinning clay. It's obvious neither George nor Alison are enjoying this at all.

'Okay, well done everyone. I want you to now make some patterns and then later on we'll give them a paint. We'll glaze them tomorrow, put them in the kiln and then you can collect them later. They're yours to keep.'

I go over and study the bright geometrical patterns of the Ndebele huts. They are really beautiful. I take up a thin steel rod and try and copy the pattern on the top and base of my pot.

'That looks really good,' says Helen, coming over to inspect. 'Once you paint it, it'll look like a genuine Ndebele work of art.'

'Brilliant. I love their artwork. They have such an innate talent.' I address my words at Hattie who sneers and turns away. I complete the pattern and have to admit that pottery class, with the exception of having Hattie and Wolf around, has been great and at least it took my mind away from the painful onion layers for a while. Perhaps Helen was right. I do feel a bit better today.

## CHAPTER NINE

B ut the feeling doesn't last. The next morning I sit cross-
legged on the marshmallow duvet, my head clasped in my
hands. The literature from the group class lies by my bedside. I
sigh and pick it up. The first page lists the six Ds of depression:
despair, discouragement, disinterest, distress, despondency and
disenchantment, and it goes on to extol the benefits of cognitive
therapy. I know it's the trend at the moment but I feel it's just
more psychobabble. It's obvious that negative emotions have
their roots in your thoughts but it's naïve to think you can retrain
your brain to dwell only on the positive. I'd like to meet one
person who can always control their thoughts? I laugh out loud. I
suppose that thought's negative already.

I throw the page aside. It's not like it's telling me anything
new. I pull a face and move to the window to stare out at the
rolling lawn. I don't know if this is going to work. This
patronising preaching is just irritating me. Why can't they give
the doom and gloom a miss for a while? It's enough to drive me
to drink.

The thought makes me long for a cool glass of Chardonnay or

maybe a double Johnny Walker. My chest tightens. It's just making me feel trapped and claustrophobic. My hands moisten and my breathing grows shallow. I throw my head back and shout up at the ceiling: 'When the fuck is it going to get easier? When?' But instead of an answer, Mom walks back into my mind. *You need to be careful about drinking, Melissa.* She'd said this as I finished one bottle of Chardonnay and opened a new one. *How dare you talk to me about my drinking...* I'd spat back. A sad shadow had flitted across her eyes before she walked away. It's only now I realise she was trying to warn me. Poor Mom. I've really misjudged her and been such a bitch. She needs help as much as I do.

Heaviness covers me. I screw up the pamphlet and throw it in the bin. I don't want to think. I don't want to remember, face my demons, or do some stupid moral inventory. What's done, is done. I can't go back. I look at my watch. Shit, it's time already for the morning session.

As I head down the corridor, I notice Karlos behind me. At least thinking about him takes my mind away from the past. I'm glad I chose to wear my tight Levis this morning. I can hear his breathing behind me and, without even meaning to, I find myself wiggling my bum and can sense his appreciative eyes and smile to myself. No harm in a bit of flirting to distract from all this angst.

'This is on causes of stress and how not to turn to the good old brandy to relax,' he whispers, coming up on the side of me.

'Mine was Johnny Walker.'

'Classy,' says Karlos, looking down at me with a smile. 'But on the serious side, if you need to talk, I'm here.' His fingers brush against mine and linger so that their warmth oozes through. Excitement flutters in my stomach.

'I'm okay... just been a bit of a roller-coaster... that's all,' I stammer.

'It'll get better,' says Karlos. His tone is confident. My body tingles. There's blatant interest in his eyes.

As we enter the room Nic looks at me, then Karlos, and then back at me like he's at a tennis match. There's an empty chair next to him but I ignore it and head to one on the opposite side. I smile to myself as I sense Karlos following behind. He settles down with a satisfied sigh on the chair next to me, his long legs stretched out in front, and he places his arm across the armrest of mine. I keep my face set but a flutter of excitement ripples through me. I lean back in my chair with a nonchalant air and cross my legs. I lean my arm against the side of my chair just millimetres from Karlos. I can feel the heat of his body. Nic is watching with a set expression and hunched shoulders. A twinge of guilt tightens in my belly. I don't like him, but at the same time I must stop being such a bitch. Although I can't deny the lovely warm feeling it gives me from winning the power play for a change. Set one mind game to me; nil to Nic.

Hattie and Wolf are seated next to each other at the end of the room. They've got their heads close together and are whispering and sniggering about something. She's still clad in the same pink tracksuit and probably stinks as much as he does. The sores on his arm are glowing red and crusted over with mercurochrome which I suppose poor Helen had to do for him. We ignore each other.

Dr Brink enters. 'Good morning, everyone.'

'Howzit,' shouts Hattie.

George enters and remains frozen near the doorway, twisting his hands and sweating. His chest pants up and down and he's obviously having a panic attack. Karlos pats the chair next to him with a loud thud. 'Howzit, George. Sit.'

Relief flashes across George's face and he jerks over to Karlos on thin legs. Tick for Karlos. That was a nice thing to do.

'Hello,' I mumble as he sits down, while Nic acknowledges

him with a tight, 'Howzit.' His jawline jerks and he clasps his hands together. Maybe he finds him repulsive too?

'Alison's not well enough to join us today,' says Dr Brink, taking a wad of clipboards out from the cupboard near the door. 'We're going to fill in another form, I'm afraid, but the questions should help,' says Dr Brink. He hands out a clipboard with a form to each of us. 'Don't worry, you don't have to share them with the group if you don't want to.'

My shoulders sag with relief at the no-share option.

Karlos leans over to me. '*Agh*, that's a shame,' he whispers. 'It would be nice for you and me to share.'

I give a low laugh but keep my eyes focused on my clipboard.

'If you could take about ten minutes or so to fill it in, that would be great.'

'*Agh*, I've done this one already?' Hattie sniffs loudly and leans back in her chair with the clipboard resting on her lap. 'Can't I take a smoke break?'

Dr Brink shakes his head. 'For you and Karlos, here's another form which is different, and it's important you do it, please.'

Hattie sniffs. 'Ja, okay… with the fucking H-man I probably need to do two.' She picks up the clipboard and shifts on her chair with her shoulders back and head up as if she's suddenly embarked on some important mission.

Karlos and I exchange a look and raise our eyebrows at each other. She's enough to make me throw up, she really is.

I read through the ten questions. Some more painful layers to peel off, no doubt. The first question asks me to focus on how my mental and physical health was affected by my drinking. Like an impartial observer I think back on my alcoholic days. There were so many times I exercised poor judgement, suffered anxiety, gave into negative thinking, even had the tremors, headaches, a sore body; not to mention the psychological suffering of guilt, shame and the loss of contact with my family and friends. How can I deny that it's more an enemy than a friend? There's nothing 'happy juice' about it: in reality it's evil, or as Nic put it so succinctly, 'fucking dangerous'.

The questions go on to deal with the problems of shame our drinking has caused. The harsh words of that bitch of a neighbour, Cynthia McKenzie, ring again in my ears as she screamed at Mom and Dad, calling them drunks because they'd reversed into her roses. Elsa had been blood-red just like me, so had Nat. I guess it must've affected all three of us. Maybe that's why I drank even at that young age? Maybe it was some twisted way of giving McKenzie the finger, and proving there was nothing wrong with having a bit of happy juice, so how dare she treat Mom and Dad that way?

As I let my mind pace back through the dusty rooms of my past, open its creaking doors and look again into those darkened rooms with their yellowed walls and ceilings, I see myself repeating Mom's mistakes. I'd also woken to a sour room stinking of old wine and sick on more than one occasion, and turned into Miss Superbitch plenty of times, wallowing around in my own special brand of drunken self-pity. What a joke. It's only now, almost as if cataracts have been cut from my eyes, that I can see so clearly that all the things I'd condemned and hated in her as a child, I've actually done myself as an adult. We do follow in our parents' footsteps despite thinking we never will. The generational curse is certainly alive and well in our veins and doing its shitty best to repeat its sordid cycle of history.

As the old alcoholic memories stagger through my mind, a surprising feeling of relief at being at Shaloma eases over me. I smile sardonically. Despite how I felt a few hours ago, I am glad I came to the meeting today. I can't deny, I'm slowly regaining some self-respect and my sobriety has helped wash away some of those chains of shame from the past. Hopefully, the longer I stay sober, the better it will get. Perhaps I should mark off the days somewhere, like a prisoner. They say it takes three weeks to break a habit – I wonder how long it takes to forgive yourself.

'Anyone want to share their thoughts?' says Dr Brink.

Karlos self-consciously clears his throat. 'I will.'

Dr Brink turns to him and nods. 'Thank you, Karlos.'

Karlos leans forward. He rests his elbows on his knees with his hands clasped in front and stares down at the carpet for a few seconds. Silence fills the room as we all turn to him with expectant eyes. He looks slowly round the group and clears his throat again.

'I used to drink two bottles a day, you know... I lost my farm, my family...' He puts his head down and shakes it from side to side before continuing in a low voice, 'My parents, *agh*, they were so ashamed of me. My old father, he is still broken over it.' He pauses and swallows. 'My wife, she died also from too much drink. She was pregnant...' His voice falters on the last word. I stare at him with a hollow pit in my belly as he goes on. '*Agh*, when they died I just drank more and more.' He falls silent and holds his head in his hands before looking up again at each of us in turn. 'I was so bad that I got the DTs... ja, man, I saw these hallucinations of an old woman coming at me to steal my bottle. I was just like some old, mad tramp shouting and screaming at everyone. People were scared of me. *Yslike*, when I think of it now, I can't believe I sank so low.'

Karlos rubs one of his hands back and forward across his cheek before hunching over in his chair, head down and eyes focused on the carpet. I shift in my seat, uncomfortable at his show of emotion. I feel numb inside. Poor guy. He's had such a hard time, even worse than me. Karlos wipes his thick fingers across his eyes and sits back in his chair, lips clamped together, staring straight ahead.

Nic narrows his eyes at him and looks serious while Hattie and Wolf sit with sneers on their faces. I glare at them. How the hell can they sit there and snigger at someone else's pain. How dare they!

Dr Brink's voice breaks into the stiff silence which descends on the room. 'Anyone else want to share?'

No-one answers. My pen scratches as I start filling in my form.

'Well done, everyone. Please keep your forms,' says Dr Brink as we finish. 'They will be useful for you to look back on as you progress through the course.'

I fold mine into a small square and push it inside the pocket of my Levis. Karlos crumples his up and hides it in his fist. Dr Brink pats his shoulder as he gets up.

'Well done,' I whisper as we shuffle out of the door.

'*Agh*, thank you.' Karlos looks down and gives me a wry smile. 'It felt good to talk.'

As we enter the hot sunlight he gives my hand a squeeze. It sends a flash of warmth through my body. My thighs are tingling again. He keeps his hand lingering on mine. It's firm and strong, waves of arousal pulse through me. I bite down on my lower lip. It's a while since I've felt like this. It must be his earthiness, that musty male smell, like the circus lions I'd squatted next to and breathed in as a child. Men like lions are so much more exciting than the Aramis-drenched pretty boys like Mike. No wonder Elsa likes their type.

Karlos seems like a rare breed; a macho man with a heart. I admire him for being so honest about his past. It takes a lot of guts to spill your guts so to speak, especially if you're a guy. I glance out of the corner of my eye at Karlos' broad frame as he strides next to me and think back to the Karoo and Aunty Yvonne's farm. It's a good life. Uncle Piet's similar to Karlos. He's quiet, but a good man and a loyal husband to Aunty Yvonne. They're both so happy and content with their lives. If you're living that type of life with the right person and enough money and security, it's probably as close as you can get to heaven on earth.

We enter the lounge and make our way to the 'business class' couches. A tray of tea with shortbread biscuits is waiting on the table.

'Let's sit,' says Karlos.

'Thanks,' I murmur as I sit down on the first couch. He plonks himself next to me, making the faux-leather squeak. Nic enters and looks at Karlos and me through half-hooded eyes before sitting down on the couch opposite. The room thickens with silence as the raw emotion of the session returns.

Karlos turns to me and clears his throat. 'You okay?'

I give a small laugh and nod. 'I never thought I'd say I'm glad to be here, but I think maybe I'm getting that way.' I surprise myself at my own confession.

Karlos laughs. 'Ja, it's leaving here that's worrying me. That's why I've stayed for a second time, like Hattie and Alison.'

'You're nothing like Hattie or Alison,' the words shoot out before I can stop them. Nic's eyebrows rise and I see his jaw stiffen. 'But I know what you mean. I don't know if it'll really prepare anyone for outside if you leave too soon.' I frown at my use of 'outside'; surely I'm not institutionalised already? Imagine what I'll be like in five weeks' time?

'Don't worry, they'll teach us,' says Nic, with a hard edge to his voice as George and Wolf join us.

I turn and scowl at him.

'It's in the programme,' he says with a patronising smile.

'Well, the test will be if it works. It's easy to write up loads of self-help directions. Not so easy to make them work.'

Wolf plonks himself down next to Nic and pulls a cigarette out from behind his ear and lights it.

'A mate of mine vent to rehab a few years ago,' he says, through a mouthful of foul smoke. 'Still thought he could handle von or two. Not fooking true. You have to stop completely. That's the only vay.'

George remains standing next to the couch, his head forward and his arms stiff by his side. 'I think it's best to attend regular meetings,' he says, pausing after each word as though he's reciting a mantra, but still flicking that awful tongue.

He's really creepy with that awful lizard tongue – he must be on the spectrum and I don't particularly want him as part of our extended group therapy. Karlos gives me a conspiratorial smile as if he senses my irritation.

'I think we all know that, George,' he says, 'probably forever if you need to.'

I burst out laughing at the image of us all, old and grey, still gathering here for our weekly meeting. 'A lifelong sentence; oh, the joys of being an alcoholic, hey!'

'If we don't, we'll all end up dead,' says George in a monotone voice.

'Ah yes,' says Nic, raising his eyebrows in mockery. 'It's a fatal disease. Never forget that.'

'I remember being told there're as many alcoholics as drinks,' I snap. 'I'm sure they don't all lead down the road to death!'

'Oh yes, they do,' says Nic with a smirk. 'We'll be reading about all the stages and eventually if you stay around to reach stage four, the end is shuffling off this mortal coil.'

I clench my jaw and ignore him. They're all pissing me off now. I just want to be alone. 'I'm going to the garden,' I say, looking at my watch. 'There's still twenty minutes before the next session.'

'Can I join you?' says Karlos.

'Yes, if you want,' I say, enjoying the look of distaste on Nic's face.

We step outside onto the grass.

'*Agh*, ignore Nic... he's an arsehole.'

I shrug. 'Yeah, I know. I guess we're bound to have a few personality clashes, but the worrying thing is it's still the first week.'

Karlos laughs. 'Ja, but don't worry, it goes fast, although...' he clears his throat and bends towards me. 'I think I want time to slow down.'

I smile and try to hide the flutter inside. We walk over the grass in silence and I steal a sideways glance at him. He's staring out towards the rich green of the Milkwood trees with a wistful look.

'You've had a hard time. I'm sorry,' I say quietly as we reach the dappled shade.

Karlos pulls a wry face and laughs. 'Ja, you could say that.' He settles himself down and pats the grass next to him. 'But I've survived.'

'It must be bad to get the DTs.'

'It was hell.' He shakes his head in disbelief and clenches his jaw. I watch as his jawline jerks up and down.

The sun is curving downwards and splattering us with puddles of light, but the air is still warm. Karlos picks up a blade of grass and twirls it between his fingers before placing it in his mouth. 'I'm okay now, don't worry,' he says, looking straight in my eyes. 'We have to just take what life throws at us, I guess.'

'Life sure can throw shit at times.'

Karlos laughs. 'Ja, and it's an ace shot.'

He nestles his body down onto the soft grass. I stretch my legs out in front, pressing them deep into the soft blades and lean back on my elbows. I squint up at the patches of clear blue which flicker down at me through the waxy green leaves.

Karlos tilts his head in my direction and I feel his eyes wash over me like a lazy river. I keep my eyes focused on the rich green leaves as the patches of sky merge with them into a turquoise haze. I freeze my mouth in a half-smile while warmth spreads across my stomach. I'm glad I did the full makeover this morning. I know I look and smell good. I smile more broadly as a comfortable cushion of silence nuzzles down between us. I feel like I've known him for ages rather than barely a week. Who'd have thought I'd meet a kindred spirit in a place like this, and who'd have thought in a million years it would be an Afrikaner? He's right; I also want time to slow down. Five more weeks is not very long.

Karlos pushes himself up and leans over towards me. 'So, Liss, tell me about your family. I want to know everything about you.' He smiles as he stresses the 'everything' and let's his eyes streak down my body. 'Are your parents still alive?'

'My Mom is.'

# CHAPTER TEN

My body vibrates as Dad's Hilux bumps over the potholes along the long Transkei road. It's a part of the country I've never visited before and I'm so glad I talked him into letting me come along. I look out the window at the vast, undulating hills dotted with grazing cattle, goats and Xhosa huts which stretch out on either side. A young boy is driving a herd of reluctant cattle in front. I watch as he hits one of the rebel cows with his nimble switch. Funny to think Mandela was once a herd boy here just like him.

The copper sun is beginning to fall and cast crimson shadows over the far horizon. It's such a beautiful area and I should feel at peace looking out at it, yet I still can't shake off the tension of Flagstaff as we'd driven through. The crowd packing the dirt pavements outside the stores in the town's main street had visibly stiffened at the sight of our white faces, turning on us with eyes full of bitterness and hatred. To them we are despised whites; how could they possibly know we are on their side?

'Much further?'

Dad squints ahead and gives a small shrug of his shoulders as we near the signpost for Lusikisiki. 'Fifteen to go.'

'I think this should be the last drop you do.'

Dad keeps his eyes fixed on the long, pot-holed road while the air thickens between us. He shakes his head.

'Dad... please.'

He turns. 'I shouldn't have let you come.' His voice is low and I see his knuckles whiten on the steering wheel.

'It's just that things are getting so much worse.'

'More reason to help.' Dad keeps his eyes fixed on the road.

I sink back against the bench seat and mutter. 'You can help in other ways.'

'Enough, Melissa.' The harshness of his tone cuts through me. I stare out at the rolling green hills as they blur past. A cow rears up from the roadside slope, its flank glistening and its nostrils flared. It lurches towards us.

'Damn!' Dad swerves violently to the side, flinging me into my taut seatbelt. The cow darts skittishly to the side of us with a loud baying.

'Bloody cows.'

We look at each other and laugh. I switch on the radio. The deep harmony of Ladysmith Black Mambazo and Paul Simon singing *Graceland* blares out. The irony of our ungracious land doesn't escape me, but the rhythm soothes my nerves.

A Mazda 323 screeches past and just misses a bus coming towards us on the opposite side. Dad slows and rattles over the dirt verge, sending small stones shooting out and splattering against the back window.

'Bloody fool.'

We come around the bend and straight into chaos about two hundred yards ahead. A crowd are blocking the road. They have their backs to us and are shouting and jostling around something or somebody in front of them. The Mazda 323 and two Hiace taxis are parked on the side.

'Shit, what's happened?'

Dad hits the brakes, slowing the Hilux down to a crawl. 'I

don't know.' He pulls over onto the verge about a hundred yards from the mass of people. 'Stay here,' he says.

'Shouldn't we turn back?'

Dad shakes his head. 'I need to get the papers to Lusikisiki tonight.' He gets out and takes a few steps towards the crowd. I squint at the crowd through the windscreen. It looks like it's adult men. Most of them are holding sticks or knobkerries high in the air and stamping and shouting abuse around whatever's in the front of them.

Their angry shouts fill the air. I swallow. This can't be just an accident. I get out and join Dad in front of the Hi-lux.

Dad frowns at me. 'I told you to stay put.'

I touch his arm. 'I think you should get back in.'

Dad grips the car keys and stares at the crowd with narrow eyes, but says nothing. Suddenly the crowd lets out a roar. I step backwards against the bonnet. Rolling plumes of black smoke and crackling flames have shot up. The men hoist their sticks high into the air as the billowing smoke rolls skyward. *'Bhuhba, bhuhba!'* they shout. Their murderous roar fills the air as the smoke thickens and swirls upward in black mounds, darkening the sky and filling the air with the acrid stench of molten rubber and petrol. Bright fiery flames rise up, and the smoke reels towards us.

'Shit! It's a necklacing. Move!' Dad pushes me hard towards the door of the Hi-lux before running around to the driver's side. 'Hurry!' he shouts.

A scream of raw pain cracks through the noise of the chanting crowd. I clamber into the cab and retch. 'Oh God, how can people do this to someone? How can they?'

Dad shakes his head from side to side. 'He must be an informant... we're trying to stop this... God. We have to stop it.'

Dad and I sit frozen, staring through the windscreen with horror at the chanting crowd as they lift their knees high in a toyi-toying dance. My head is light. Nothing feels real. A gap reveals a flash of the writhing, burning body screaming from the flames of its melting tyre necklace in the centre of the circle. *'Bhuhba, bhuhba; BHUHBA, BHUBA,'* they chant as they dance around him. Their cry grows louder and louder, shrill laughter mingling with the war cry, while others point their knobkerries at the burning, screaming figure and lift their knees in toyi-toying victory.

*'Aieeuuuu... aieeuuu, nceda... NECEDA... AIEEEEEEEE...'* The scream of pain and plea for help from the burning man grows. I put my hands against my ears to shut out its raw agony, but it's no good. It continues to tear into my soul despite the closed doors of the Hi-lux. I bend forward in the cab and clutch at myself and retch again.

When I look up one of the men has turned his head and is looking straight at us. He stops dancing and points: *'Nomlongo!'* he shouts, *'Nomlongo.'* The circle of men turn around. They fix us with hate eyes and hoist their sticks and knobkerries into the air. One man whistles his knobkerrie through the air with its dull, hard ball pointed directly at us; the others follow suit. Their shrill warning screeches in my ears.

*'Nomlongo,'* the man shouts again, *'Ukubalala nomlongo.'*

The crowd roars and begins stomping forward towards us. *'Bhuhba... bhuhba,'* they shout, pointing their waving knobkerries directly at us, *'BHUHBA...BHUHBA.'* The cry grows in intensity. They march closer in an ox-horn formation like a horde of warring Zulu impis.

'Shit!' says Dad. 'Shit...' He shoves the key into the ignition and turns it with trembling fingers. The *'BHUHBA'* cry grows closer. It rings in my ears as I sit, wide-eyed and frozen, staring through the windscreen at the advancing horn of men. The white hatred of their eyes is clearly visible.

'Oh God... oh God!' I can't breathe. My heart pounds against my chest. 'Jesus, help us... please...'

The Hi-lux's engine splutters to life. I draw in a shaky breath as Dad screeches it around in a squealing U-turn. A shower of gravel pummels the side as he puts his foot down flat and heads back with smoking tyres towards Flagstaff.

I turn and look out of the rear window. The men are running after us, their faces frozen in grotesque screams of hate as they point and shake their sticks and knobkerries into the air and shout their curses. '*Ukubalala nomlongo, ukubalala nomlongo.*'

I swallow and turn back to look at the long winding road stretching out in front of us. The hot air of the cab is pressing in around me. My whole body is tingling and my head spins. I feel like I've left my body. This can't be happening, surely it can't be happening? Dad's face is pale. His jaw-line jerks up and down as he glances frequently into the rear-view mirror. He keeps his foot flat as we catapult along the potholed road. I squeeze my eyes tight and pray silently. 'Please, don't let them come after us, please.'

I look back. The Mazda 323 is gaining on us. Two men are hanging out of the passenger windows. Dad looks back at the rear-view mirror and keeps his foot down. A loud explosion shatters our rear window. My ears fill with a loud ringing, and Dad's body jolts forward onto the steering wheel. I stare at him as a bright fountain of blood gushes out of the back of his shattered head like a broken water spout. The Hi-lux shudders back and forth across the road as his foot slides off the accelerator. Dad's breath rattles out of him as the car judders onto the dirt verge before collapsing on its side with a crash.

'Dad, oh God... Dad!' I scream, as I'm flung against the crumpling side.

# CHAPTER ELEVEN

Dad's funeral is the first one I've ever been to even though I'm twenty-three. I stare down at his pale face tucked above the white lace collar of his burial gown. I'm numb as wax; worms have eaten my soul and I can't feel any more. I can't believe he's gone, but there he is. There's the irrefutable evidence. My beautiful Dad is murdered and for some reason fate decreed I would be merely bruised, lying frozen in that wreck until the police came. Why? Why was it Dad's time and not mine? Why did he have to die like that?

My breath comes out in short, sharp, shallow gasps. He'll never hold me, speak to me, and be with me again. He was so wise, so full of love. 'Why God? Why him? All he was trying to do was help people... help this country. Why didn't you protect him, Jesus, why?'

But Jesus doesn't answer.

Nat takes my arm. Elsa puts hers around Mom and so does Aunty Yvonne. We move away from the coffin and sit down heavily on the front pew.

'*Agh*, this is the saddest day ever,' says Aunty Yvonne. She takes out a white hanky and dabs it across both her eyes. Her black hair matches the black mood of her suit. 'You must all be strong. That's what Jon would have wanted. You must mourn, but stay strong.' Aunty Yvonne puts her fat arm around Mom's taut shoulders and gives them a pat. Mom remains still, staring forward, her eyes never leaving Dad's mahogany coffin. Her pain seeps towards me and joins forces with mine.

The robed priest paces solemnly up to the pulpit. He clears his throat.

'We have come this morning to honour and celebrate the life of Jon Kenneth Windsor. Loving husband of Maria and father of Elsa, Natalie and Melissa...'

My ears shut out his voice. I can't listen to this. I can't listen to someone shouting at me that my Dad is dead.

I see myself again, crumpled, dazed and bruised in the broken cab; Dad's heavy, lifeless body dangling down onto me, his hot blood pumping, pumping onto my cheek, dribbling down my neck and arm, and sucking out my soul along its way. Why did I survive? I was there for hours and hours until the police cut me out. So many hours that Dad had grown cold. I shouldn't have survived. I wish they had just left me there until I'd joined him.

The priest finishes and Thabo moves with slow steps to the front. His eyes are red and swollen. He stands silently looking at the coffin, bows and then turns to face us.

'Jon was a man who cared for all South Africans,' he says. His hand clenches and he swallows back the tears. 'He was our brother and our comrade. A man who was prepared to put his own life on the line to help his fellow man to gain equality and freedom. Many of you are unaware of how much he helped the ANC in its fight. You had to be. But now that he is gone I will not stand in fear, but rather proclaim his role and his goodness. It is such an irony that Jon had to die is this way; my spirit reaches out to you all. I am so sorry... so sorry.'

Thabo lowers his head and silence fills the chapel. He keeps his head down for a full minute. He clears his throat again. 'Death is so common in our country, but to lose someone like Jon blows my soul apart. There will never be another like him and I will miss him every day. It was an honour to be his friend.' Thabo bows his head again as his words echo around the chapel.

I'm too numb to cry. If I give in now, I'll never stop. Mom leans forward, her head with its neat, blonde bun held in both her hands and her black-clad, humped back trembling. Aunty Yvonne's arm tightens around her shoulders. '*Sterkte*, Maria,' she whispers, '*Sterkte.*'

Elsa watches Thabo with narrow eyes full of intensity. My stomach lurches. Please don't let her start getting involved. Just now they'd kill her, too. If she'd been there to smell the burning rubber and blood, she'd think differently. Hate just breeds hate; why can't we see that? I glance at the back, half-expecting to see the police. Thabo's publicly declared Dad a comrade; they're sure to hear about it and start watching us. They could even storm in right now and arrest Thabo, it wouldn't surprise me.

A low moan rises up from deep inside me. I hold my head between damp hands as the chapel begins to spin. I swallow and stare down at the carpet. I draw in a long, shaky breath. What did blowing apart Dad's life achieve? He was helping them, for fuck's sake. He was on their side. Are they so blinded by hate that they can't even realise it?

What a country! So much violence and pain: white against black, black against black, it's all human against human at the end of the day, and what for? So families all over this country are devastated by loss that etches deep ravines into their souls forever. How can we ever stop hurtling towards destruction under this façade of a 'state of emergency'? Oh God, how could they have murdered my Dad?

The palms of my hands grow sticky. The organ starts and we stand to sing *The Lord is my Shepherd.*

I stiffen and hope the chapel won't start to spin again. I must stay strong and be dignified. 'Please help me,' I pray. And as we begin to sing about the green pastures and still waters, I think my prayer is answered for a deep womb of peace suddenly surrounds me and numbs the pain. I draw in a deep breath and shudder as salt tears of pain, sorrow and guilt all flow out in one cathartic rush.

# CHAPTER TWELVE

The house oppresses me. Every room hurts. The dark pain is everywhere, eating into my soul. Even Aunty Yvonne senses it. Her face is pale and puffy, her eyes red-rimmed and sunken. I want to run away, far, far from everything. Where's Dad's smell? Why isn't his aftershave lingering in the air? Why aren't his clothes sprawled on the chair in the bedroom? How do you refill a shell when the yolk's been ripped out?

I look out at the fragile blossoms of the frangipani trees. Dad planted them. He loved that delicate fragrance which now reaches up to me but gives little comfort. I shut my mind against the horror of his loss. 'Nomlungu' had been the surprised cry of the Transkei policeman as the crumpled metal gave way and they yanked my still conscious body from the wreckage. They'd left me lying there, covered in Dad's dried blood, on that hard soil verge while they pulled out his limp and broken body. I shut my eyes against the memory of the cheap, black plastic covering. It was my Dad lying under that flapping plastic and I'd never again be able to speak to him, hold his hand, laugh with him or tell him that I loved him. A cry shudders up from deep inside and floods through me.

I look over at the place near the front door where his shoes always sat. It's bare now. Aunty Yvonne must've hidden them. Probably just as well. I felt like I'd been stabbed when I saw them. Strange how seeing someone's shoes when they've gone can hurt so much.

'Maybe you should all come to the Karoo for a bit,' says Aunty Yvonne. 'Or see a counsellor after what you've been through, Lissa.'

I shake my head. 'We're too busy... I can't leave the lab.'

Aunty Yvonne clears her throat as the silence thickens. 'I'm so sorry for your experience, my girl. I'm so sorry.'

I force back my tears and swallow. 'I'll be okay, Yvonne. I'll see someone if I have to.'

'Good girl.' Aunty Yvonne gives my waist a squeeze. 'I'll talk to your Mom, maybe she can come.'

I nod. 'Good idea.'

'Let me open another bottle of Chardonnay. Can I top you up?'

'Please.'

Aunty Yvonne brings me back another full glass, and I gulp it down, letting out a shaky breath as it courses through my veins. The edges of my pain begin to blur.

---

The sun's streaming in my bedroom when I wake. My head's pounding and my mouth is foul. Shit, I'm still fully dressed. I shouldn't have stayed up so late with Yvonne. I can't even remember how many bottles we drank. I roll out of bed and pad through the silent house into the kitchen. The walls spin. I need water. I get a glass, turn on the tap and glug down a pint with a trembling hand. I clench my hand around the glass as Aunty Yvonne comes in, but the trembling persists. I hope she doesn't think I'm a drunk.

Aunty Yvonne puts her arm around me and gives my waist a squeeze. 'I've spoken to your Mom and she's agreed to come back with me for two weeks.' Her voice is measured but with a higher pitch than normal. She's slurring slightly. 'We might go on to Cape Town for a week or so after and then she can fly back to Durban from there.'

I turn with raised eyebrows. 'Good work. I didn't think she'd go.'

'*Agh*, I've good persuasive powers when I need them.'

'I've got such lovely memories of that childhood holiday.'

'Ja, the space is good for your soul,' says Yvonne. 'I wish you could come too, Melissa. I really do.'

I shrug. 'We're understaffed.'

Aunty Yvonne nods. She puts her fat arms around me again and gives me a fierce hug. I try to chase away my pricking tears with memories of those golden fields of mealies and the wide desert spaces of her farm. She's right. The Karoo is so healing. I'd love to breathe in its hot earth again, watch the dancing dust devils, and walk around in sun-drenched sandals. It would be so good to be far away from all this pain. Maybe I'll go when my leave falls due.

---

They wave goodbye the next day with Aunty Yvonne strong and capable behind the wheel of her four-wheel drive.

'It'll be good for Mom. I'm glad she's agreed to go,' says Elsa.

'Yes, it will,' says Nat. She turns to me with earnest eyes. 'You sure you'll be okay on your own? Don't you want to come stay?'

I shrug. 'No, I'll be fine.'

Her blue eyes narrow. 'I'd rather you...'

A knot of irritation lodges in my chest. 'It's okay.' The words spit out. Nat flinches and draws back.

'I'm so sorry,' she whispers, 'I'm so sorry you were there.'

'I'm not,' I snap back. 'I'll never get him back, but at least I was with him to the end.'

Nat's eyes cloud over.

'I'm sorry,' I whisper. 'I know you miss him too.'

'You'll need to see someone,' says Elsa, in a measured tone. 'The trauma won't go away on its own.'

I bite back the urge to swear at her.

'I know that... I just don't want to talk about it yet.'

Elsa clears her throat.

'Liss, you've been drinking too much for a long time... this is just going to make it worse.'

'Please go,' I snap. 'I'll be okay. I just want to be on my own. I'm sure Greg is waiting for you at home.'

The air in the room grows hot. I can read their thoughts. I know they're judging me.

Elsa picks up her handbag. 'I'll phone later. If need be I'll come stay. Greg will be fine on his own.'

'Me too,' says Nat. 'Dave won't mind.'

I turn back to look at my sisters: Nat hunched and tear-stained, and Elsa, stiff, erect, jaw clenched and feet apart. Part of me wants to run into their arms and cry out our communal pain, but the other part can't. They don't understand. They weren't there. It's not the same for them. I shake my head and try to give them a half-smile.

'I promise. I'll be fine. Thank you anyway. I appreciate the offer.'

Nat comes over and gives me a hug, followed by Elsa.

I wait until the security gate clicks closed and sink with weak legs onto the carpet. My tears break free. The sobs wrack through my body and rise in intensity until they merge into one long wail of pain. I let it out until my body's as empty and light as my spilled wine glass.

Later, as the sun falls fast behind the horizon and darkness cloaks the world, panic covers me. Maybe I was stupid. I should've let them stay. I walk my eyes around the darkening lounge. I don't know if I can be alone in this house of shadows. I snap on the light as Dad's blown-open skull fills my mind. I mustn't think about it. I mustn't. I pace into the kitchen and yank open the fridge. I stab in the corkscrew and pull the cork from a half-drunk bottle of Chardonnay. It pops through the silence of the house.

Why is it so eerily quiet in here all of a sudden?

I walk back into the lounge and switch on the television. *The A-Team* blares out. I take a slug of my wine and pull down the sides of my mouth as I watch Mr T aim his gold-ringed knuckles at some baddies' faces. If only it were that easy. I stare unseeing at the screen until the bottle's finished and then go back to the kitchen for a fresh one. I feel better now. My whole body's deliciously warm and my mind's growing numb. I settle on the couch and take a large slurp. This is class wine; fruity, cool and sweet. Aunty Yvonne has good taste, expensive taste. Good for her. She really is my favourite aunt. The knot in my chest has unravelled. My breathing is deep and slow. Thank God. At last I'm safe.

'*gh*, Lissa, that is too terrible. No wonder you drank.' Karlos is sitting up next to me, his eyes still narrowed with the same intense concern they'd shown the whole time I poured out my pain. I squeeze back the tears. My chest feels like I've been stabbed. I've never spoken to anyone fully about Dad's murder, not even Nat or Elsa, and yet with Karlos it felt so natural to just let it all come out. A deep sigh shudders through me. Karlos moves closer, puts his arm around my huddled frame.

'Sometimes you just need time to pass... you're lucky they didn't shoot you, too.'

I give an ironic laugh. 'I guess it wasn't my time.'

Karlos' arm tightens around me and we sit in silence for few minutes. I push my fingers through the short green blades of grass and breathe in their fresh lawn fragrance. The blades tickle softly against my flesh and the dappled sun is warm on my bare head. I close my eyes and let it wash over me. My head is light and my whole body has become weightless. When people say a burden is lifted off your shoulders, it's true. The loss of heaviness which has held me down is tangible. I guess I've carried the burden of Dad's loss so deep inside for the last five years, deeper and more hidden than I ever thought, and now it's as if a big, heavy black lid has been yanked away.

Karlos is still holding me tight. It's so long since I've felt a man hold me like this, a gesture of pure care and concern with nothing sexual. My cheeks warm. I can't believe I've told him all this when we hardly even know each other, and yet it felt so right. I guess when you meet someone you really click with, time is irrelevant. Bonds come from a spiritual connection not a material one.

I draw in a long, slow breath and feel it ease through my veins. I open my eyes and look sideways at Karlos. He's chewing on a blade of grass and staring out into the distance. I glance back up at the house. I'm sure Hattie is spying on us and no doubt sniggering with Wolf, but who cares?

Karlos looks down at me. 'It's bad when the man goes.' He clears his throat. 'Was your mom okay?'

I shrug. 'Not emotionally. She kept the Lieberstein wine factory in business.'

'Agh, no,' says Karlos. He gives a laugh. 'But at least you weren't left poor.' He pauses. 'That happened to my ma. Her father… he was also murdered.'

'Was he? I'm sorry.'

'Agh, it's okay. I never knew him. Some blacks came on the farm and murdered him.' Karlos falls silent. 'They lost the farm. Everything. Ay, my Ma said it was hard. They had to even beg for food.' He pats my thigh. 'But I'm glad that didn't happen to you. Your Dad left you guys alright?'

I nod and give a sad smile. 'Something to be grateful for, I guess.'

'Ja, it helps. He sounds like a good man.' Karlos looks up at the window of the house. 'Shit, Helen's just come in the lounge,' he whispers, drawing his arm away from me. He grunts and gets to his feet. 'We'd better go.'

I grimace. 'We're probably going to be told off.'

'*Agh*, so what,' says Karlos, giving me a wink.

I smile and brush the flecks of grass from my jeans. We exchange a brief conspiratorial look as we make our way back to the lounge. Helen narrows her eyes and gives us a fixed smile as we enter, while Hattie smirks. I keep my back straight with my head held high, return Helen's smile and ignore Hattie. I know this thing with Karlos is all happening a bit too fast, but at the same time, what the hell. It's not every day you meet a kindred spirit and at least it'll make this time in Shaloma palatable, and who knows, maybe even fun?

'You two have a good time?' Hattie's rasping voice drips with sarcasm. She lights up a smoke and holds out the pack to Wolf. He helps himself and lights up. They move over to the bar and stand smirking at us through a pall of grey smoke.

I ignore them and pour two glasses of water. I hand one to Karlos.

'Alison was looking for you,' says Wolf, still smirking.

'What for?' Karlos snaps.

'Aren't you friends?' sneers Hattie.

The door opens. Alison stands framed in the doorway. Her head jerks back when she sees us. A mottled pink rash spreads across her neck and upper chest.

Hattie smirks. 'He was outside with Melissa.'

Alison's mouth twitches and her eyes dart from Karlos to me and back to Karlos. Her hands ball into fists and she turns abruptly, leaving the door slamming behind her.

'*Agh*, shame,' says Hattie. 'I think she's upset.'

'Ja, you broke her heart,' says Wolf.

'Fuck off,' says Karlos. He scrunches up his face and leans towards Hattie. 'Stop stirring. She's just a girl.'

'Ja, and she thought you fancied her.' Hattie looks at me as she spits out the words.

My chest tightens. What a bitch she is, but I'm not going to give her any satisfaction if she thinks she can get to me.

Helen looks down at her watch with a grim face. 'I think you all know the rule on relationships. It's time for exercise class. Why don't you go and change?'

Karlos pulls a face, while Hattie and Wolf remain lolling against the bar and smirking.

'Good idea,' I say. I smile at Karlos and strut past Hattie and Wolf with my head held high. I smirk as I sense her burning eyes following me. Wait till she sees me in my gym gear.

# CHAPTER FOURTEEN

The next five weeks pass as quickly as a fast-setting African sun. Despite my cynicism, the daily session and recitation of the *Twelve Steps* has helped. I don't even mind the group therapy any more. I haven't aired all my dirty linen, but why should I? I've told Karlos everything and he understands without judgement, and that's the only group therapy I need.

An autumn shower has left the air heavy with humidity. I uncross my legs and get up off the bed to push the window open to its widest. I lean my head against the burglar bars and draw in a deep breath. The air is thick with the scent of honeysuckle and the lawn has taken on a beautiful, bright post-rain green. I roll my gaze across it towards the hedge of purple hydrangeas rising proudly in the distance and giggle like a schoolgirl at the memory of the kiss Karlos and I shared behind them yesterday evening. He suggested a different place every evening for our goodnight kiss to stop Hattie and Wolf from surprising us with their spying. I smile to myself. We're one step ahead of them every time, and I'm enjoying the game. I draw in another deep breath of honeysuckle air and briefly close my eyes. All the angst and self-doubt which has haunted my mind for so long has dissipated. At last I like who I am, in fact I even have a glimmer of self-respect. I guess Merry Melissa has defeated the Miserable one. I'm sleeping well, probably from all the art therapy and exercise, but best of all the craving for alcohol has gone. I haven't thought about a drink for at least a month. In fact just the thought of a glass of Chardonnay or Johnny Walker makes me feel queasy. I don't need it any more. I don't want to ever feel out of control like that again. I really don't.

I look down at my watch. It's nearly time for the late afternoon session. I wonder if Karlos will be in the lounge? Ever since I shared that terrible time of losing Dad, we've experienced a new kind of closeness. I've never felt so at ease with a man. I smile as I relive our daily conspiratorial glances and little touches, as well as our stolen kisses. At least tomorrow we'll be free to show our love to the world and no-one will be able to say anything against it. We just need to arrange where to meet. A tiny drop of fear trickles through me. Dr Brink's agreed I'm okay to go; I just hope he'll do the same for Karlos. I shake the fear away like an unwelcome fly. Of course he will. He's done a second round of treatment, so why wouldn't he?

I touch up my make-up before heading out at a fast pace to the lounge. I push open the door and click my tongue. Hattie's sitting on a chair near the bar nursing a glass of Coke with Alison as the only other occupant. Surprisingly she's sitting hunched in a chair near the bar instead of being hidden in her usual corner. The air is thick with stale smoke. Hattie stares at me through the haze with stony eyes. I blink away from her and head for the bay window and settle in the armchair facing away from her and Alison. I grimace as I feel her eyes burning into the back of my head. At least I've only got one more day of putting up with that pink monstrosity and the revolting Wolf.

The door creaks and I turn to see Karlos. He strides straight towards me and squats down by the side of my armchair. 'It's okay,' he says, breaking out into a big grin. 'I'm leaving tomorrow too.'

'Great,' I whisper, ' I was hoping it would be okay.'

Karlos nods. 'Ja, it was just a formality really. He can see I'm good now.' He moves his head a little closer to mine and whispers, 'Thanks to you.'

'I'm sure you would've made progress anyway,' I whisper back, but my stomach warms with his praise.

He smiles and gives his head a shake. 'I don't think so.'

The scrape of a bar stool breaks through the air and we both look over at Hattie as she gets up and stubs out her cigarette.

'Meet me outside after the session so we can arrange what to do when we're out. Nic and Wolf are also being discharged tomorrow, Hattie too. I don't want them around with us. I need to see you alone,' whispers Karlos quickly, as Hattie flicks back her exploding pink hair and heads in our direction. She throws us a knowing look as she saunters past.

I wait until she's out the door before asking, 'Of course. Where?'

'By the Milkwood tree,' says Karlos, giving my hand a squeeze.

Leather squeaks as Alison squirms in her armchair and draws her knees up to her chest, hugging them with thin arms. She rests her chin on her upturned knees and peers from Karlos to me with narrow eyes. Karlos and I raise our eyebrows at each other.

'She's a strange one,' I whisper, 'but I feel sorry for her. Dr Brink has ruled she needs a third round of treatment.'

'Ja, probably George, too,' says Karlos, giving Alison an irritated glance. 'I'm sick of her staring at us…'

'Me too, but I think it's because she fancies you…'

'*Agh*, she just irritates me.'

'I can see that.'

The door opens and Karlos quickly straightens and steps away from me. Helen stands framed in the doorway.

'You okay you two? I think Dr Brink's waiting...'

'Just going, Helen,' says Karlos, moving towards the door.

'This is your last afternoon session, make the most of it,' she says as he saunters past. Helen looks at me with set eyes while I move in silence for the door, trying to avoid her gaze. It's obvious she suspects something, but who cares. They can stick their 'no relationship rule' and all the other ones that go with it tomorrow. One more session then... freedom. These last six weeks have certainly been quite a ride.

'These are hand-outs which will help you keep on the sober track. The first danger sign is a dip in confidence. If you don't nip that, it will trigger the pattern of denial, followed by over-confidence in your sobriety and judging of others. It's vital you keep up regular visits to us,' says Dr Brink, as we sit dutifully in our circle around him.

I stare down at the thirty-seven points. Thirty-six is *controlled drinking* which leads to uncontrolled drinking because for us alcoholics, of course, there's no such thing. I grimace. So much for my freedom. It really is a lifelong sentence.

'This is depressing,' I whisper to Karlos.

'Ja, but at least we're in it together. We'll keep each other strong.'

I smile. A delicious warmth spreads through my body. He's right. At least we understand each other. We've both been in the pit of shame; we don't need to feel frightened as long as we're together.

'Ultimately, it's up to you.' Dr Brink looks at each of us in turn. 'It's your journey and your choice. You've all learned where the path of substance abuse leads to. For your own sakes, every day, every minute if you have to, you must urge yourself to stay sober if you want a future.'

The room falls silent. Hattie's pink head is downcast, her knuckles white around the hand-out. For the first time I feel pity for her. Alcohol's a hard thing to beat, but heroin must be hell. Alison has made the session but remains still and silent in her chair; her face moth-white. Poor girl, I wonder if she'll ever be ready to leave? She glares at me constantly, but I don't take offence. Nic's jaw is clenched, while Wolf's brow is pulled together in an angry frown. I guess none of us wants to hear this eternal truth.

'Lean on your Higher Power; don't try and do it on your own strength.' Dr Brink's voice is soft with compassion. 'This is a chart which will show you how you can start building up a problem again if you're not careful. It outlines danger signs to look out for. Put it on your fridge, your cupboard, anywhere you'll see it often, so you don't forget.'

I swallow. Oh the joys! No doubt the craving demon is going to be back to attack me. This is going to be a long, hard road.

Wolf throws his head back and lets out a dry laugh. 'At least this is better than that Addington rehab. They treated me for Valium addiction and then gave me a fooking Valium prescription when I left. That stuff is bad. It drove me *mal*.'

'Mad fuckers,' says Nic.

Dr Brink lifts his eyebrows, but says nothing.

'Ja, it's like them giving you Methadone to get off the fucking H-man. It's doesn't help. You're still an addict; can't they see that?' She pulls back her top lip like a snarling pit-bull. 'There's only one way – and that's to stay the fuck away. It's the same with the booze, man.'

Dr Brink nods. 'Yes, I'm afraid it is and that's why you do need to keep an eye on your chart. Now, I want you to fill in this questionnaire. It's got some scenarios you might encounter on the outside and how to combat them. Once you've filled them in you can go. Keep them with you so you can read through them anytime you feel the temptation's getting too much.' He pauses and looks at us with eyes filled with kindness.

'Well, Hattie at last you're ready for discharge and you too, Karlos. Well done both of you.'

Hattie smirks with the praise, while Karlos gives a small nod of appreciation.

'Ja, I've told the H-man to fuck off at last.' Hattie lets out a crude laugh and winks at Wolf.

'Ja, well done you,' says Wolf, putting his rancid arm around her.

'Yes, Hattie, but the test is now to keep him away, and the best way for that is to make sure you attend the weekly classes.' He surveys the rest of us with a serious expression. 'That applies to all of you. I'm very proud of each one of you and it's just going to be an *au revoir* from me rather than a goodbye. I'll look forward to seeing you all every Tuesday evening 7.30 pm sharp.' He smiles and turns to George and Alison. 'Don't worry you two, I'm sure before you know it you'll also be ready to leave. We've got some new patients arriving later, but I think we'll keep you two together on a separate course so that you can both get more intensive treatment.'

Alison stares at him, but George shuffles his feet and mumbles, 'Thank you.'

Dr Brink walks over to George and bends down. 'Have you had your Trithapon this morning?' he whispers. 'You look a little agitated.' George nods and his cheeks turn pink.

I read through the questionnaire and can't help scowling. It makes us sound like outsiders, as if the world out there is so different from us. People out there drink just as much – they've just been lucky enough not to lose control, that's all.

I fill it in quickly with my head full of Karlos, rather than the questions, and tuck it into my pocket before standing up and giving Dr Brink a smile. 'Thank you, Dr Brink, I appreciate all your help.'

'My pleasure. I'm thrilled with how much progress you've made, Melissa. I'm sure you'll cope well as long as you keep to the weekly classes.'

I suppress my irritation at the continual reminder. 'Of course,' I mutter. 'I think I'll just go sit in the garden for a bit before supper.'

'Good idea,' says Dr Brink. 'It's a lovely evening.'

Karlos glances up as I walk past. 'See you just now,' he whispers, scribbling away at the paper without even looking at it. I nod conspiratorially.

I slip off my sandals as soon as I reach the garden to let the grass creep up deliciously between my toes. I smile as it tickles and head for the shade to lie back on the soft, warm grass. I close my eyes while the last bit of sun dances with the clouds, sending a pattern of light, dark, light, dark, light again across my closed eyelids – like my life. As I take in a deep breath the air passes easily into my belly, not like before when the only way I could breathe was in short, shallow pants which left me in a state of perpetual tension.

My body's alive with sexual craving as I wait for Karlos. I can't stop thinking about him, dreaming about him, wanting to rip his clothes off. I bet he's really good in bed, takes control, knows just how to please, unlike Mike who was always more concerned with pleasing himself and showing off his pathetic phallic trophy, which was nothing to write home about. What a relief to have met someone decent at long last, someone who really likes me for me, who's looked into the shame of my soul and still wanted me because he'd also been there, done it, bought the million T-shirts. That's where Helen and Dr Brink are wrong. You do need someone who's also hit rock-bottom; no-one else can understand. I breathe in the memory of Karlos' musty scent strong in my nose.

The scent grows stronger. My eyes flick open. Karlos eases down next to me and bends his head. 'Liss, I'm not going to play games,' he whispers hoarsely. 'I really need to be with you when we leave.' His body is taut and his chest moves up and down with short breaths.

I press my lips together to try and control the smile of triumph which wants to march across my face. I knew it was a given we'd see each other, but I've been waiting for him to verbalise it. 'I want to see you too. Where're you going to stay?'

'Phew,' says Karlos, wiping a hand down his cheek, 'I was hoping you'd say that.' He shrugs his shoulders. '*Agh*, I don't have a place yet, but it's alright. I'll probably find a room somewhere. I just need to see you, that's all.'

I place my hand on his arm and feel him shiver. I love the fact he's so open and honest. He's right. Why waste time? It's not everyone who's lucky enough to meet someone they just know is right. Why play games? I keep my hand resting on his arm and give it a small squeeze. 'You could stay with me? I've got plenty of room in my place.'

He looks at me with narrow, glittering eyes. 'You sure?'

I nod. 'Of course. I've got a three-bedroomed house.'

'Thank you,' says Karlos, letting out a sigh of relief. 'I won't expect to stay for nothing. I'll help pay the rent.'

I give him a smile. 'It's okay. I own it, courtesy of my Dad.'

'You sure?'

I laugh. 'Of course I'm sure.' I take his hand and give it a squeeze. 'It's okay. I've got enough money for both of us for a while. I know you've had a hard time...'

'I'll try and help. I promise...'

I place my fingers against his lips. 'I told you, it's okay.'

'*Ahrrh*,' he groans, taking both my hands in his and squeezing them so I flinch. 'We must go in otherwise I will take you right here in the hydrangeas.'

I giggle like a naughty schoolgirl and take my hands away to smooth down my hair and pick out the bits of grass which have lodged in it. 'Better not go in together. You go in first.'

Karlos winks at me and gets up to stride nonchalantly back towards the building with his hands in his pockets. I look down at my watch and give him a minute before stepping lightly back across the grass. It feels as if I'm walking on marshmallows.

Nic gets up as I enter the lounge. 'Lissa, can I talk to you?'

'Sure.' I shrug my shoulders.

Nic looks down at the pine wood floor. 'I don't want to interfere and I know I've irritated you somewhat…' He clears his throat. I see a faint pink blush wash over him like sudden rosacea, highlighting the thin network of capillaries on his cheeks. 'I just wanted to say I really don't think it's a good idea for you to get involved with Karlos.'

Anger tightens my chest. 'It's none of your business,' I snap.

'I'm sorry. It's just… it's going to be hard out there.'

'What's your case? Are you trying to say Karlos doesn't have genuine feelings for me? Actually, if you must know he's the most genuine person I've met; all the other men in my life have been fickle, good-looking bastards like you who've just fucked me over.' I vomit out the words in a voice full of bile and bitterness, but I don't care. He's got no right to try and keep me and Karlos apart.

Nic retreats as if from a spitting cobra. 'I'm sorry that's what you think and I'm sorry you've been hurt. I just wanted to say be careful.' He pauses and stares at me for a few seconds before muttering, 'I wish you all the luck in the world.'

He turns abruptly and exits the room with heavy steps. I stand tense and panting as the door bangs shut behind him. Maybe that was a bit harsh of me. He looked really hurt. I must sound like a complete bitch. Perhaps I've misjudged him? Still, who's he to judge Karlos? He doesn't even really know him. Karlos is a far better judge of character than him.

# CHAPTER FIFTEEN

I click my case closed with a mixture of fear and excitement. Shaloma has given me hope, just like its slogan says. I shake my head and let out a wry laugh. It's only been six weeks, but no more drunken caterpillar for me.

I give the rosy room a final sweep and pick up my suitcase.

Out in reception, Karlos is waiting. Helen gives me a wide smile but can't hide the quizzical gaze in her eyes as she looks from me to Karlos. 'You all set?'

I nod. 'We're giving Karlos a lift.' I flinch at the high pitch of my voice.

Helen holds my gaze for a second in a disbelieving smile before handing me a leaflet. 'These are our meeting times: every Tuesday at 7.30pm, but there are also others you can join if the need is urgent. It's really important for you both to attend regularly.'

'*Agh*, thanks. I'll be there. You too hey, Liss?'

'Of course.' I take the leaflet with a frown of irritation. I don't need any reminders to spoil the moment. I'm quite aware it's a lifelong sentence; they've told us that often enough.

Elsa pulls up outside, and I shake Helen's hand. 'Thank you for everything. I'll see you Tuesday.'

Elsa runs up the stairs to hug me, followed by Nat. She takes my suitcase and waves her thanks to Helen. They both look alive with excitement and I'm so grateful to them for being here. I follow them to Elsa's BMW. It's all moving so fast for introductions but Karlos stays behind me. Both Nat and Elsa turn and look at him with frowns etched across their faces.

'This is Karlos. He's coming to stay with me for a bit.'

Nat gives me a startled deer look and utters a surprised, 'Oh?' Elsa continues to frown.

Karlos smiles and offers them both his hand to shake, but it's all received curtly. He looks uncomfortable and I feel a ripple of anger in my belly. One minute we're all happy and excited, and now they're back in their protective mommy mode and being rude. Why do they still have this ridiculous need to look after me? They've got Greg and Dave and their cosy little homes so why the hell can't I have someone, and why the fuck do I need their approval?

I glare at Elsa and turn to Karlos. 'Put your case in the boot.'

'Ja, of course. Let me put Lissa's in first.' He takes the case from Elsa with a smile which she doesn't return and puts it in the boot before edging his next to it. We climb into the car in silence, and I bite my tongue to stop from cursing them for spoiling the joy of this moment.

We speed down the leafy driveway and along Musgrove Road with its white mansions before joining the busy crush of cars and belching diesel buses along Umgeni Road. I stare out the window at the many NP, ANC and DP election posters clumped together on the lamp-posts. A smattering of ACDP posters sit on some. There's a tangible smell of excitement in the air.

'Election's here,' says Nat, turning back to me with a wide smile. 'It doesn't seem possible, hey?'

I raise my eyebrows in agreement and glance at Karlos.

'It feels like we've been on another planet,' he says. 'I'd forgotten all this was happening.'

'Me too,' I say with a twinge of guilt. Given my family's fight against apartheid it should've stayed foremost in my mind, but it didn't. How could it really? I guess we were shut off from the outside for a while, but I can't deny how good it felt. Karlos' leg moves closer to me and presses into mine. He intertwines his fingers around my hand and gives it a tight squeeze. My whole body tingles. I feel like a silly schoolgirl holding hands with her first love in the back of the car. It's so intense, so beautiful, so erotic even. I return the squeeze and smile at him. I feel so lucky to be alive. There's a deliciously sober thought.

———

That night it's everything I thought it would be. Karlos is snoring softly next to me, his tanned body proud and naked in the warm air. We've left the fan on and its tickety-tockety rhythm is rocking me deliciously towards sleep. I draw in a deep breath and exhale slowly. Mike and I shared a lot of passionate panting and writhing but somehow it always left me feeling dirty. I guess it was because deep inside I knew he was using me. I look back at Karlos' naked body and relive the passion of our love-making.

# CHAPTER SIXTEEN

I wake early as election day dawns. The calendar has a bright red circle surrounding the 17th April. It's hard to believe that all South Africans are going to be making that historic little black cross together. Unbelievably, South Africa has done it! Apartheid's coffin will be nailed for good. 'Thank you, Lord, and thank you, Mandela,' I whisper, as I think back to the fragile government of national unity which has been teetering along for the past four years. We very nearly didn't make it. I don't blame Mandela for losing his patience. Just as well Roelf and Cyril found common ground in fly-fishing of all things. We are a mad country. It is a miracle we've got here at all.

The curtain flutters, ushering in the early morning air smelling like newly mown grass. Excitement tingles through me. I bet the whole country's already awake, well, most of it anyway except for the AWB racist bastards who probably find this end of white domination their worst nightmare. Who would have thought it even as little as four years ago? No doubt they'll try to stage another great trek into the great beyond, but I don't think there's anywhere left for them to run. I feel deliciously smug at the thought that justice has come around at last. At least what Dad worked for is coming to fruition.

I remember him and Thabo huddled over a pile of papers and envelopes the night before we left for the Transkei. It's only five years ago, but hope of change seemed impossible then. *'Things are getting worse in the townships,'* Thabo had said, his face as furrowed as an eroded field. Dad's posture had mirrored his. *'Winnie's not helping...'* he'd said, and Thabo had looked just as broken as he agreed, *'Eitch, to kill a child like that.'* He was right. How could Winnie be behind that murder of little Stompie? Her radicalisation must have broken Mandela's heart.

A brooding silence oozed through the room and the air had grown heavy. I can still see Dad so clearly, shuffling through the wad of papers before taking out a pile and placing them in a brown envelope. *'I'll get these to the Lusikisiki cell first thing tomorrow. This violence must end,'* he'd said, little realising that the next day his own life would be ended by that terrible violence. *'Yebo,'* Thabo had replied, clearing his throat and pushing himself up from the couch like someone decades older than his fifty-three years. A mix of fear and heaviness had lodged itself in my spirit. I feared that the police must be getting suspicious of Dad's frequent trips to the Transkei and that they'd be sure to be watching us, especially since the recent explosion at Natal Command. I felt deep inside that all this suffering, blood and violence would destroy us all in the end. And it has. It's destroyed so many, including Dad.

I rub my hand across my forehead and blink my eyes to chase away the threatening tears. I'm sure Dad's watching us from heaven and smiling down on this. He must be so proud to see the newspaper headlines proclaiming *'Vote the Beloved Country'* rather than cry for it. I think back to Alan Paton's book which ate into my soul when I'd read it as a fifteen-year-old schoolgirl. Now at last the green rolling hills he wrote about will be able to stand proud in all their glory. Shame he's also not around anymore to see it.

I shake my head to chase away the bitter memories and pick up my white satin gown from its untidy position on the chair. This is a day of celebration and we must go forward and not dwell on the past. I slip my feet into my matching satin slippers and pad over to the window and draw back the curtains to let in a slither of pale, early morning light. A light breeze ruffles my hair and I straighten and draw in a deep breath of the early morning freshness. I can't remember a time when I felt as together as this, as strong inside and in control, but above all, so happy. I've been out of rehab a whole month without even the slightest craving and without any need for the silly weekly meetings. I really have defeated the bastard demon at last.

My thoughts of Shaloma jump to the memory of seeing Nic in the parking lot at La Lucia Mall, then again at the beachfront last week. I frown and shake away the feeling of unease as his face flickers through my mind. I swear it was also him yesterday when I went into the chemist – he always seems to be lurking somewhere in the background, watching us. It can't be coincidence that we're always in the same places. I bite my lip. Maybe I should tell Karlos he's stalking me. He'll probably smash his teeth in. He's a farmer with the muscles to prove it. He knows how to throw a punch, and Nic's nothing compared to tackling a powerful cow or even a sheep for that matter. Karlos would floor him before he knew what hit him. I can't help the smile that slides across my face; two powerful kudu bulls locking horns and pushing and grunting to the death over me for a change, not Elsa; it does feel good.

I press my head against the burglar bars and stare up at the slowly lighting sky. It's still very early and the full moon surrounded by a smattering of fading stars is still visible. The lower horizon is streaked with pink and orange and looks so beautiful and full of promise. A fitting start to this historic day.

I smile and turn to look at the sleeping figure of Karlos snoring under the covers. Nat's harassed voice invades my peaceful thoughts. *'It's too soon,'* she'd said. *'When it's right, it's right,'* I'd answered, straightening my back and looking directly at her. *'I've never been so sure of anything in my life.'*

*'Liss, you don't know him that well. Perhaps you need someone who hasn't had a drinking problem?'* I'd become angry and shaken my head. *'No, that's where you're wrong. You need someone who understands completely. We can help each other.'*

*'Can't he find somewhere else to stay now?'* Nat had asked with that stupid frown on her face. My anger had increased as I spat the words out. *'No. He'd have to board somewhere and I'm not having that. I'm not a child. Let it be.'* But she hadn't, and Elsa had called the same day, also anxious and going on about the quick affair.

I click my tongue at the memory. I feel like a rebellious teenager fighting with Mom. What is it with my sisters and their protectiveness? Why can't they just trust my judgement?

I leave Karlos snoring, unlock the security gate and pad outside. I kick off my slippers and let my feet sink deep into the damp grass. The early morning dew is cold against my bare feet, but I don't mind. I want to feel the grass between my toes and the soft soil under my feet. It makes me feel so grounded. The haunting call of a lone hornbill fills the early morning air mixed with the croak of waking frogs. God must be happy with us. *'If you humble yourselves and pray,'* he promises, *'I will heal your land.'* And he has. The miracle we all never thought would come, has actually happened. My body tingles with excitement. I'll make coffee and wake Karlos. There'll be a massive queue at the voting station. It'll be better if we get there early.

---

As I stand next to Karlos, pressed in among the squirming snake of bodies waiting at the Red Hill polling station, my head grows light. I turn and look up and then down the packed queue with all of us, African, Indian, Coloured and Whites, pressed up against each other. There must be thousands of people here, all looking excited, triumphant and happy in the hot morning air. An old African man with grey coiled hair catches my eyes. He's clutching his ID book in both hands. I'm sure he woke long before the sun had even thought of rising and quite possibly walked miles to get here. He's wearing a white open-necked shirt, brown trousers and highly polished black shoes and looks so smart. His brown eyes are serene and bear the deep wisdom of age. He holds up his book at me and smiles. I feel a sob rise in my throat as I hold up mine in return and for a moment it feels like our souls have left our bodies and touched each other. There's such a sense of joy of solidarity between us. There's no resentment or cynicism in his face. He's another Mandela with that incredible depth of forgiveness or *Ubuntu* which cannot be of human origin. I think of Mandela's words, *'Forgiveness frees the soul.'* It's so true and it's been a hard lesson for me to forgive myself. I pray that despite the awful suffering of the past it will happen. If they don't forgive us this new dawn will be short and bloody. The PAC slogan of, *'One settler, one bullet'* reverberates through my mind. This new foundation is very fragile. There're a lot who really hate us, and I can't say I blame them. I shake my head. No, I must stay positive, especially on a day like this. I close my eyes and utter a silent prayer. 'Please let them listen to Mandela... please.' If he can forgive after twenty-seven years on Robben Island, let's just hope they can too.

'Iconic day.' I turn to see Nic standing beside us.

My mouth drops open.

Nic shuffles his feet and clears his throat. A faint blush colours his cheeks. 'I... just saw you guys. I'm up there.' He points to the front of the queue. 'I asked someone to keep my place so I could say "Howzit".' His blush deepens and he looks directly at me. 'I know this is a special day for you, Lissa... I just wanted to say... enjoy.'

I frown at him. 'Thanks.' I give a curt nod. 'It's special for a lot of us, especially Africans.'

'No more racist addiction for Mandela's new South Africa,' says Nic, with a sardonic lift of his eyebrows. 'Let's hope he wins.'

Karlos gives a snort. '*Agh*, of course he'll win.'

Nic gives a nod and then narrows his eyes at us. 'Ja, I know. I was only joking.' He shoves his hands in his pockets and clears his throat again. 'You guys have missed the meetings.'

I shrug. 'I don't need them anymore.'

Nic purses his lips. His eyes flicker from me to Karlos and back at me. 'Well, good for you.' He keeps his eyes on me for a few seconds more before pushing out his hand towards me. 'Can I shake and wish you luck?'

I offer him a limp hand. 'Good luck,' I murmur.

His hand is damp and I can feel it tremble against mine. He lets go and holds his hand out to Karlos who gives it a curt shake. Nic's cheeks redden and he turns abruptly away and strides back up the queue.

I wipe my hand against my Levis. 'He's creeping me out. I'm sure I keep seeing him.'

Karlos tenses and looks down at me with a frown. 'Think he's following us?'

I shrug my shoulders. 'I don't know. Maybe I'm just paranoid, but I'm sure I've seen him at least three times in different places. Unless it's his evil twin.'

Karlos clenches his jaw and looks back up the queue to where Nic has squeezed himself in. 'Why didn't you tell me?' He scowls down at me.

'I wasn't sure it was him,' I stutter.

'Don't do it again,' says Karlos in a fierce voice. He closes his eyes for a second and then puts his arm around my shoulders. 'If you think you see him again, tell me straightaway.' I nod but his anger ignites a queasiness in my stomach. Damn Nic. Why the hell did he have to spoil the moment.

But as I hand across my ID book and place my hand out for its ultra-violet stamp all traces of negativity disappear. When it's my turn, I walk straight-backed with firm steps towards the voting box and close the short black curtain behind me. I scan my eyes down the eleven political parties displayed on the voting slip and pick up the short stubby pencil provided. As I twirl it between my fingers, the memory of apartheid's bizarre pencil test creeps back into my mind. Who'd have thought something so innocuous as a pencil could tear a family apart, but it did. I remember Dad's anger as he told us about Thabo's sister being taken away from the family because she'd failed the test in court.

'How can they use a pencil to test if she's white,' Elsa had demanded, her eyebrows drawn angrily together.

Dad had shaken his head for a few seconds. 'Words fail me,' he'd said. 'Words fail me.'

'Poor Thabo,' I whispered, still unable to believe that just because the pencil that the judge had put in her hair hadn't stuck, he'd said she must be white and he'd given her to a white family to look after. My mind had jumped to the new girl with thick, black curly hair, who'd just joined our class. I was sure a pencil would stick in her hair. I'd looked up at Dad while my young mind spun round and round, trying to make sense of it all. 'Does it mean anyone with curly hair is coloured?'

Dad had shaken his head and looked down at me while sad shadows played across his eyes. 'No, Lissakins. It was only because Thabo's mother is coloured.'

'We must be the laughing stock of the whole bloody world,' said Mommy, as she stomped angrily into the kitchen to get more Lierberstein.

'Not any more, thank goodness,' I whisper, as I look back down at the voting sheet and carve my charcoal cross deep into the white paper. 'Viva Mandela at last. Viva!'

# CHAPTER SEVENTEEN

A breeze rustles the closely drawn dusty-pink curtains allowing yellow slithers of early morning sun to shiver through the wrought-iron burglar bars and penetrate the darkness. I blink against their brightness.

I push a limp strand of hair away from my cheek. My staccato breath breaks through the silence. I put my hand up to still the intense thudding which drums inside my head. My mouth is desert dry. I swallow hard. What's happened? Why do I feel like this? I try to push aside the obvious answer. I've no recollection of touching any, but deep inside I know that doesn't mean anything.

Maybe Karlos and I were celebrating the miracle of the new South Africa? Maybe I caved in and had a drink? But where did I get it from? I don't remember buying any. Fuck, I can't remember anything. I must've had a lot. I push myself up, hiding from the bloated face and glassy eyes which taunt me from my dressing-table mirror. I smooth down my ruffled hair. Did I really get drunk? The question's rhetorical; of course I had. No-one feels like this and can't remember, unless they'd got paralytic!

'Karlos... Karlos?'

The empty house mocks me with its silence. I try again. This isn't funny. 'Karlos... where are you?'

Still nothing! My heart thuds in my ears. What if he's walked out because I'd become ugly; all slackened jowls and bitchiness. I hadn't been drunk since before rehab. He's never even seen me drunk. He's probably repulsed!

'Never again,' I whisper. 'Please God, never again.' I shudder out a sigh as I see Karlos' brown cable-knit sweater and khaki pants tossed across the rocking chair. His pair of veldskoens sit neatly together under the chair. Thank God! He must be here somewhere. I'm being stupid. He's probably outside in the garden and if I was drunk then maybe he was too? Perhaps he's got his own guilt and needs a smoke.

I push out on shaky legs and take a few tentative steps. The room begins to heave. This is the worst hangover I've ever had. I swallow back the waves of nausea and narrow my eyes towards the bathroom.

I fumble through the drawer for aspirin and glug them down with tap water. I splash my face with a shock of cold water, then squeeze a blob of peppermint toothpaste with trembling hands. I must get rid of this puffiness and look half decent before Karlos comes back. Nausea floods through me. My mouth fills with the bitterness of bile and I retch. Perhaps I'll feel better if I make myself sick?

Suddenly my legs collapse. My head cracks against the tiled floor. A vicious spasm shoots up my spine and jolts me into the air. I lie still for a second and then my legs convulse. I stare forward; bits of white flecked foam dance like sea-froth before my eyes. The spasms come again. They jerk my body viciously, again and again, until a final, fierce paroxysm pounds through me and stops.

I lie still. *What's going on? Please God, what's happening to me? Karlos? Nat? Elsa? Please, someone come and help me... please.*

# CHAPTER EIGHTEEN

'Natalie, Melissa, she is very, very bad. Her body, she is jumping too much and there is white froth by her mouth. I think the spirits, they are taking her.'

Oh, thank God. It's Eunice... phone the ambulance, Eunice... not Nat. Phone them now! Terror prickles through me as my body jerks. Maybe, she's right... maybe I'm dying. Oh God. Phone the ambulance, please phone them.

I hear Eunice pause and give a small sob. 'Please, you must be quick.'

She puts down the phone and walks back to my jerking body. I can see and hear her as she bends over me, but I can neither speak nor respond. Please God, let Nat be phoning the ambulance. Please, let them hurry, Lord... please.

Eunice clucks her tongue as tears fill her eyes. 'Houw,' she whispers, 'Houw!'

Despite the horror of what's happening I find comfort in her African expletive. Yes 'Houw', I can't say it better myself, why is this happening? I can't possibly have drunk enough to cause this.

I watch from the corner of my eye as Eunice walks over to the rocking chair and moves Karlos' clothes onto the floor. The chair creaks as she sits down. Her large bulk looms to and fro in my peripheral vision. She prays, calling on *Yesu* to help, and if not him, then send back the spirits of my ancestors to fetch me. Her incantations must be working for my jerking eases.

I lie shuddering, with Eunice rocking rhythmically next to me, for what seems like hours until the screech of tyres, followed seconds later by the wail of the ambulance. The front door thuds open and footsteps clatter down the hallway. Nat enters, her long hair flying behind, and runs up to my twitching body.

'Oh Liss… Oh God… what happened?'

'The men are here.' Eunice places her hand gently on Nat's shoulder as two burly men in fluorescent green jackets tramp into the room and lean over me. One is bald and looks about fifty. The second is tall and thin with thick blonde hair and looks about my age. He carries a small oxygen canister under his arm. Their faces, as they look at my jerking body, are calm and indifferent.

'We need to work on the patient, please,' says the bald one in a heavy Afrikaans accent. 'Sorry, ma'am, you must move away.'

Nat nods and Eunice leads her to the rocking chair. The bald-headed paramedic brings out a syringe and oxygen mask. Again spasms break out and convulse through my frail body. I feel their hands press down on the mask, pushing back on the spasms in a black comic break-dance.

'Oh God…' Nat says, as her face shudders over me. Embarrassment washes over me as I feel my body splutter like an engine trying to come to life. I scream silently for blackness to come and cover me and take all this horror away, but my plea is ignored and instead I remain fully awake.

'You must come to the kitchen. I'll make the tea.' I listen to the pad of Eunice and Nat's footsteps past me. 'We must leave the men to work.'

'Where's Karlos?' I hear Nat demand as they recede down the corridor towards the kitchen.

Yes, Nat's right, where the hell is he? I've been so absorbed in my pain that I've forgotten him for a moment. If he's outside surely he'd be in by now with all this commotion. Why isn't he here? Has he gone like I'd first feared?

'*Angazi*,' I hear Eunice reply. 'They were both in the house when I finished the work yesterday. I have only seen the Johnny Walker whiskey bottle today. I don't know where Master Karlos has gone.'

'Damn Karlos. Damn him! When did she start drinking again? He never said anything,' shouts Nat. 'How many bottles, Eunice? Oh God, how much has she drunk to get like this?'

'*Angazi*, but the bottle was empty.'

'Oh God,' moans Nat. 'We'd better look for more in the cupboard. She might have hidden them.'

The blonde paramedic calls out. 'Lady, we've got your sister stable enough to keep the mask on. Addington's ICU is full. We're going to take her to King Edward's hospital...'

'Kind Edward's? Surely you can't take her there?'

I flinch. Nat's right. I can't go there. Why doesn't she tell them I've got medical aid? Why can't they take me to Parklands? 'Tell them I'm covered, Nat... tell them,' I want to scream, but nothing comes out.

'It has a good ICU,' says the paramedic. 'We need to get her there fast. Do you know the way?'

'No.'

'Okay, you can come with us.'

'I must phone my other sister first. She can meet us there.'

'Okay. Wait here until we have her in the ambulance.'

Nat obeys and stands still, staring down at me until Eunice brings her tea.

'Thank you.' Nat gives Eunice an apologetic smile as she takes the mug of tea with a visibly shaking hand. 'Thank you for phoning me... I need to phone Elsa.'

Eunice looks at Nat with sad brown eyes. 'I will come with

you to the hospital. If they cannot help her I will call the *Sangoma*. She can call on *Yesu* to tell the spirits to come to help.'

Nat nods while Eunice goes to fetch the cordless phone. My body jerks again. I need Jesus more than a psychic *Sangoma*, but where is he?

# CHAPTER NINETEEN

The paramedics wheel me out and rush me in through the emergency double doors towards the A & E corridor. Nat and Eunice run at my side.

'Ladies, go to reception. You can come to ICU afterwards,' shouts the paramedic.

The strong stink of antiseptic, tinged with blood and pus, hits me as the paramedics wheel me further down the long corridor. There are streaks of blood smeared across the ceiling and the air smells like iron. I feel bile rise in my throat. My eyes are wide open and I try to ignore the people at my side, crammed along the corridor. A young child screams, while a man with a thick blob of congealed blood on the side of his head reaches out to stop the gurney. The paramedic pushes him roughly away. I cringe at the awful reality of all the suffering and anger. What the hell am I doing in King Edward's hospital? Two nurses saunter towards us, talking loudly in Zulu and laughing.

'Mind!' barks the bald-headed paramedic. 'This is an emergency.'

The nurses give him a dirty look, but move to the side so they can wheel me past.

I see the notice board for the ICU rear up as we approach the end of the corridor. They wheel me into the industrial lift and seconds later we're surging upwards.

In ICU, the air is cold. The smell of bleach catches the back of my throat. Machines hum like wasps as the ventilators breathe their mechanical life into their patients, but the ward feels strangely silent. The steady rhythm of the ventilators draws me in and for a second I feel I've strayed onto an alien mothership where some weird mechanical life will experiment on me.

The paramedics lift me onto the bed and hand a file to a tall Indian doctor who stands over me.

'Convulsions,' says the bald-headed paramedic. 'We've managed to control them some. We've moistened the open eyes, but she's not responding.'

'Good man. Thank you,' says the doctor.

The doctor studies my file while another young man slices away my sweat-drenched pyjamas, totally oblivious to the fact that despite appearances, I'm conscious. He sticks material patches all over my chest and instantly the heart monitor springs to life. The fast, steady beeps mean the thin blue line is beating. Can't they tell from my fast pulse that I'm awake? My legs jerk and I feel a wave ripple through my body. A fat nurse attacks me with needles; first on one hand, then the other. I watch, frozen, as she mounts the infusion bag and opens the taps to let the liquid drip life into my body. My jerking eases. She tightens a blood pressure monitor around my arm.

'It's low, Doctor.'

He nods and shines a light into my eyes. His face blurs. His hands are cool against my chest as he examines me. At least it feels like he cares. He squeezes some liquid into my staring eyes and the room dissolves for a few seconds into a dense mist. He closes my eyelids and tapes them down.

My pulse quickens and I try to still my mind from the panic

which seeks to invade it. I hear the swoosh of the ICU swing doors.

'Ladies, you can come in now. Please just put on these covering shoes and cap and wash your hands. I'm Dr Rajeet.'

Footsteps pad towards me.

'She's stopped fitting now but is not responsive.'

'Will she be... okay?' Nat's voice breaks mid-sentence.

'We don't know yet. Her brain has gone a long time without oxygen. I'm sorry, lady, it's still touch and go. We will just need to wait and see. You can sit here by her and hold this hand.'

I hear the scrape of a stool and sense someone sitting down next to my bed. Someone takes my limp hand and gives it a gentle squeeze.

'Houw,' whispers Eunice. She clicks her tongue, 'Houw!'

'Can you hear me, Liss?' whispers Nat. 'Elsa and me are here, so is Eunice. Don't worry, you're going to be okay. Squeeze my hand if you can hear me.'

I will myself to respond to Nat's touch and manage a slight squeeze.

'She just squeezed my hand. Feel, Elsa... feel.' Nat lets go my hand and I feel another hand close around mine and give a gentle squeeze. I respond.

'Nat's right,' says Elsa. 'She just squeezed mine too, Doctor.'

'Probably a slight muscle spasm. She's in a deep coma. She won't be able to respond.'

'She just did. Don't discount it,' Elsa snaps.

'We'll keep a careful eye on her. She's hooked up to the latest machinery. You can see that.'

Dr Rajeet's tone holds a hint of disdain.

'We need to make sure we do everything we can for her. She's our... baby sister.' Elsa's voice cracks as she utters the words.

'I promise we'll do everything we can. Does she suffer from epilepsy?'

'No.'

'How long was she drinking?'

'She'd been to rehab… she was off it until this…' says Elsa.

'It's easy to give in,' says Dr Rajeet. 'I'm sorry to say it, but it's probably drink which has caused this.'

'Surely she would have had to be doing it again for a while,' says Elsa. 'She's only been out of rehab four weeks. Eunice, have you seen her drink anything in that time?'

'*Akukho*, only see the empty whiskey bottle today. Nothing before that since Melissa come out of the drink hospital.'

'You see!' demands Elsa. 'She hasn't been drinking for weeks or anything like that!'

'If she had a great deal in one night then it can do it, especially if she has a history. The pyjamas we cut from her stank of alcohol. She must have had a lot. We will test for liver and other organ damage and also X-ray her brain. How old is she?'

'Twenty-eight,' says Nat. 'But my sister's right. If she'd been drinking again for a while we'd have known. I've seen her nearly every day since she came out. She was stone cold sober every time. I promise you she was.'

'We need to examine every possibility, Doctor. Can anything else besides alcohol do this?' Elsa's tone is clipped and official, and she's obviously in lawyer mode.

'Ja, there's a few things. Do you know if she took drugs?'

'No, I'm sure she never took any,' says Elsa.

'Okay, we'll look back at her records. We'll leave you for a while to sit with your sister and then I'm sorry, you'll all have to go. We'll phone you if anything happens,' says Dr Rajeet.

'You mean if she dies?' whispers Nat. 'She's not going to die, is she…?'

Dr Rajeet remains silent and my pulse quickens. *I don't want to die. Please God, don't let me die.* I hear the double doors swoosh open again and footsteps hurry in.

A nurse calls out, 'You must put on a cap and slippers first – and wash your hands.' The footsteps stop and seconds later hurry in my direction.

'What's happened to Liss? What happened?'

Oh Lord! I don't want Karlos to see me like this. I really don't.

'I thought maybe you could tell us.' Elsa's voice is filled with bitterness. 'Where the hell have you been?'

'I just went to the gym at 5am... when I came back Lissa was gone. The neighbour told me about the ambulance. H... how is she?'

'Not too fucking good, actually,' Elsa's tone is hard and condemning.

'I'm sorry... I had no idea she was drinking. I don't understand what has happened. I really don't,' mumbles Karlos.

'Well, she apparently was drinking. Eunice found an empty whiskey bottle in the house. Weren't you with her?' demands Elsa.

'I never saw anything... I don't know... but maybe she was...' Karlos' voice rises and fills with anger. 'Maybe she hid it from me. I don't know. Alcoholics do that, you know. I never gave her any.'

My mind whirls with confusion. I don't remember drinking. When did I even buy it? How could Karlos think I would hide that from him? I just don't know... But Eunice found the bottle and my pyjamas stank of booze . Did I drink? Did I hide it from Karlos? Oh God, did I?

'You cannot shout in here,' says the nurse sternly. 'I think you must go now. Say goodbye and please go. We will call you if we need to.'

They fall silent and I smell the Aramis aftershave I bought Karlos as he leans over and his lips touch my forehead. 'Get better soon, Liss... please get better,' he rasps, breaking into a loud sob seconds later. A mix of hopelessness and gratitude washes over me. I can hear from his voice that he really does love me. He sounds so broken, so distressed. How cruel, that just when I had one shot at real happiness again, this has to happen. Why did I have a drink? Why have the cards of time dealt me another joker? Wasn't the last card bad enough? Where the hell's my pack of *Happy Families*?

# CHAPTER TWENTY

A shudder passes through me as the tape is taken from my eyes and I blink rapidly as the misty ward comes into focus.

'She is waking doctor.'

'Thank you, Pumza.'

Hands tug at my gown. Something's pressing down on my throat; it moves. I stare blurrily up at the ceiling. The blades of a white painted fan rotate over me, their steady beat blending with the 'beep, beep, beep' of the heart monitor. The air smells so sharply of antiseptic, I can taste it. I glance to the side. The doctor's hand comes in to view and rests on my throat. I feel a surge of movement. My throat closes. Shit, I'm not breathing. I try to move my hands but they lie lead heavy at my sides. My heart thuds in my ears. Why can't I move? Why?

A face comes into view. 'Welcome back. I'm Dr Rajeet. You've been in a deep sleep for six weeks. Your family will be very happy to see you back.'

Dr Rajeet pushes his hands down on each side of my ribs and then checks the tube rising from my throat. 'Your body did not want to breathe on its own,' he said. 'We've given you a tracheotomy. We must hope that your brain will sometime tell your body to breathe again. These things take time.'

My legs jerk involuntarily and the doctor glances over at them.

'You're still convulsing a little; I'm afraid you'll find you can't move your arms and legs yet, but you should have feeling from the neck up. We'll take you down to the General Ward later today. Try and rest now.'

Sardonic laughter trembles through me. I can hardly do anything but rest, if all I can move is my head. Everything is surreal. I'm like the living dead. Have I really been brought out of my coma for this? A cloud of darkness descends and I squeeze my eyelids closed. Oh God! I don't want to live like this.

'I am going to give you something to calm you. It won't hurt.' Dr Rajeet holds a syringe, ready to attack.

'*Of course I won't fucking feel anything if I'm paralysed.*' I feel like screaming at him, but of course talking, like walking, is not an option. The depth of helplessness swamps over me. I just want to die. '*Please God, take me,*' I scream inside as the panic of my paralysis prickles over me like an uncontrolled bush fire. I lie burning for a few seconds, screaming inside, before a welcome womb of blackness rises up and covers me.

When I next open my eyes, I'm being wheeled down a long, dirty corridor with footsteps clip-clopping loudly behind me.

Elsa's earnest face, framed by her high advocate collar, peers down at me from the side of my trolley. She must've come straight from court for my grand exit from ICU. 'We're taking you down to the General Ward, Liss.' She tries to smile but can hardly manage it.

Nat's voice is locked in a high falsetto, but I can hear the tears behind it. 'We're both here with you, Liss. Don't worry it's going to be okay…' She scurries up on the other side of me and gives me a false smile.

Despite their pained expressions, they both look so normal,

so clean and smelling of bloody Chanel! I, on the other hand, am in an ugly hospital gown and undoubtedly look and smell like shit. Oh the joys!

'You'll be okay. It'll just take time, that's all,' says Elsa.

'Yes, you'll be okay.'

I snap my head to the side. Karlos has joined us. Can it get any worse? He's the last one I want here. I don't want him to see me like this: a half-human, damaged thing. I'm no longer capable of being his girlfriend. I close my eyes to shut him out. This can't be real; it can't be happening. It's just got to be a nightmare. One fucking, gigantic living nightmare!

I open my eyes again as they wheel me into the General Ward. It's filled with groaning, writhing bodies and third-world chaos. We wheel towards a bed tucked away in a far corner, past a young woman whose bloodied bandages cover her arms and head. She's groaning to herself and obviously in great pain. I look away. I'm obviously one of the privileged few because I still need a drip.

'We can't leave her here,' whispers Nat. 'We can't. It's too awful.'

'Ja, I agree,' says Karlos. 'But the doctor said she must stay in case she needs to go back to ICU.'

'So much for Mandela's new South Africa! This wasn't what I envisaged. Why didn't they take her to a private hospital, for goodness' sake?' Nat's voice is tight with anger.

'They didn't know if she had any medical aid. That's why they brought her here. You phoned the ambulance, Nat, not me.'

'They didn't ask me about medical aid or money. I would've told them it wasn't a problem.' Nat's eyes fill with tears. 'They just said they had to bring her here and I was in too much shock to argue,' she snaps. 'If you'd been there when the fitting started, Liss might never have got this bad.' She glares at him and slaps the tears off her cheeks.

My face grows hot. I wish I could just tell them all to 'Shut the fuck up'. How dare they talk about me like I'm not even here? Why don't they all just go? I just want to be alone.

'I phoned Hillcrest Hospital this morning. They may have space,' says Elsa. 'Dr Rajeet said he'll get her records over to them. They're a specialist hospital who'll give her the best.'

Karlos' voice rises. 'When is she going?'

'I don't know,' snaps Elsa, glaring at Karlos, 'As soon as the doctor says she can. Probably tomorrow if she's still stable when he checks her later. We're not letting her stay here one second longer than she has to.'

'Thank God for that.' Nat's face crumples with relief. 'Let's hope it's tomorrow.'

Elsa narrows her eyes at Karlos. She lowers her voice and speaks in a voice filled with venom. 'I want to make something very clear...' She pauses and moves closer to Karlos. 'I don't know how the fuck Liss has ended up like this, but you tell those other rubbish from the rehab to keep the hell away. Dr Rajeet said that some woman with pink hair and two men wanted to see Lissa when she was in ICU. Said they knew her from Shaloma. Luckily I'd told him no visitors except us. The last thing she needs is that type coming here.'

Karlos' eyebrows lift in surprise. What the hell were they doing here? Come to gloat no doubt? I look at Elsa with relief. Thank God she didn't let them see me.

My sisters and Karlos stand at my bedside looking down at me. I screw my eyes shut to escape their pity. 'Please God, save me from this living hell,' I plead silently, 'or at least give me a drink.' If ever there was a need for a case of Johnny Walker, this is it.

Karlos' lips touch my forehead in a hard kiss. 'I'll see you later, before I go to the meeting.' I open my eyes, but already his broad frame is marching out of the ward.

Nat pulls a face and Elsa bites her lip as they look down at me. 'Mom and Yvonne send their love,' whispers Nat, bending over me. 'Mom's too distraught to come. We'll bring her to Hillcrest as soon as you're there.'

An old African woman next to me suddenly starts singing loudly to herself.

'Looks like she's having fun,' whispers Nat, giving me a wry smile. 'Hope she won't keep you awake.'

Despite everything, my mind smiles, convinced that it has to be some kind of a black comedy. This ward of overflowing broken bodies and me. It can't be real. It can't be.

'We'll see you tomorrow, Lissakins. Don't worry. We'll make sure we get you to Hillcrest ASAP. I promise,' whispers Elsa, kissing the top of my head.

Her words make me yearn to be young again. I squeeze my eyes tight. I just need someone to help me, to take care of me, and the only one who can do that now is God. My mind drifts back to the first time I met Him at that revival meeting. He was real then. Please let him be so still.

# CHAPTER TWENTY-ONE

D ad puts his arm around me as we walk away from the car
park and across dark, crunchy grass to a big tent with
lights around it. The air is warm and the dark sky is filled with
millions of stars. A round, yellow moon shines down on us. I turn
and look back at Nat and Elsa who're walking with Mom.

The sound of drums and loud singing and clapping, mixed
with guitar music, thumps out from the big tent. Dad pushes
back the canvas flap. It's as big as a circus tent inside and is so full
of people that I can smell their sweat. *'Hallelujah to the Lord'* rings
out in song, while a band with guitars and bongo drums plays
loudly from a stage in front. An old white man in a wrinkled
brown suit pushes through the crowd, waving his hand and
smiling at us.

'Len Furnwood. Welcome, brother. Welcome, sisters,' he
shakes Dad's hand. 'We've still get some seats at the back.'

Dad introduces us and we follow him.

I hear Nat giggle behind me. 'What's with all this "brother,
sister" stuff?'

'Weird,' says Elsa.

I follow behind Dad and Len until we get to a row of orange plastic seats on the other side of the tent.

'There should be space for you here. May God bless you in the service.'

'Thank you,' Dad says. He puts his hand behind my back and helps me squeeze past an African man and a fat woman to get to our seats. The woman's wearing the green and white uniform of the Zulu Zionist church and the man is dressed in a black suit like he's a priest. They smile, and it makes me feel warm inside. I thought all the Africans would hate us because of what happened to those children in Soweto. The horrid picture from the TV of Hector Peterson covered in blood from police bullets flashes through my mind. It pushes bitter water into my mouth, making me retch. Dad says it's because the government was forcing the children to have their lessons in Afrikaans and it made them riot so the police started shooting at them. He says it's disgusting and Mom says the country is going to explode now like a grenade. I shiver inside. How could the police shoot children? I look around. The tent is filled with white, Indian and African people. Everyone here is happy together, singing loudly, and some even have their arms lifted up and their eyes closed. Lots of others clap to the music. Why can't all churches do this?

On the stage is a big wooden cross and a man about Dad's age. He's quite handsome and tanned, with thick black hair which looks like it has been slicked back with oil. His eyes are closed and he sings loudly.

The smell of beetlenut is strong. It reminds me of the Indian shop that used to be at the top of our road before the government made them move. There's a row of Indian woman in bright saris of gold, red and peacock blue in front of me. They're holding their hands high in the air and shouting out 'Jesus, Jesus, Jesus'. Then they sing 'Angels bow before him' in loud voices. More African women wearing the clothes of the Zionist church woman stand near the front, waving their arms in the air and dancing.

The tent shakes from all the singing and I'm not sure if I should also sing with my arms up high. I can only see five other white people.

I grow warm inside, like I did when I first tasted the gin. It's so nice to be in a tent with all these different people, but at the same time it feels a bit weird. A trickle of fear runs through me. I hope the police don't come in and arrest us. Mom thinks that they'll be breaking down our door to take Dad away if he doesn't stop helping Thabo and Isaac. Goosebumps prickle over my arms and my heart jumps to my ears. I look up at Dad. He looks happy and doesn't look scared of anything. He's watching the stage where the band with guitars and bongo drums is playing. I let out a shaky breath; it must be okay if he's not worried. The song changes and everyone begins singing, 'What a mighty God we serve, what a mighty God we serve,' and clapping loudly. Then they start to shout out the name of Jesus, and praise his power. Many of them are shaking like they're really cold, and one of the Zionist church women moves into the aisle to dance, still shouting out the name of Jesus.

The air buzzes with invisible power. I shiver and take Dad's hand. The pastor talks in a strange language, shouting out as he walks across the stage. His head is thrown back and his eyes shine. Other people in the tent lift up their arms and call out in the same strange language.

'What're they saying?'

Dad lifts his eyebrows. 'I don't know.'

Elsa stands very still. Her face is like wood and her blue eyes are serious. Mom shakes her head and sits down in her seat. I'm beginning to wish Dad had listened to Mom. I don't know if I want to stay any more. I sit down and lean back into my chair.

'This is a different kind of church, hey, Liss,' Nat says.

'I don't like it.'

Elsa turns sharply to me. 'It's nice to be in a multi-racial service.'

I pull a face but stay in my seat. The pastor begins to talk. He thumps the pulpit.

'You must be born again,' he shouts, looking at us with fierce eyes. 'You know not the time or the place. Jesus will come like the thief in the night, and if you're not ready, it will be too late. Don't let it happen.' His eyes fill with tears. '*Nkosi* loves us; all of us. He wants to save you. All you have to do is ask him into your heart. Don't play with eternity. Don't play with your soul. Don't go to an eternity of damnation in hell because you are too proud to admit your sin.'

His words hit into me and my heart pounds. My mind jumps back to Aunty Yvonne's farm and the gin. I'd pinched more of it at home without anyone knowing. I know in my heart it's wrong. I don't want to do that again. I don't want to go to hell.

I take Dad's hand. 'I don't like this.'

'It's okay,' Mom says and glares at Dad.

The gin memory's so strong in my mind that I can smell it. The tears prick behind my eyes. I try and blink them away before Mom sees them. I know the pastor is talking about me. I know he is.

'*Nkosi* is real,' he shouts. 'He's the same yesterday, today and forever. He's a *Nkosi* of salvation and a *Nkosi* of healing. Come to him for rest... come drink from the living water. Come and be healed. Have the courage to give your life to Jesus. Ask him into your heart. Come now.'

His voice fills the tent and rings in my ears. I want to run away but know I can't. The band plays as the people sing, '*Leave it there, Leave it there. Take your burden to the Lord and leave it there.*' Some people press out from the rows and into the aisle so that it looks like a long snake of squirming bodies. They push forward with small steps. Some of them are on crutches, and some are wearing dark glasses with people helping them walk forward. Some of them are crying.

A young Indian girl steps onto the stage. Her hair falls in one long plait down her back. She looks about twelve and is wearing a dress covered with bright pink roses. The pastor puts his hands on her head. The tent is very quiet. I hold my breath.

Then he shouts, 'In the name of Jesus, loose this child from the spirit of deafness. Go! Go now. In the name of Jesus, I command you.'

The girl shakes, her legs shivering so that the pink roses on her dress dance around her. The pastor clicks his fingers close to both her ears.

'Can you hear this?' he says, bending towards her and staring straight into her brown eyes. 'Can you hear?'

He clicks his fingers again. Her eyes grow wide and her face lights up like our caravan gas lantern. She jumps up and down shouting, 'Yes, I can hear, I can hear... Jesus has healed my ears! I can hear.'

The tent grows noisy and everyone starts to shout, 'Praise you, Jesus, praise you.' My tummy does a tumble. An old African man, dressed in brown trousers full of holes and a dirty grey jersey, is next on the stage. He's bent over and thin and walks with a stick. His hair is grey, like peppercorns. The pastor lays his hands on his head and the old man lifts his shaking hands high into the air. The pastor calls out to Jesus to heal him from his pain and the old man's body shakes like it's gone mad and he falls backwards. Two men catch him and help him onto the floor. Another man comes and covers him with a red blanket as he lies there, shivering like a jelly.

I feel like the tent is falling in on me. Something strange is happening. This isn't a pretend church, it's real. Maybe God isn't just a story; maybe this pastor is right and Jesus is real? He must be. I've just seen him heal these people. I can feel his power all around me. He is alive. Why haven't we met him at our Methodist church?

Pins and needles cover my whole body as the pastor shouts, 'God is speaking to you... listen.' Tears stream from his eyes.

'Jesus is calling you. Don't leave it too late. Softly and tenderly he is saying, "Come my child. Come let me help you. Let me cleanse you from your sin…" Please, don't ignore his call.'

The pastor's words march through my mind. My heart's beating so hard that I think it's going to explode with bullet holes like Hector Peterson's body. My breath comes out in short pants and I clench my fists so tight that my knuckles turn white. I can't run away. God will know. He sees everything.

'I'm going up,' says Elsa.

She pushes past Nat and joins the snake of people.

'Me too,' says Nat. 'You coming, Liss?'

I nod. I also want to be saved and meet with Jesus. I need him to forgive me for my sins. I take Nat's hand and jiggle into the queue behind her and Elsa. I look back at Mom and Dad. They're still sitting in their seats, but Dad gives me a small smile.

My hand grows sweaty and I slip it out of Nat's grip and wipe it on my white skirt, leaving a brown stain like the sin the pastor talked about. The queue shuffles forward. The people who had fallen on the stage are being helped off, and we're halfway there. I swallow and wish that I'd stayed in my seat, but then I feel Nat squeeze my shoulder which helps. The pastor is commanding that cancer leave the liver of a woman in a bright pink sari. She screams and then falls backwards. The air grows hot around me and my head becomes dizzy. What will God do to me when I get there?

'Nat, I think I need to go back and sit down.'

'It's okay, we're nearly there. Just take a deep, slow breath.'

I suck in some of the hot air and close my eyes. We move forward some more and before I can run away, it's my turn.

'Praise God,' says the pastor as I go up the steps. He takes my hand and guides me to the middle of the stage. 'Praise God that you have answered his call.' He puts his hands on the middle of my head. I hold my breath and keep my eyes fixed onto the floor of the wooden stage. His hands press down onto me as if he is trying to push me into the stage. The air around me grows hot. The pins and needles grow stronger. They move up from my feet to my head so that my whole body is tingling and my mind is going round and round. My breath comes out short and fast as my heart whooshes in my ears.

'Lord Jesus, come into this young life. Fill her with your cleansing power. Guide her life and make her whole.'

I close my eyes tight and cry out silently to Jesus. 'I'm sorry for getting drunk. I'm sorry for being so horrible to Mommy and my sisters. I'm sorry for all the things I've done wrong. Please take my sins away. Please save me from hell.'

My ears buzz and then my whole body grows hot and for a minute I feel like I'm back in the Karoo. I can feel God's power. It comes over me like the strong waves in the sea at North Beach. My head is going around and I feel like I'm drunk even though I haven't stolen any gin today. My legs start to wobble. I try and make them stiff, but I can't. They're wobbling so much now, I think I'll fall. I lift up hands. They shake like the other peoples' have.

As I shout the words in my head I feel like God has suddenly put a big warm blanket around me and is hugging me tight. My legs stop wobbling and the horrible drunk feeling goes. I feel so happy I want to cry. I know that Jesus has come into my soul and is soaring through me like an eagle. His blood is washing me clean. I bend my head.

'Thank you, Jesus,' I whisper, as the tears trickle down my cheeks. The blanket grows warmer and sobs ripple through my body like little waves. Then it is over. The pastor takes his hands from my jelly head. I feel so different inside, like I've been thrown into a giant washing-machine and come out clean. Jesus is real. He's saved my soul and I won't be going to hell any more.

# CHAPTER TWENTY-TWO

I blink out of the memory and look out at the darkening ward. I guess I can be grateful that at least I'm still alive. Although I don't know if this living hell's much of a life. Maybe I'd be better off dead and, as long as heaven's real, I should head for it. My nose wrinkles. The air is rank with a mix of putrid infection and antiseptic. At least it didn't stink this badly when Karlos was here. I hope the Shaloma meeting helps. I'm glad he's gone there. He'll have to keep strong and not take that first drink. A night light shines dimly near the nurse's station at the end of the ward. The wall clock's illuminated at ten past nine. It's later than I thought.

The stench assaults my nose again and my stomach contracts. I try to focus on the staccato rhythm of the patient next to me as she snores. I have to hang on to the hope of getting better. I have to. I turn my head towards the snoring woman. It must be her bandages that smell. They look yellow and rotten and are stained with brown blood. I shudder out a long sigh. A patient further down the ward lets out a long moan. How the hell can I sleep in this stink and suffering? I think back to that revival tent. We really did see miracles happen that night and many times afterwards. I close my eyes as the pain of my paralysed reality stabs me deep in the belly. Maybe God will grant me one now… maybe he will. I squeeze my eyes tight. 'Please God, help me… please.'

But no miracle comes. God's obviously not listening, or maybe it's that I don't deserve one. I guess the only thing I can be thankful for is that hopefully I'll be going to Hillcrest Hospital – even if it's only for bloody geriatrics. Surely anywhere has to be better than this hell hole. Maybe God will help me there? Perhaps I'm going to be one of those slow-burn miracles you sometimes hear about.

The stink of the ward grows worse. A nurse two beds away is unwrapping a foul bandage from an old man's chest. She throws the dirty dressing on the floor. He groans and writhes on the blood-stained bed. The stench of rotting flesh grows worse. Nausea floods through me. Fuck, this is the reality of the third world. I think back to our teenage years when Elsa campaigned against forced removals to Lime Hill and we collected blankets for the poor Africans who'd been taken from their tribal land and stuck in a camp on a desolate hill. We were so proud of ourselves for helping. We thought we knew what racial suffering was all about, but in reality our liberal perspective was so narrow, we knew nothing. How can the black hospitals be so different from the white ones? How could we have allowed people to be treated so differently? I think back to when I'd been in Parklands Hospital as an eight-year-old having my appendix out. It was like staying in a hotel with the menu brought round every day so that I could choose my meals. The nurses were lovely and constantly pandered to me. My bed-linen was changed daily with everything sterile, fresh and clean. I could even buy sweets from the trolley whenever I wanted and spent most of the time watching films. It was more like a holiday than a hospital stay.

I look around at the humped, groaning bodies piled around the ward because there aren't even enough beds for them all, let alone nurses, clean bed-linen and decent food. It's hard to believe that others were going through this while I was in Parklands – and twenty years later it's still so bad. I let out a long sigh. It's going to be a long, hard road to achieve true equality in this new South Africa. I turn as footsteps approach and hope it's Karlos.

'Good evening, Melissa. How are you doing?'

Why's Dr Rajeet so late doing the rounds? He smiles down at me, but I can only glare back. How the hell does he think I'm doing? I can't talk, can't breathe, I'm hooked up like some kind of freak to a tube, about to be sent off to some geriatric hospital for possibly the rest of my days. '*Oh fucking marvellous, thanks,*' I want to scream. I close my eyes to shut him out. I need God to heal me quickly, otherwise this well of bitterness and self-pity is going to suffocate me.

'I have good news for you. I've had a look through your progress and I think you're stable enough to go to Hillcrest Hospital tomorrow.' He beams down at me. 'So, this is your last night here. Karlos asked me to phone him if you were going tomorrow. I've done so and asked him to tell your sisters we'll take you there around nine o'clock in the morning. Hopefully that tracheotomy can be closed in a week or so and then you should be able to speak. I've already sent your records to Hillcrest. You'll have the best of care there. I'm sorry you've had to be down here at all.'

Relief floods through me at the news. Thank God it's only one more night in this hell ward, but as I open my eyes I see Dr Rajeet pull up his nose in disgust as he scans the ward. What's he sorry about? Does my white skin make me that different? Actually, now I really think about it, the rest of them have to stay here so why shouldn't I see a bit of the real world? Dad's face drifts back into my mind. I think in a strange way he'd be proud I came here instead of Parklands. You can't profess equality for all and then want the best for yourself while the majority suffer. Dark despair rises up again and covers my soul, but I try and push it away. I felt God when I was young and I need to try and feel him again. There has to be a plan and purpose in all this somewhere. There has to be.

'I'm going to give you a sedative. It'll help you sleep and when you open your eyes, it'll be morning and time to go.' He gives me a smile. 'You should live to a ripe old age.'

Dr Rajeet wraps a band around my arm and there's the sharp prick of the needle while I feel mocking laughter at the thought of ripening to old age like some blackened banana. Dr Rajeet pats my arm.

'Sleep well.'

# CHAPTER TWENTY-THREE

My head spins as a bright flash of white light flares up. I know this is no sedated sleep. That flash was the moment of my death. It was my crossing over. I'm certain of it. What the hell happened to my ripe old age prediction?

I'm strangely calm, relieved even at the fact that I'm still conscious and that the spiritual life I'd always believed in is true. I look around expecting to see heaven in all its glory or at the very least see the welcoming light of an angel greet me. Instead I'm shrouded in mist and completely alone in the pulsating vastness of space. I have no answers for what's just happened, only memories which flick through my mind like an old cine film. Oh God. How fast it's all been. The only thing I can be grateful for is that at least I'm standing again and breathing on my own. Looks like I finally got my miracle.

Someone whispers my name: 'Lissa. Lissa...' the voice sighs and is joined by others until it grows into a chorus all calling out my name. A door of light opens to reveal my broken family huddled in mourning outside the cold stone entrance of St Martin's Church.

People sometimes imagine with a macabre sense of glee what

it's like to be shown your funeral and let the pain of others feed their ego. The process bears nothing positive. Elsa, Nat and Mom stand pale and hunched like broken puppets next to a tearful Aunty Yvonne and Eunice. My earthly life is over. I'm an ex-human now, just like Monty Python's cold, stuffed parrot. Sadness covers me as this truth hits home. My pain deepens as a distraught Karlos joins Nat and Elsa. His hair is unbrushed and he looks so uncomfortable in his black suit and tie. He's even wearing black patent shoes, which I know he'll hate. His jaw is clenched and his eyes are red-rimmed. My spirit aches. Life is so unfair.

The hearse draws up. Six dovetailed men from the funeral parlour pace my mahogany coffin with its sprawl of red roses into the church. I glare at them. Why didn't Karlos, Greg and Dave help with the carrying? Why do I have these anonymous, sombre penguins? The moment of watching my own funeral, knowing that in that polished box lies my own earthly body, is so surreal that I want to laugh out loud. Is this whole thing just an LSD hallucination; a mirage like the ribbons of water I thought I saw on that long Karoo road?

But as I look at my broken family, I can't deny the reality. Mom's eyes are shrouded by dark glasses. She's hunched and sheathed in black, her face pale against the high-necked, black lace blouse and her knuckles cemented white around her crumpled, white linen handkerchief. Eunice is a picture of pain in her green and white uniform of the Zionist church with her wide, black armband proclaiming the brutal fact of my passing. Guilt eats into me at the pain I've caused and grows as I watch Nat break down in tears. She turns to Aunty Yvonne and clutches her with clawed fingers as the sobs wrack through her body. Aunty Yvonne envelops her in strong, fat arms and pats her loudly as if she's winding a baby.

'I can't… believe… she's… gone.' Nat's words spill out staccato-like between her sobs.

'*Agh*, Natalie, I can't either. Neither can your poor Mom. I just wish I could have helped. I just wish I had been here for you all.'

Nat pulls back and looks up at Aunty Yvonne with a tear-stained face. 'It was so unexpected... we were taking her out to Hillcrest the next day... Dr Rajeet said she'd made good progress... I just don't understand it... I really don't.'

'Neither do I,' says Elsa, taking Nat's hand. 'Come, let's get Mom inside.'

Greg stubs out his cigarette and signals for Dave to follow. They stand behind Elsa as she puts her arm around Mom and guides her into the church. Eunice takes Mom's free hand and gives it a squeeze. Dave ushers Nat and Yvonne inside, his face thin and wan. He's a good guy and I'm glad Nat's got him at home with her. Karlos watches them as they pass through the wide doorway but he remains standing alone at the end of the paved church path. Why hasn't my family included him? He shouldn't be left all on his own. Poor Karlos, he must be so hurt by it all. Can't they see it'll help them all if they pull together rather than push him away? He was part of me, no matter how brief that time.

Karlos looks at his watch and does up the button of his suit jacket before walking with slow steps and a downcast head into church. More people arrive: I see Thabo dressed in black with a black armband on his upper arm like Eunice. A sob of gratitude sighs out from me. I'm so touched he sees me as family. Another car arrives. I recognise Dr Pillay, Joshua, Amos and Mia from the lab. It feels like a lifetime ago that I worked there, even though it's only a matter of months since I resigned. They walk into the church with serious faces. So, they've thought of me, but Mike obviously hasn't. My spirit flinches. Bastard, after all the pain he caused me, he can't even have the decency to come to my funeral. He obviously didn't care for me at all.

A white Mercedes pulls up to the curb. A serious faced Dr Brink sits behind the wheel with a grim-faced Helen next to him.

Nic and George are in the back seat. The door opens and Nic gets out. He's wearing a smart, black pinstripe suit and a white shirt, looking like the lawyer he said he'd been in his previous life, but he's lost weight. I flinch as I look at his eyes; they're red raw with pain. He waits for George to exit and then makes his way into the stone church with hunched shoulders. George follows behind with shuffled steps, looking as miserable as I remember him. I hardly had anything to do with him so why is he even here? No sign of pink bitch Hattie or the Aryan Wolf, but no surprise there – they're the last people I want to be here. I'm surprised at the pain on Nic's face. Perhaps I've misjudged him? He's a good-looking guy and a probably a player, but maybe he wasn't stalking me and genuinely cared for me? He looks even worse than Karlos.

My mahogany coffin with its golden handles rests beneath the altar draped with red roses. The priest steps up to the pulpit and speaks in a sonorous voice about the resurrection and the life, and of how death is not the end. I hope my family take comfort from those words, but I wish it could have been Pastor Jorge taking my funeral, not this nameless priest who didn't even know me. I'm flooded with an overwhelming desire to pass through the doorway and tell them I'm still here and that death is just an illusion, but of course I can't.

The priest leads them in the singing of *Psalm 23* followed by *Amazing Grace* before Dr Pillay goes up with slow steps to the front and tells of how efficient I was in the lab, what a good colleague and treasured employee I was, and extols my untapped potential. I smile at his kind words. He was a really good pathologist and a true gentleman. I remember Monica Moodley, his unrequited love: 'Don't pillay with me; I'm not in the moodley', Mia and I used to joke when she rebuffed him again and again.

The church falls into a sombre silence until the priest gives the final blessing and my mourners file behind the slow-paced penguins and my coffin. The hearse leads them down to Red Hill cemetery, and I watch them drive through the red brick gates of the wide, tarred driveway. Cement tombstones with chipped angels and crosses are dotted around the green expanse like stone flowers. New graves with mounds of red earth line one of the boundary fences. I remember friends of ours who lived nearby telling us about the AK-47 bullets which cracked through the air during the ANC burials of the early 1990s. At least now, only four years later, things look peaceful. The procession winds along the drive like a heavily fed python. It stops near an open grave which lies like a wound in the red soil.

The penguins carry me with serious faces and set steps. They look like something out of *Oliver Twist* and for a second I want to giggle. What a job! They must spend their whole lives walking around with miserable faces, looking like they've just swallowed a hive of wasps, but my amusement quickly fades as I look at my family and friends just as miserable and their bodies hunched. Loss is such a hard thing to deal with and don't I know it.

They stop a little way from the empty hole and wait while the robed priest moves, clutching his Bible, to the head of the grave. The poker-faced pallbearers hoist me onto the wide straps straddling the grave and begin to carefully lower me down. Nat, Elsa, Yvonne and Mom break into sobs as I disappear in my mahogany box, deep into the open arms of the damp earth. Dave stands stick straight, his arm tightly held around Nat to support her. Greg shifts from one foot to the other and bites his bottom lip as clods of damp earth drop down on my coffin.

Eunice ululates while the priest intones, *'Dust to dust, ashes to ashes.'* He sprinkles a light rain of red earth down onto my coffin. Nat helps Mom, her shoulders hunched and her eyes hidden by dark glasses, throw down a red rose. It lands like a spilled drop of blood on the top of my coffin. Mom moans and turns around to clutch at Nat, while Nat looks over at Elsa with pain-filled eyes. Elsa's face grows grim and then crumples as she throws in her rose. Greg goes to put an arm around her, but she stands immobile, staring down at me, while Nat, Yvonne and Eunice add their roses. The petals spread their crimson across the mahogany top for a few minutes until the soft, damp earth smothers them.

Karlos stands stoically to the side. He waits until they've finished, before moving closer and picking up the bouquet of red roses which had sat proudly on my coffin in the church. He walks to the top end of my grave, kneels and places the bouquet on the soft earth. The rest of the funeral party stand, heads bowed, as the miserable penguins pile the earth over my coffin so that it becomes one with the red soil. I smile. Just as well I'm not really in it. I don't think my claustrophobia could take it.

The last clod seals my grave and penguin-man pats the hump of earth smooth with the back of his shovel, taking care not to upset the roses. The finality of my earthly end shudders through the still afternoon air. My family stand in front of the newly covered grave with lowered heads. Nat lifts hers after a while and looks up for a brief second at the empty blue sky. I see her shoulders shudder and her deep sigh echoes through the surrounding silence. Elsa keeps her head lowered. She takes Mom's limp hand and gives it a squeeze. Eunice and Yvonne stare down at the humped soil with Thabo behind them. My spirit aches. It's such a painful last step, this ritual of closure. I remember the bullet holes in my own soul when we lost Dad. I had to take it one day at a time, wrapped in numbness, until one day the tide of sorrow was unleashed. I'm so sorry I've caused them so much pain.

'Hamba kahle,' says Eunice, showering the grave with another sprinkle of fine red earth. She gazes down with soulful eyes until Thabo pulls her away.

My family walk away with a mourner's pace.

'We'll see you at your Mom's house.' Yvonne takes Mom's arm and steers her towards the Land Rover.

Karlos turns to Nat and clears his throat. 'I won't come to the house… it's too sad.'

'Okay,' Nat says, and she and Elsa watch him with narrow eyes as he makes his way to my Golf and drives off.

They walk towards Nat's Honda.

'What the hell's this?' says Nat as they reach the car. She snatches a small white piece of paper which is tucked under her wiper. She reads it and turns open-mouthed to Elsa. 'This is weird.'

Elsa examines it with a frown. 'Is it some kind of sick joke?' She turns and looks around with fierce eyes at the now deserted cemetery.

'What's wrong?' asks Greg.

'It's a blank prescription from Dr Clark…'

Greg snatches the paper. 'So?'

'He was our childhood doctor. He's dead…' Elsa says.

'He's been dead seven years…' Nat says.

'It's probably another doctor called Clark,' interjects Greg, crumpling up the paper.

Elsa's brow furrows. 'It's our Dr Clark's address…'

'Come on, enough, let's go,' says Greg, opening the back door and ushering Nat and Elsa in. He exchanges a look with Dave who quickly heads for the driver's door and seconds later they speed out of the cemetery.

I feel a moth of unease flap through me as I look down at the crumpled piece of white paper lying on the path. What if it is our Dr Clark? Why's there a blank prescription from him on Nat's car?

The fluttering in my spirit grows in intensity. 'Absent from the body, present with the Lord' the Bible says. Mine was no normal crossing over. This is not how it's meant to happen.

# CHAPTER TWENTY-FOUR

I blink and shake my head. I'm in Elsa's hallway, just outside her closed dining-room door. One minute I'm watching my funeral and now instantly I'm back on earth.

I run my fingers through my hair. Fine strands break free and nestle against my cheek. My fingers are warm against my skin. I pinch a small area of flesh on my arm and flinch. The sensation is no different from when I was alive – or whatever alive really means. I guess I'm some kind of paradox. Alive and dead at the same time - a ghost, spirit, ethereal being, but one which still has a beating heart. The only real difference is that my senses are heightened. I can both see and hear the buzzing energy of the life around me.

I think back to those burnt-out addicts from church Elsa had tried to help. I remember eavesdropping from the bedroom window while one of them sat in the back garden telling Elsa how acid had changed his perception and helped him see into an unseen world of spinning colour and energy. His brain was so fried with acid he thought he was a peacock in a pear tree instead of a partridge because of the vivid colours and energy he saw. Maybe he was seeing a glimmer of this exciting reality? Perhaps the acid in some weird way freed his spiritual eyes? Except, of course, instead of waiting for death, he frizzled his brain and turned into a cabbage.

The low mumble of voices penetrates the door. I move through it as easily as through air. I smile to myself. I might be somewhere in space, but I'm obviously not bound by it. I can move through things, just like the risen Christ. But the joy of wonder at my new-found being evaporates as soon as I set eyes on Nat and Elsa.

They're hunched around the dining table, both their faces carved deep with pain. A surge of longing mixed with sorrow swamps me. I can't believe I'm actually seeing them again, face to face, but their terrible distress is my fault. Why am I back? There's no clear answer. Maybe it's a gift, a small slice of time back, for us unlucky few who've been torn away before our time so that we can guide our loved ones in their grief and lead them down the pot-holed road to closure?

Nat's fingers fiddle with the linen placemat in front of her.

'Do you think it was some kind of sick joke?'

Elsa tucks a strand of long blonde hair behind her ear and gives her head a small shake. 'It's probably just another Dr Clark, like Greg says.'

Nat pulls a face. 'It's pretty strange, given the circumstances.'

Elsa gives an angry shrug. 'Maybe.' She falls silent and stares ahead, her blue eyes washed with sadness. 'I think we're just making a connection which probably means nothing.'

Nat pushes her lips together and traces a circular pattern over the placemat with her finger. I move forward until I'm standing right beside her. I only need to put my arm out to touch her, but she continues to trace the pattern, completely unaware of my presence. The rasp of her breath assaults my heightened hearing and I can see the darkness of her sorrow. I reach out my hand and rest it lightly on her bare forearm. She flinches as if aware of my touch and looks down at her arm with twitching nostrils. I watch as a swallow of fear sticks in her throat. Her nostrils twitch again, like a rabbit's, while a deep frown etches across her brow. I continue to stand there with our faces barely a foot away from each other. If only she knew.

'Els,' she whispers.

Elsa looks up and narrows her eyes. 'What?'

'Can't you smell it?' Nat's voice is low. She sniffs again.

'What?'

'Lissa's perfume. I'm sure I can smell it.'

Elsa's nostrils twitch. She frowns. 'I'm sure it's nothing.'

I let go of her arm and she rubs the space as if conscious of my disappearing touch. She turns to Elsa with wide eyes. 'I can definitely smell it… it's really strong, and I'm sure… I can sense her.'

Elsa pulls down her mouth and gives a slow shake of her head. 'It's just your mind playing tricks because you miss her so much.'

'No, it's not… I…'

'You're imagining it,' snaps Elsa.

Nat frowns and clenches her fists under the table. She breathes in deeply and continues to stare straight at me.

Am I wearing Royal Secret? I don't remember having it on in hospital and surely they don't spray you with perfume in the morgue? I lift my wrist to my arm and breathe in a strong whiff of its signature sandalwood scent. Nat's right, I am, although how it got there, I have no idea, but at least it's a subtle sign of my presence, a scent of my ongoing life for her to know, and I'm so grateful she's spiritually in tune to smell it.

Elsa's scowls at her. 'Nat, when you're dead, you're dead. You have to accept that.'

'I don't.'

Elsa sighs and shoves her hair behind her ears. 'You need to.'

Nat's mouth turns to scorn as Elsa utters each empathic word and she shakes her head as soon as Elsa finishes speaking.

Elsa stares at her in silence for a few seconds. 'I miss her too.

In fact, I miss her like hell, but we both have to accept she's gone and is never coming back; it's important for closure.'

Nat ignores her and stares straight ahead.

'For goodness' sake, Nat. We all want to believe in immortal life, but it isn't real, it doesn't exist! Liss is never coming back. Can't you see that?' Elsa's face reddens with intensity and she bangs her fist down on the table.

Nat clenches her lips together and continues with twitching rabbit nostrils to stare straight at me, while ignoring Elsa's irritated gaze.

'Oh, stop being stupid,' says Elsa. She gets up and flings back her chair. 'I'm going to make some tea.'

Nat says nothing, but as soon as Elsa leaves the room she whispers, 'Liss, are you here? Are you...? I can smell your perfume. I can sense you. I really can.'

I hesitate. I want to ease her pain and show myself, although I'm not sure how. At the very least I want to speak to her and tell her that I'll always be here with them all, whispering into their thoughts, lingering with them in the forests of our shared memories, but how's she going react if I do? It's all very well to wish someone back but quite different, I'm sure, if you actually see them manifest in front of you. Nat's nostrils continue to flare. She shifts uncomfortably on her chair so that the leather squeaks. She rubs her hands against her jeans and a mottled pink rash breaks out across her chest.

'I'm here, Nat,' I shout before I can stop myself. My words echo in my ears, but Nat's expression remains unchanged. A heavy sensation lodges deep in my belly. She may be able to smell my perfume and sense me, but she can't see or hear me, so why have I been sent back? What the hell is really going on?

# CHAPTER TWENTY-FIVE

I find myself in Nat's bedroom, watching her deep in sleep. Where have I been since seeing her and Elsa in the dining room? Why is it just a blank? As a buzzing covers my ears, I don't need an answer. I'm entering Nat's dream and this time I'm sure she'll hear me speak.

Elsa's also there, the three of us sitting cross-legged on a red and green tartan blanket around a large piece of burning driftwood, on the soft sand at Beachwood, the sea air moist and smelling strongly of wood smoke and salty fish. The sun has long since fallen into darkness but a glowing full moon is throwing its silvery light in ripples across the lapping Indian Ocean. We're holding steel skewers with pink and white marshmallows perched on their ends and prodding them into the dancing orange flames until they transform into burnt bits of sticky sweetness. We fill our mouths with them like in a game of chubby bunny, leaving our lips dotted with delicious bits of melted marshmallow.

We look up as bright veins of lightning streak out across the night sky, setting it alight, and then hear the thunder crash and roar.

'We'd better go,' shouts Elsa, but as soon as we begin to collect our things the lightning stops. I stare up at the night sky. A host of thick, dark clouds have swallowed the moon. The blackness closes in around us and a fierce wind whips the waves into a white frenzy that heaves forward to crash upon the sand and race towards us. The foam fingers snatch at our marshmallows, drawing them back into the dark, swelling waters until they bob away to nowhere.

We grab our blanket as more waves rush up over us. Nat and Elsa claw themselves away, but the current is too strong for me. I throw back my head and scream, my hands clutching out towards Nat and Elsa, as the wave drags me deep into the dark, roaring ocean.

'Liss... Liss!' scream Nat and Elsa in chorus as I'm pulled under only to emerge seconds later, holding high in my arms a bedraggled white rabbit. Elsa and Nat run down the beach and lunge madly through the crashing waves towards me. Their heads bob across the surface of the dark, swelling water as they try to frantically swim. Simultaneously, they grab hold of the rabbit's foot.

'Oh God, Liss... oh God!' they scream, as they pull and pull at the dangling rabbit's foot to try and get hold of my arm, but the foot breaks away and they fall backwards into the swelling waves with the ragged stump lying across their open hands. Bright red blood pumps out in a fountain. The bright red clots of blood emerge across the crest of the waves and wash over me, covering my arms and face red. I stretch out my arms to Nat and Elsa, but it's no good. The blood is too thick and choking. Its rank stink is suffocating me and I can't escape. All I can do is surrender as it draws me further and further back and soon Nat and Elsa are nothing more than small dark dots on the far, distant horizon.

A second later, I'm back standing beside Nat and watching her restless movements under the sheets as she twists and kicks her legs. She lets out a low moan and half-opens her eyes.

'Oh God, Liss,' she whispers. Her voice cracks and a small tear trickles down her cheek. She throws her hand across her forehead and begins to sob.

I stand shaken by the dream, the iron taste of blood still strong in my mouth and making my stomach heave. I didn't speak to Nat like I hoped, so what the hell was all that about? Isn't this whole experience surreal enough, without having to share Nat's nightmare? The bizarreness of it all makes me hope for one brief second that this is all just some drug-induced, bad acid trip, given by mistake in the third-world chaos of King Edward's and none of its real. But the hope is short-lived, extinguished in one breath by my rational mind.

No matter how much I might wish it, deep inside I know my death happened. I've seen my funeral, watched it play out across the loops of time, seen the pain of loss impressed upon my family's faces, and I know there's no going back.

———

Nat's dressed in black trousers and a white shirt and sitting on the couch with her arms huddled around her bent legs. I might be back in time but I'm certainly not part of it, nor can I control it. It's moved me forward again and the sun is streaming in the window, but Nat appears oblivious to its heat. She shakes as she recounts her nightmare to Elsa.

'It was so vivid. I just can't stop thinking about it. I can still see that awful rabbit... even smell the blood...' Nat grips her knees tighter and leans forward.

Elsa's forehead creases and she looks at Nat with narrow eyes. 'Dreams are always a mix of things from our subconscious. I guess we're both still in shock about the whole thing.'

Nat lifts her head. 'What do you think the blood means?'

Elsa shrugs but says nothing. She places a strand of hair in her mouth and chews on it, eyes deep in thought. The room fills with the ticking of the wall clock.

'Well?' says Nat.

Elsa sighs and turns to Nat.

'I really don't know, but blood means death so it's maybe not that surprising. As for the other parts, I guess we did have some great fires on the beach with toasted marshmallows.' She gives a wry laugh. 'The only rabbit memory I can think of was when we stole the school bunnies.'

Nat gives a small laugh. 'The three bunny burglars - I'd forgotten about that,' she says. Suddenly her expression falls. 'We didn't really help them much though. Dingaan and Shaka ripped them to shreds. We should've thought about the dogs before we put them in the garden.'

Elsa frowns at her. 'Hmm, I know, but maybe that's why you dreamt about the blood and the foot coming off.'

Nat shudders. 'Maybe. It's just there're so many weird things happening, Elsa. I know you don't believe me, but I really did sense her yesterday and smell her perfume, and now this nightmare. I don't know, but inside I just have such a strong feeling that something's not right in all this. I really do.'

Elsa looks at her with serious blue eyes. 'Nat, there are no such things as ghosts. People don't come back. You've got to remember, you're still in shock and that will colour how you experience things, as well as what you dream about.'

A long sigh judders out of Nat. 'Lissa's not gone. None of us truly die.'

Elsa pulls down the corners of her mouth. 'You know my stance on that but...' She glances down at her watch and flicks away a dog hair from her trousers. 'As far as I remember from what Pastor Jorge taught, only familiar spirits are supposed to come back, not the real person.'

Nat clenches her fists and frowns. 'Maybe you're right,' she whispers. 'I know she's in heaven.'

Elsa gives Nat a sad smile, 'Well, like Shakespeare says, more fool you for mourning our sister, who's in heaven.'

'I *did* sense her,' says Nat, 'I'm not making it up or imagining things.'

'Okay, let's just leave it. I don't want to argue.' Elsa clears her throat and fumbles through her briefcase. 'I need to get these papers to the Executor - you sure you're okay on your own?'

Nat tucks her hair behind her ears and nods. 'Yes, I'll be fine. I'll see you later.'

'Take it day by day.' Elsa gives Nat a hug, 'That's all we can do.'

Anger prickles through me as I think about Elsa's words. She's right to a point; I should be in heaven, not here. Who's controlling all this and why won't they at least let me give them some sign?

# CHAPTER TWENTY-SIX

I t's early morning and I'm back in Elsa's dining room with no idea of how many days have passed. Karlos sits at one end of the table. My legs grow weak and my hands tremble as I move towards him. Seeing him this close up, smelling him, taking in every little detail, the short brown hairs of his beard, his rugged tanned arms, his brown eyes, is too much. The noise of my longing is deafening. I've wanted to see him again so badly, but I expected it to make me feel happy, not raw. Why was our time together so short? It's so incredibly unfair. Before I can stop myself, I'm right next to him and running my fingers through his hair, wishing that my energy could join with his so that he can sense me, or at the very least smell my perfume like Nat did. But he is oblivious to any part of me. Nat isn't. Her nose twitches and she frowns as her eyes flit anxiously around the room. Why can she sense me, but Karlos can't?

Elsa flicks, straight-backed, through the wad of papers with her red nails. She takes one out and reads through it with lawyer eyes. Seconds later she slams it down with a sigh and looks up. 'The Executor will see us again next week.' She turns to Karlos. 'She'll notify you as well. Lissa's divided everything between the three of us.' She pauses and studies him in silence for a few seconds. 'How come Lissa changed her will?'

Karlos shrugs. 'They kept telling us at Shaloma that alcoholism was a fatal disease. I didn't make her do it if that's what you're insinuating,' he snaps. 'I also made one and left things to her.'

Elsa blinks away. 'Fine,' she says.

I think back to Shaloma. We certainly heard the 'fatal disease' bit enough times which is why Karlos suggested making one. I guess I can understand why Elsa with her cynical lawyer's brain will question me having a new one, but she needs to realise that her and Nat don't need money, while Karlos does. Of course I would include him.

Nat looks from Elsa to Karlos before searching across the room. Elsa tilts her head to one side. Her nostrils flare and she gives her head a small shake as if she can also smell my perfume. The door opens and Eunice comes in. Her face is serious and she's carrying a small parcel wrapped in brown paper. She stops when she sees Karlos and frowns.

Karlos gets up. 'I must go. You sure you want to keep those? Shouldn't I just give them to the Executor?'

Elsa looks directly at him and back down at a pile of papers. 'No, it's okay. I'll give them in.'

Karlos shrugs. 'If you'd told me you wanted them I would have brought them. I thought someone had broken in.' There's a tone of accusation to his words. 'I had no idea you had a key.'

'It's still Lissa's house. She gave me a key and I have every right to let myself in.'

The air grows tense. Nat shifts on her chair, making the leather squeak.

Karlos holds Elsa's gaze for a second before muttering, 'Goodbye.' He turns and paces towards the door, brushing straight past me but still showing no sign that he can sense my presence.

Why the hell's Elsa so aggressive? Can't she see he's in pain and feeling awkward? There's no need to take her hurt out on him.

Eunice follows Karlos and I hear the security gate click closed. She returns and pulls out a chair as if she's about to take a meeting. She plonks the small brown paper parcel on the table. 'I have spoken to the Sangoma,' she says, looking at Nat and then Elsa with a grim expression. 'She says Lissa is not at rest.'

Nat exchanges a quick glance with Elsa.

'She needs the donation,' continues Eunice. 'We must go to the river.'

'A donation?' Nat places her fingers around her gold cross which hangs around her neck and covers it with her fingers.

'The Sangoma says without it she cannot rest.'

'Eunice, I don't know about talking to the Sangoma,' says Nat.

'You must not fear her. She speaks with *Yesu* as well as the ancestral spirits.' Eunice's face grows stern and she speaks to Nat as if she's a little girl again.

Elsa's fingers freeze around the wad of papers. She looks up at Eunice with narrow eyes and sighs before biting her bottom lip.

'The Sangoma says that *Nkosi* did not make the time for Lissa to come.' Eunice looks intently first at Elsa and then at Nat. Nat swallows and her eyes widen.

The three of them sit in silence while the questions march through my mind. What does Eunice mean? If God didn't deem for me to die then who did? I squeeze my eyes closed and will my mind back to that night. I'm sure Karlos and I both had our normal cup of tea before bed that night. I can remember that much. So when did I drink alcohol? When? The memory of Karlos' comment in the hospital stabs me. I'm sure he didn't mean to say I could be hiding my drinking. I think he probably just said it because he was in a state of shock and Elsa was so angry. He knows I wasn't drinking. We spent nearly all our time together. He would've smelled it on me? Karlos was with me all night until he went to the gym at 5am, so how on earth did I wake up fitting just over two hours later? What happened between five and seven to cause something like that? Did someone knock me out and force a bottle of whiskey down my throat? Who would want to do that and how? I'd have choked on it. Nothing makes sense. Nothing!

Nat's voice is a whisper. 'What kind of donation, Eunice?' She hunches in on herself, her hands clasped together so tightly that her knuckles turn white. 'I don't know if I like the idea of talking to ancestral spirits.'

'It is no problem to talk to them,' says Eunice with a frown. 'It must be the stone with the prayer and the money that will let the '*amadlozi*' help her. I have taken the stone from Lissa's garden. We must take it to the river now.' Eunice's mouth is a firm line, her tone is authoritative and it's clear she won't take 'No' for an answer.

Nat tenses and clenches her fingers more tightly around her gold cross. Elsa gives Nat a 'Let's appease her' look and scrapes back her chair. 'Okay, Eunice, if you think it will help, then let's go.'

Eunice's face relaxes and she picks up the parcel. Nat purses her lips together and frowns, but follows them out of the house. As they reach the driveway Nat pulls Elsa to one side and whispers, 'I'm really not happy about this.'

'Oh for goodness' sake,' snaps Elsa. 'Let's make Eunice happy. It's all rubbish anyway.'

Nat's eyes narrow and she glares at Elsa. 'I'll go, but I'm not taking part.'

Elsa rolls her eyes. 'Come on, before Eunice realises you're being stupid.' She hurries towards the BMW and the waiting figure of Eunice, while Nat paces behind with a worried frown across her brow.

I'm already waiting on the opposite bank of the Umgeni River as the three of them make their way down to the edge. Elsa and Eunice move towards the water until they reach the lapping edge, while Nat remains behind on the muddy bank, staring poker-faced at the brown rolling waters. Eunice tucks her dress into her knickers on two sides while Elsa rolls up her jeans. The two of them make a strange picture standing barefoot in the soft brown silt of the river. Eunice tilts her head up to the sky and closes her eyes as if in prayer.

'Okay, Eunice?' says Elsa, 'Do whatever it is you need to do.'

Eunice nods. She holds the brown parcel in one hand and unwraps it in slow, sure movements like she's undoing a baby's nappy. The underbelly of a smooth beige river stone peeps out from a flapping white paper cover. The stone I would guess is from my rockery. The paper on top looks like a letter and is half-wrapped around the body of the stone and secured with an elastic band; the pink of a fifty-rand note flutters from under its edges. If it wasn't for the fact that they're so filled with pain I think I'd burst out laughing at the dark comedy of it all. The South African exchange rate is plummeting; just as well they don't need to donate pounds.

Eunice cradles the stone in her upturned palms. 'I will throw it far in the water and then we must kneel and pray.' She wades past a bunch of white crested reeds on the edge of the brown rippling water and moves forward until it laps strongly just below her knees. She braces herself, legs apart, and pulls back her arm before catapulting it forward. I watch as the stone sails over the flowing water until it hits the surface with a perfect plop, shooting up circles of rising water towards the blue African sky. Then I'm underwater, at one with the stone, watching it keenly as it somersaults down through the muddy brown water. The dangling roots of reeds sway next to me like ghosts, waving me on as I dive beneath them. The donation plunges deeper and deeper through the murky depths. The words of the letter drift out at me like the bubbles of a fish's breath:

'*Amadlozi*,' they proclaim. 'Bring peace to Lissa's soul.' My spirit aches as I read them; there's nothing funny about it anymore, and I close my eyes in silent agreement.

# CHAPTER TWENTY-SEVEN

Nat, Elsa and Karlos sit tight-faced in front of a desk. A woman dressed in the blue Standard Bank uniform sifts through papers. I flinch as I realise it's my will. She shoves a paper in front of Karlos and he signs it. Elsa looks at him with hooded eyes. Nat sits tense and silent, staring in front of her. The woman pushes two papers towards Nat and Elsa which they sign in silence. The room is tense and hot, despite the air conditioning.

'Thank you. Things should be finalised in approximately four months. I'll be in touch as soon as I hear.'

As they exit the building Karlos turns to my sisters, 'Stay well,' he says.

Elsa gives him a curt nod, while Nat manages a half-smile. My spirit tightens. Can't they see he's in pain? They know how much I loved him. Can't they at least try to be nice for my sake?

Elsa watches Karlos stride away. 'I don't like him, I really don't.'

'I can see that,' Nat says.

'Why's he even here? Liss hardly knew him, for fuck's sake.

How long was it? Four months? That's nothing.' Elsa gives her head a shake. 'There's something off about him.'

Nat bites her bottom lip. 'Do you think he had something to do with Lissa's fit?'

Elsa stands staring into space, her face etched in thought. 'Quite possibly. I wouldn't put it past him... I just don't know how to get to the truth.' She lets out a long sigh. 'Let's go for a drink.'

'Oh Els, please, no.'

'Don't be stupid, Natalie,' says Elsa, glaring at her. 'I don't mean get drunk. I just need something to relax me. Surely you do too?'

Nat nods. 'What an awful day... everything's so surreal.'

'Beyond awful,' says Elsa. 'That's why I need a drink. Come on, let's drive out to the thousand hills. I need some scenery and some space. We'll go and see Mom later.'

A cocktail of sadness and confusion sits deep in my spirit as I watch my two sisters walk away arm and arm and melt into the crowds. I guess Elsa's just speaking from her pain. Surely she can't think that the drink is going to help after all we've been through. How things have turned - now it's me worrying about Elsa drinking. An intense feeling of hopelessness washes over me. Why do I have to see all this like some helpless watcher? Why can't I just go on to heaven and be happy?

# CHAPTER TWENTY-EIGHT

I 'm standing barefoot in a sea of soft, swaying grass the colour of the Granny Smith apples I used to love as a child. The sky above is a cloudless indigo and the air is heavily scented with a mix of rose and honeysuckle.

Perhaps God's realised it's too painful for me to be back on earth, or perhaps Eunice's donation has done the trick and moved me on? I see Elsa and Nat on the far side of the field. Our eyes meet. Relief floods Elsa's face. Her whole being smiles out as she lifts up her hand and waves. It's so good to see the sadness gone. I smile back from across the apple-green field and lift my arm to return the wave, while I scan the horizon behind them, half-expecting Mom to also come to say goodbye, and then to turn behind me and see Dad waving his love to us all and calling for me to join him.

I try to step towards Elsa and Nat to give them one last hug goodbye, but my feet refuse to move. Elsa sees my effort and tries to come towards me. Nat does the same. We stare at each other, all willing ourselves to move so that we can just touch for one last time, but something's holding us back.

A loud crack deafens my ears. The sky above has darkened

with thick black clouds. They roar closer and closer, smothering with their gloom, swallowing the living colour and turning it to ugly sepia brown.

Nat and Elsa's faces cloud in fear as the shadowy figure of a man swirls above. Another resounding crash of thunder booms through the air, and the shadowed man clouds over me. I scream as dark liquid drips in burning drops from his fingers. My body jerks. Oh God, I'm convulsing again. I watch transfixed as white froth spits from my open mouth and drifts in front of my eyes like lost sea-foam.

I jerk away from the horror of the vision. I'm in the parking lot directly in front of Elsa's BMW. My sisters sit motionless in the car, staring forward with glazed eyes. They stare for a few more seconds before Nat blinks and gives her head a shake. She rubs a shaky hand across her forehead and turns to Elsa.

'Els. I've just had another weird experience...'

Elsa blinks and stiffens. She turns to Nat and her eyes bore into her. 'What happened?'

Nat shrugs her shoulders and reddens slightly. 'I don't know, really. It was like I went into some kind of trance. I saw Liss in this vividly green field. You were with me. We were on one side and Liss on the other.' Nat frowns while Elsa pales. 'It was so beautiful. It was as I imagine heaven would look and it felt so peaceful, so serene. We tried to go to her but couldn't move... it looked like Liss was trying to get to us but couldn't, then storm clouds suddenly came. They changed into this dark shadowy figure who totally destroyed Liss.' Nat rubs her hand across her forehead and places her head between steeple fingers before shaking it slowly from side to side. 'It was horrible. Really horrible.'

Elsa's eyes are transfixed on Nat. 'This shadowy figure... did he destroy Liss by burning her?'

Nat gives a small nod. Elsa shakes her head before leaning

forward onto the steering wheel. Nat touches her shoulder. 'Elsa. What's wrong?'

Elsa lifts her head. 'I think we must've somehow shared some kind of trauma-related hallucination. I've just had the exact same experience.'

Nat jerks back like she's been slapped. She stares at Elsa. 'Right this minute?'

Elsa nods.

'What's happening, Els? What the hell's going on?' Nat's voice rises in pitch with every word. She leans over to Elsa with earnest eyes. 'I can sense Lissa so strongly again right now... something is not right. There've been so many things. The dream, that donation. Now this. I'm sure Liss is trying to tell us her death wasn't natural, Els. I'm sure she is. Otherwise, why would this all be happening?'

'Nat, I'm sure there's a perfectly sane psychological explanation for it, but at the same time, like I said, I want to find out what Karlos knew about her drinking that night. I'm sure he's hiding something and I don't like the fact he's got a third of Lissa's estate when he's only known her for such a short time. It's got nothing to do with anything supernatural.'

'I think you're just blind to the supernatural, but I also don't trust Karlos. Maybe we should find out more about him. I can't believe Liss suddenly drank. I saw her the day before and she was fine. I'd have known if she was drinking.'

Elsa sits silently in thought for a few seconds before nodding. 'You're right. I saw her two days before. I'd also have known.' She turns to Nat with a cynical smile. 'We saw it often enough, didn't we? She just needed to have one drink and I knew.'

'Do you think Karlos encouraged her to drink that night? Maybe it was the first time since rehab...'

'I don't know. He could've talked her into it. He's also an alcoholic. Perhaps he was craving some, I don't know. I guess it would explain the empty whiskey bottle Eunice found.'

'Maybe, you're right,' says Nat.

'All I know is that we need to find out a lot more about Karlos before I let him get his grubby paws on Lissa's money,' says Elsa, 'My intuition's always proved correct in the past. I don't see why it should be any different now.' Elsa stabs the key in the ignition and the BMW purrs to life. 'I think I need that drink. Let's go.'

I watch them drive off with a hollow feeling in the pit of my stomach. Deep inside I know that I've just experienced a vision both of heaven, and the reason for my death. Elsa's intuition is right. And I know why I'm back. My sisters are right. I wasn't drinking, despite the empty bottle and the stink of alcohol on my pyjamas. Someone tried to make it look that way and that someone is the shadowy figure from the vision we've just shared.

I need to find out who the hell he is. But first I have to somehow get Nat and Elsa away from suspecting Karlos. They've been biased against him from the start, but they need to know it can't be him. There was nothing in Karlos' behaviour that would ever suggest he'd want to harm me - if anything, he couldn't do enough for me. We were so happy. We hardly ever disagreed about things, never even had an argument. I know he loved me, truly loved me. Even when I was in hospital, he looked so broken by it all. Karlos went to the gym at five every morning, so it wasn't as if he'd suddenly left early on that day. If there was someone plotting to get me, all they would've needed was to watch the house for a few days to know when I'd be alone. We're creatures of habit even though we think we're not, and that makes it easy for any would-be perpetrator.

Nic stalked me. Had I ever told Nat or Elsa? I shake my head in irritation. No, I'd only ever mentioned it to Karlos. I don't think they'd even remember who Nic was, even if I somehow could bring his name into their minds. But how could he have given me anything? How could he get into my house, and why kill me and not Karlos if he was really stalking me? My mind jumps to a picture of Alison's pale, pinched face. She hated me because I'd taken Karlos away from her, or so she thought, poor girl. Who knows what went on in her sad head. Maybe the shadow man is a she rather than a he? I shake my head. No, she might have wished it, but I don't think she'd be able to do anything given her high level of anxiety. But it had to be someone who knew I had a drinking problem – otherwise why would they have made it look like I'd been drinking? Wolf? Hattie? Those scum would certainly fit the bill, but they'd have had to pour more than one bottle of whiskey down my throat to cause the type of fitting I had, and how could they have done that? No, it's got to be a poison, but how did my killer give it to me? How?

# CHAPTER TWENTY-NINE

I will myself to calm. I have to think rationally and find out exactly what caused my fitting. It's got to be some kind of drug or poison. My first thought is to find a medical dictionary which lists substances that might cause seizures. I hadn't taken any prescription drugs at Shaloma and I know Karlos didn't. We both hated anti-depressants and tranquillisers; he said he'd had a breakdown once when coming off a Prozac derivative and never touched anything after that. Wolf's ugly face with its blackened teeth rises up in my mind. He said he'd had a breakdown coming off Valium. It could quite possibly be him and Hattie using some drug they had, maybe even an illegal one. I remember Karlos saying he'd heard they'd squandered their money in less than a month and were living in some squat down Point Road. Neither of them liked us. They could've been looking for money? Drug-fuelled crazies did things like that when they needed a fix. Elsa had been angry because Hattie and two men wanted to visit me in hospital. Why would they come? Wolf must've been one. Nic, Gruesome George – he was also a dark horse. There wasn't much love between me and George, although Karlos got on okay with him. I remember Dr Brink asking him about his Trithapon, so he was taking medication, but that doesn't mean he would've killed me. We hardly spoke to each other, although he did come to my funeral for some strange reason, so I can't rule him out.

My mind spins with unanswered questions, but the more I think about it, the more I'm convinced it's got to be those drug-crazed, evil stuff-ups. I think back to the blank prescription from our long-dead Dr Clark which was left on Nat's car. Is someone helping from the other side, giving us a clue? Was it some prescription drug? But why leave it blank? Why didn't they just list what it was if they really want to help? There are thousands of poisons out there. How am I going to find out unless they exhume my body and test it, and that's not an option.

I think back to the lab and all the testing we did for toxins. Tricyclic anti-depressants cause convulsions if the dose is high enough. There were hundreds of them on the market. I remember the sad cases of fatalities of children who ingested them like sweets after fishing through their mother's handbags – we are such a pill-dependent society and doctors dole them out far too easily. I think back to my studies. An overdose of an anti-depressant affects the autonomic nervous system, as well as the central one and even the heart. You need a high dosage, but they definitely can cause seizures serious enough to cause the type of reaction I had. Damaged people are full of irrational hate. They have no morals or conscience. It has to be one of them. Why else would anyone want to harm me and make it look like I'd been drunk?

I think back to that last night in the hospital. Dr Rajeet thought I was on the road to a long life. Did one of them come back to the hospital in the middle of the night to finish off their failed murder plan? It was a Tuesday night, and Karlos went to the meeting. I'm sure they would've asked about me and he could've told them I was going to Hillcrest Hospital the next day. It would be quite easy for them to creep into King Edward's in the middle of the night. No-one would have questioned them because they were white and anyway the nurses didn't monitor who came or went. It's not impossible.

I shake my head. I can't explain the fitting, but if I think about it rationally, the most likely explanation would be that my death in King Edward's was a medical mishap. I let out a dark laugh. There're certainly enough of those covered up in the medical world. But at the same time, there's got to be some point to me coming back. If one of those scum tried to kill me by somehow forcing alcohol and poison into my veins, then they deserve to be punished. Perhaps if I can find them and see what they're up to I'll get my answer, but how to make the first move? The blank prescription and these shared dreams and visions show that someone is helping from the other side, and I have to trust they're someone on the right side of the light.

# CHAPTER THIRTY

Elsa takes out a folded paper from a large brown envelope and pushes it towards Thabo. 'His name's Karlos Beukes. He was a patient with Liss at the rehab and hooked up with her afterwards. That's all we really know about him. He was apparently a farmer from the Greytown area.'

I should've known this would happen. How will we ever find the truth behind my death if they only focus on Karlos?

'You really think he's got something to do with her death?'

Elsa shrugs. 'I just don't trust him. I don't like him.'

Thabo comes from behind the desk and puts his arm around Elsa's shoulder. 'I know it's hard. It's been such a tragic time. What did the hospital list as the cause of death?'

'Her heart stopped,' murmurs Elsa. 'But that doesn't mean something didn't cause it. You know what things are like up there, it's complete chaos. Karlos could easily have given her something.' Elsa's face is screwed up with anger as she spits out the words.

Thabo looks down at her with concern etched deep into his brown eyes.

Elsa brushes trembling fingers across her forehead before

going on. 'I've had a long think about everything. Both Nat and I saw Lissa frequently; she wasn't drinking. For her to suddenly fit like that just doesn't make sense. I know I probably sound a bit hysterical, but I just can't shake off this feeling that something's not right about her death.'

'There's so many weird things happening,' says Nat. 'Eunice said she needed a donation, both Els and I had a vision of some shadowy man attacking her. I keep sensing Liss and smelling her perfume.'

'Shh, Nat,' Elsa says. 'Let's keep it rational please.' She turns to Thabo. 'Liss made him a major beneficiary. She revised it three weeks before her death. If for no other reason, that merits we investigate him. It gives him a prime motive to want her gone.'

Thabo's eyes are narrowed in thought. He turns to Elsa and pats her arm like a father soothing a child.

'Okay, I'll ask Mannie Govender at CR Swart to look into him. He's chief detective up there and owes me a favour.' Thabo turns to Nat. 'Did you make a donation?'

Nat nods. 'We went with Eunice. They threw it in. I waited on the bank.'

Thabo purses his lips. 'And you've sensed her?'

Nat nods and looks at him with wide eyes. 'A few times.'

'I think you're right. We need to look into this Beukes more carefully. I'll get Mannie on the case pronto.'

'Thanks, Thabo. We appreciate it.' Elsa places her hand on his arm to give it a squeeze. She pushes back her chair.

I follow them out of Thabo's office with a mixture of irritation and affection. I know they're doing this out of love, but they've got to stop being so blind and biased about Karlos. If they thought about it more rationally as Elsa keeps advocating, they'd realise his feelings for me were genuine.

'At least Thabo's more in touch with the supernatural,' says Nat, giving Elsa a sideways glance as they step out into the humid air. 'He believed me.'

Elsa pulls a face. 'I'm not going to argue about that. Let's just hope this Govender will help.'

Nat nods. 'I'll see you this evening.' She heads over to her Honda.

Elsa gets into her BMW and slams the driver's door shut. She sits with both hands clasped around the steering wheel before she lets out a long sigh and drops her head forward onto the wheel. I ease myself in next to her, wishing I could just communicate, tell her not to worry, that it's okay, I'm here and I'll find out the truth. It doesn't have to all rest on her shoulders any more, it really doesn't.

Her head jerks away from the steering wheel. She turns to stare wide-eyed at the empty passenger seat where I'm sitting. Her nostrils flare and she lifts her wrist to her nose to sniff it, before wiping it across her nose. She screws her face up in a picture of pained concentration. I smile at her detection of my scent. She can smell my perfume just like Nat, but I don't think her rational mind can deal with it. I lean towards her. *'Elsa,'* I whisper directly into her waiting ear, *'it's me. Can you hear me?'* I wait for her reaction but she remains frozen. It's no good. Elsa sits for a few more seconds in the thick silence, broken only by the distant roar of the passing traffic. She lets out a shuddering sigh and swings the engine into life.

# CHAPTER THIRTY-ONE

I 'm outside Shaloma and for the first time it's somewhere I've really wished I could be. I move with ease though the warm night. The humid air, thick with the sweet smell of damp vegetation and the happy chirruping of the night crickets, is soothing. I look up at the glittering expanse of the night sky. The richness and beauty of an African night is hard to beat. I trace the Southern Cross and Sirius, the Dog Star. Even as a child I loved to scan the night skies for those special stars. I remember lying in the darkness on the cool, damp grass of the caravan park at Dragon's Peak with Dad, Nat and Elsa, and all four of us trying to pinpoint the constellations. Thankfully Dad pointed them out. When he died, I'd looked up at that host of stars and cried out to him that I loved him, missed him, and yearned for him every day.

I reach the familiar white walls and edge around the building until I'm directly outside Dr Brink's office. I move into his darkened room with a feeling of power and control. There's something to be said for not being bound in space when you're trying to find your killer. I push my hand through the aluminium drawer of the filing cabinet and push apart the atoms forming the lock. The drawer clicks forward and I sift through the files one by one. Valium is listed on Wolf's and Methadone on Hattie's. I run my fingers down the page of Nic's records and lift my eyebrows: Prozac for anxiety and depression – he hid that well. His ravaged face at my funeral comes back into mind. He did look genuinely upset. Maybe I need to give him the benefit of the doubt? My gut feeling is he's not my enemy and I don't even dislike him anymore, but still I won't rule him out altogether. I'll just put him at the bottom of the list.

I pick up George's file. The Trithapon Dr Brink spoke of is listed. I frown as I read the name. Thinking back, I'm sure that's not a tranquilliser, I'm sure it's a neuroleptic drug. Maybe George is psychotic? He was always so quiet. I hardly spoke to him, although he used to watch me a lot with his lizard eyes, but most of the time he just faded into the shadows like Alison. Pity they didn't get together. They suited each other. Although I think she obviously fancied Karlos. Poor girl, she probably misread the signals when he was just being kind.

I close my eyes and draw up memories of George. I see him again sitting on the leather couch clutching a cup of tea, his pockmarked face pale and drawn, the jawline jerking and his tongue peeking in and out like a gecko's. I should have picked up on the fact that there was more of a mental illness aura around him rather than just alcoholism, especially with that tongue. I should've twigged as soon as Dr Brink mentioned the Trithapon. I don't know why I didn't. *Still waters run deep*, and it's true. It's often the quiet ones who you have to watch the most.

Did George secretly harbour a hatred for me? Did I resemble someone in his past that he wanted revenge on? If he's psychotic, he could easily have had delusions about me, or even Karlos, and want in some way to harm us. As a neuroleptic drug, Trithapon is likely to cause serious fitting, especially with an overdose. I need to find out what George is doing now, and Hattie and Wolf for that matter. Who knows, maybe she turned Wolf onto heroin as well? You can't get much lower than squatting in Point Road and craving for your fix. I can't rule them out.

I look back through George's file. I need to see if his doctor has the name Clark, then the blank prescription would make some kind of sense. I run my finger down the page. The doctor's name is listed as Dr Bond; first name James, no doubt. Is that really his doctor or is he lying? I scan again through Nic's, followed by Hattie's and Wolf's. None of them have a Dr Clark listed. I pick up Karlos' file. My chest contracts and a dull pain edges itself across my chest. It feels so strange looking through pages from his life before me. There's no doctor listed. The only medical establishment given is Greytown Hospital. That makes sense. He said he'd been a mess and not wanting to see anyone before he was admitted, so it stands to reason he wouldn't have had a regular doctor. No drugs are listed other than alcohol.

I find the weekly meeting record. Karlos is missing from all of them other than the one on the night of my death. My heart sinks, and I hope he's not drinking again. He needs to sense my presence, smell me like Nat and Elsa can. If he can just grasp the fact I'm still here, maybe it'll help him cope with the pain. I read through the rest of the attendance record. Hattie and Wolf are missing from the last three weeks, but George is still going regularly, so is Nic. There's someone called Mike on the list now. Won't it be poetic justice if it's bastard old boyfriend Mike, but I guess that's being a little too hopeful? Alison it appears is still an inmate, even though she attends the meetings. Her pale face rises like a sick moon in my mind. Poor girl! I wonder if she'll ever reach the recovery stage?

# CHAPTER THIRTY-TWO

E lsa and Nat sit stiff-backed across from Inspector Mannie Govender as he filters through the files littered across his desk. He pulls one out from the bottom, untidy writing scrawled along the side in black marker pen. *Melissa Windsor – deceased.* The cheap brown cardboard cover is so ugly, like an insult to have documents about my life filed away in that.

'There's no way we could exhume her body without proper evidence,' Inspector Govender says in a measured tone, almost irritated at having to investigate what he so clearly believes is a no-win case, purely as a favour to Thabo.

Elsa looks directly at him with hard eyes. 'I'm aware of that. What does her file say?'

Inspector Govender frowns at Elsa. Nat touches Elsa's arm as the Inspector scans down the first page.

'The only report we have is from her first admission. It details the seizures and coma. Her cause of death is listed as sudden heart failure.'

'Didn't they do a post-mortem to find out what caused the failure?' Elsa asks.

Inspector Govender turns over the page. He shakes his head.

'Why not?' demands Elsa.

Inspector Govender looks at and her and pulls down his mouth. 'You'll have to ask the hospital. There's nothing listed.'

'We need Karlos' medical details. We need to see what drugs he was on and if they can cause fitting. If he's on something which can, we could have a connection to start on,' snaps Elsa.

She leans towards Inspector Govender as the air in the bleak office grows tense. 'I am very aware that murder is commonplace and this is not a high priority to you, but I need to make very clear to you that we expect this case to be investigated fully.'

'If there is proper evidence then of course it will be.' Inspector Govender shuts my cardboard file with an angry jerk and shoves back his chair.

Elsa's eyes harden. 'I'll be sure to tell Thabo how helpful you've been.'

They lock eyes like warring buffalos before Elsa turns to Nat and motions for them to leave.

Inspector Govender stands up and shuffles through the pile of brown files on his desk.

'Well, are you going to ask for Karlos' medical records from Shaloma?'

Inspector Govender looks at Elsa with half-closed eyes, like a hooded cobra. 'I will send a detective as soon as I can. Now, I'm sorry, I'm very busy.'

Nat and Elsa fling him a dirty look and slam the door behind them. Their heels clop loudly on the hardwood floor.

'What a useless arsehole,' says Elsa as soon as they step out into the humid Durban air. 'No wonder the country's descending into criminal chaos. He doesn't give a damn.'

Nat nods. 'If that's how he acts when he owes a favour, I'd hate to see what he's like when he doesn't.'

'Fucking idiot. I'll speak to Thabo about him.'

Elsa yanks open her car door. She gets in and waits for Nat to sit in the passenger seat. 'Maybe we should just employ a private detective and get this bastard ourselves? The police aren't going to make it a priority, not unless we can provide proof that it's murder.'

Nat bites her bottom lip and nods. 'Perhaps we should.'

Elsa stiffens her face in resolve and swings the engine into life. She squeals away and I watch the red blur of her BMW disappear among the darting, hooting cars with a mix of irritation and despair. Maybe getting a private detective will be the best move. At least he'll be objective. You can't solve a murder if you start off with a bias.

# CHAPTER THIRTY-THREE

I stand stiff in the counselling room at Shaloma and watch Dr Brink and Helen sift through a pile of papers. The seats are arranged in a circle with the television in front. Outwardly, nothing's changed. Life goes on without me and I guess the longer it carries on, the less I'll be missed or remembered.

Nic enters, his face tight and drawn. I look in surprise at his loose Wrangler jeans and pale arms. He really doesn't look well, nothing like the good-looking, tanned surfer boy I first encountered.

Helen gives him a welcoming smile. 'Good to see you, Nic. How are you doing?'

'I'm here.' Nic shrugs his shoulders and sits down. His whole body looks like it's shrunk.

George enters, staying in the doorway, pale with his pock marks even more pronounced. His lizard eyes dart from Nic to Helen to Dr Brink and back to Nic. I see him swallow and clench his fists by his side while his chest rises and falls in short, shallow pants. I wonder what's going through his mind. Looking at him now it's fairly obvious that he's got some type of mental illness. Both he and Nic look worse than I remember. Were they always like this, or was it only because I was down there with them in the pit of addiction that they didn't look so bad?

Dr Brink looks at the clock. 'I've tried to contact Hattie and Wolf to no avail I'm afraid, nor Karlos. We'll give them a few minutes and if not we'll have to start without them. Alison's not well tonight and nor is Mike, so they won't be joining us.'

My heart drops at the sound of Karlos' name. I so want him to be here, but at the same time I can understand that maybe coming here is too painful. The desire to see him again swamps me. His bearded face fills my mind. We could have had such a good life together. Why is life so horribly unfair!

'Can I give anyone some tea? Water?'

Nic shakes his head at Helen, while George stares forward and says nothing. My eyes burn into him. He shifts uncomfortably on his chair as if he senses my hate. There's something just so off about him, but why would he have something against me? I look back to Nic. He's sits with his head held in his hands and his shoulders hunched. Did he do it? Is that why he looks in such a bad way? Is he consumed with guilt at his crime? Nic has got to be on the list. I wasn't imagining his stalking - Nic could easily be a murderer.

'How has the week been, George?'

George is sitting on the edge of his chair, hands clasped together and his chest still rising in fast pants. He shakes his head and murmurs, 'Not, good. They're trying to say O.J. murdered his wife.'

'Yes, I saw it on the news. It's tragic.'

George nods and swallows. His hands twist and turn as he mumbles, 'It was her fault.'

Dr Brink narrows his eyes at George. 'Did you have a drink?' His voice is calm and empty of accusation.

George shakes his head. 'Nearly. Someone was trying to force me. I think it might be them.'

'Oh.' Dr Brink and Helen exchange a glance.

'They're in America George, not here.'

George stares ahead without responding.

Dr Brink looks at George for a few minutes before speaking. 'I think it might be best if you stayed with us for a few days. I want to refer you to another doctor who I think can help you. Can you do that?'

George's head jerks up. He looks at Dr Brink with his gecko tongue half out before giving a short nod. Nic is looking sideways at George with his mouth slightly open. He looks at Helen and raises his eyebrows in question. He's obviously in the dark about George's condition. Why the hell was a patient with psychosis allowed in with us? George shouldn't have been there even if he was on medication.

Helen gives a small smile and asks in a quiet voice, 'How have you been, Nic?'

Nic shrugs. 'Been a hard week, but I've held out.'

'Well done. The longer you do that, the easier it will be,' says Helen.

George jerks and begins hitting out madly at the air around him. 'Leave me alone. Don't sit near me. I know you're trying to hurt me. Bitch. Bitch! You always want to hurt me.' He jumps up, his face contorted and thrashes his skinny arms around like a flailing fish trying to escape the fisherman's net. His eyes are narrow and glazed, filled with a dangerous cocktail of madness and fear. He's definitely seeing someone. Is it me? I move back towards the door. There's something so dark about him. His eyes remain transfixed on the space in front as he continues to hit out and scream. It can't be me he's seeing.

Dr Brink grabs one of George's flailing arms and tries to catch the other one as he flings it around in front of him. 'No. Don't touch me, you bitch! Don't touch me!' George screams. 'I can't do this anymore. Leave me. Leave me!'

George tries to yank his arm from Dr Brink's grip. Saliva dribbles from the sides of his mouth and his whole body shakes.

Dr Brink manages to grab the rebel arm and I see the flesh on it turn white as he closes his grip around it. George's legs buckle under him and Dr Brink draws him forward towards the floor.

'Help hold him down, Nic. Quick.'

Nic jumps up to help Dr Brink wrestle the squirming body of George onto its side. George goes rigid and I see his back arch. He twists sideways and pushes back his head while letting out a gut-wrenching scream and sending forth a torrent of flying saliva. Dr Brink and Nic draw back with wrinkled noses. Helen, syringe in hand, kneels next to the struggling George, while Dr Brink holds his upper arm still so she can plunge the needle into the thin flesh. George continues to writhe and twist for a few seconds more, before his mouth goes slack and his eyes roll inward, showing only the whites. He lies like that for a few more seconds before his lids close.

Helen takes a tissue and wipes away the streams of salvia which have dribbled down his chin. The writhing shudders to a stop. Nic lets go of the flaccid arm and sits back on the carpet looking like a shell-shocked soldier. His hands tremble and his chest moves up and down in fast pants. Hardly a session to help keep you off the booze. Poor Nic, I wouldn't blame him if he didn't bother coming back.

'Phone the Psychiatric Ward at Fort Napier, Helen. They'll have to take him in. He must be off his Trithapon.'

My eyes rest on the now prone form of George. Why the hell is he off his meds? They know he's got serious psychiatric problems, so why is he even back here? I look at his inert body. The gecko tongue is limp and lolling out from the side of his mouth. It's quite possible he's my killer. A psychotic is capable of anything given their condition. I think back to the first time I met him. He'd done a double take when he first saw me. Maybe I reminded him of some woman in his past, someone he obviously hated?

I frown back into the time before my sudden fit. I'd seen Nic, but I can't remember ever seeing George. Nonetheless, just because I didn't see him, doesn't mean he couldn't have been there. He's the last person I would've thought of, so why would I even notice him if he was somewhere in a crowd? Killers often look ordinary, just like that Boston Strangler or Yorkshire ripper bastard, Peter Sutcliffe. Time and time again they're revealed as little grey men with huge issues in their blackened souls. George is as grey as they come. He could quite easily be a killer for whatever dark reasons he carries in his sick head.

# CHAPTER THIRTY-FOUR

Thabo clicks open his briefcase and takes out an envelope. 'I'm sorry Mannie wasn't helpful, but he's passed me copies of Lissa's medical records from Shaloma as well as those of Karlos.'

He hands the sealed envelope to Elsa. 'Hopefully this'll be better than the one from King Edwards,' she says.

Nat sits straight and tense as Elsa expertly slices open the brown envelope. The room is thick with tension. Elsa takes out some stapled sheets of white paper. They crackle through the silence as she pages through them. Finally, she places the pages on the table. 'Nothing. Karlos was admitted to Greytown Hospital for alcohol dependence, but no medication's listed.'

Thabo looks intently at Elsa. 'You think he could've given her some medication?'

'It's possible she was poisoned in my opinion. I've spoken to some doctors and they feel it's unlikely to be just alcohol to cause that degree of fitting. My instinct is that if Karlos wanted to kill her, he gave her some drug and then mixed it with the alcohol. The question is, how?'

'And what drug,' says Nat.

Elsa pulls down her mouth. 'Nothing he was prescribed, unfortunately.'

Nat raises her eyebrows and then shrugs. 'Still doesn't mean he didn't do it that way. He could've got something from another doctor.'

'*Yebo*,' says Thabo, 'That's possible.'

I watch with frustration and exasperation at my sisters' attempts to play detective. I need to get them to look at the others and not fixate on Karlos. Elsa slits open the second envelope. She scans through another wad of white papers until her eyes become frozen on the second page.

Thabo frowns and lean in towards her. 'What's wrong?'

Elsa stares at the paper. 'Liss was on a daily dose of a drug called Trithapon. Why didn't Shaloma or the hospital tell us?'

Did she really say Trithapon? Why would Trithapon be on my record? They must be looking at George's file not mine. My head begins to spin. Am I psychotic and just can't remember? My eyes blur. I strain to hear Nat and Elsa, begging them silently to confirm I'm not psychotic.

Nat takes my records from Elsa. 'That's a drug prescribed for psychosis. Dave's cousin takes it.' She looks up at Elsa with wide eyes. 'Was Liss psychotic?'

'Don't be stupid, Nat. We would've known if she was.'

Nat remains po-faced with doubt clouding her eyes. I stiffen as she turns to Elsa. 'Phone Dr Rogers and ask him. Perhaps she just hid it from us.'

Elsa scrapes her chair back on the white tiles. Thabo and Nat sit in silence, intent as listening lions, as Elsa demands to speak to Dr Rogers. She scribbles down notes as the doctor's muffled voice ripples out from the phone into the silent room. She thanks him and turns to their waiting faces. 'Nothing on her record about Trithapon. He's as surprised as we are. He says he hadn't even seen Liss for at least two months prior to her admission to rehab and even then it was just for a throat infection. If Shaloma had prescribed anything or thought there was any sign of mental illness like psychosis, they would have notified him.'

'What the hell's going on?' Nat puts her face into her hands and shakes her head. 'If Lissa wasn't psychotic, what the hell's an anti-psychotic drug doing on her record?'

The hurt of Nat's doubt still lingers in my gut, but did Dr Brink put it on by mistake? Or was he giving it to me without my knowledge? I think back to our sessions. He gave me a glass of water to drink on several occasions. It could well have had something in and I wouldn't have even noticed. Does it have a strong flavour? Probably not. I shake my head. Did George put it there? Did he want to hurt me for some reason, or was he just trying to get out of taking it himself? He's psychotic, after all. It's quite possible he could've imagined Dr Brink was trying to kill him and so he passed it on to the first file he could find. My mind paces back through the surnames. Alphabetically our names would've been close together, but was it Trithapon that caused my fitting, or was it something else?

Thabo's face is creased in a frown. He rubs his fingers across his forehead. 'I'll speak again to Mannie. Her death is not as cut and dried as he thinks. He'll need to speak to the doctor at the Shaloma as well as the hospital. I'll do what I can to help.' He pauses and then looks intently at Nat and Elsa. 'You would not be sensing Lissa's spirit if there wasn't something wrong, and the Sangoma would not have said she needs a donation. We need to get to the bottom of it. Your father would expect nothing less from me.'

'Thank you, Thabo. We appreciate it,' says Nat, her face a mix of sadness and confusion.

'We're going to employ a private detective to look into Karlos' background. I bet he gave her something, maybe this Trithapon, I don't know, but I do know that somehow we'll nail the bastard. I promise you that,' says Elsa.

# CHAPTER THIRTY-FIVE

A thin man resembling a ferret and dressed in a crumpled beige linen suit sits opposite Nat and Elsa. He clicks open his briefcase and takes out a brown file. What is it with all the boring brown? He sucks in his cheeks and surveys a tense Nat and Elsa. 'I'm still trying to gather information on Mr Karlos Beukes. There are records of a Greytown farmer by that name, but I want to find out a bit more about him.'

He flicks open the file with thin fingers and long, yellowed nails. 'These are copies of the records of the other patients admitted to Shaloma at the same time as your sister. I've found an interesting one.'

He pushes across a paper with yellow highlighter slashed midway across the page like a rising sun. Nat and Elsa lean in together and stare wide-eyed at the paper.

'Whose record is this?'

'George Mannering. He was admitted two days before your sister. He's a diagnosed psychotic. He's on that drug you asked me to look for.'

Elsa snatches the file out of Ferret-man's hands and flicks stiffly through it, her eyes scanning fiercely down each page.

'What the fuck was he doing there?' she demands, her face screwed up in anger. 'He should have been in a psychiatric ward, not a rehab.'

'Do you think he gave Lissa something? If he's psychotic he could do anything.' Nat looks up at Ferret-man.

'Could be,' he says, pulling down the corners his mouth.

Elsa shrugs and slams down the file. 'I don't know. Why would he? We've never even heard Liss mention him.'

'I don't know either, but I really think we need to look into him more; maybe it's him and not Karlos,' says Nat.

Elsa pulls a face. 'No, I want Mr Fletcher to focus on Karlos.'

Nat lets out a sigh and raises her eyes briefly to the ceiling, while Ferret-man's eyes scan from Elsa to Nat and back to Elsa. 'I don't think we must ignore the listing of the same drug, especially since Mannering's psychotic, but are you sure your sister wasn't prescribed it?' He stops and leans back in his chair, putting his fingers together in a steeple position. 'Maybe she had this hidden condition and you didn't know about it?'

Elsa leans across the desk and slaps the top of the file so hard that the desk vibrates. 'I think we'd know if there was a history of psychosis with her,' she says through clenched teeth. 'She was an alcoholic, nothing else. Her death is suspicious. Let me spell out the facts: her GP says she has never been psychotic, so the Trithapon on her record at Shaloma is suspicious; King Edward hospital's record shows no post-mortem so we don't know what caused the sudden heart failure. And this happens right before she was about to be transferred to a rehabilitation hospital because she was making such good progress? Yet, she suddenly died. If there wasn't a strong case for looking into her death, and the police weren't so fucking useless, I wouldn't be employing you.' Elsa's voice has risen manically with each phrase and now she's shrieking and spitting at Ferret-man.

He leans back into his chair and pulls his head down into his neck like a tortoise. He wafts a wiry hand up and down in front of Elsa as if calming a child. For a second I think she's going to slap it, but she gives an angry shake of her head and sits back in her chair and begins chewing hard on a strand of blonde hair.

'Yes, of course. I'm sorry, I had to ask. Personally I don't see anything of alarm in Beukes at the moment, but I'll keep looking.'

Elsa leans back in her chair, her chest still heaving with emotion. Nat looks pale, probably as shocked as I am at Elsa's uncharacteristic loss of control. Poor Elsa; this is really getting to her and it's all my fault. Nat places her hand over Elsa's clenched fist and gives it a squeeze. Elsa reddens slightly and gives a slight smile. She stiffens her shoulders and moves back into the chair.

'You might not see anything of alarm but my gut feeling is him. I want you to concentrate on Karlos.'

Ferret-man does little to hide the sneer which slides across his face.

'Maybe we should also look at the others Els, especially George,' Nat says.

Elsa frowns while Ferret-man clears his throat and starts shuffling the papers together. 'I think your sister's right. If you want, I can look more into Mannering, just to make sure. Two of the other patients are living together in a squat down Point Road - a Harriet Beauchamp and a Wolfgang Schmidt. She's a heroin addict and he's an alcoholic. If your sister had been robbed they'd be high on our list. The other one's a Nicholas Davis, an ex-lawyer. Do you want me to look at all of them?'

'I think we should,' says Nat.

Elsa grits her teeth and pushes back her chair. 'You need to let me lead, Nat. Focus on Karlos and find out more about George Mannering. I just want those two for now. If we find evidence to write them off, we'll look at the others.'

'Okay. It should take me a few weeks but I'll get back to you as soon as I can.' Ferret-man places the file back in the briefcase and clicks it closed.

Nat sits tense and tight-faced while Elsa stands up. 'Thank you,' she mutters.

'Wait until I have more information before you pass this on to the police, if you don't mind.'

Elsa nods. 'Will do. Let's go.'

Nat scrapes back her chair without looking at Elsa. She holds out her hand to Fletcher. 'Thank you. We'll wait to hear from you.'

'Yes, of course,' says Fletcher, scrabbling to his feet and offering his yellow-nailed and limp-wristed hand to her. He turns to Elsa who barely returns the offered shake before marching out of the office with Nat, stiff-backed and silent behind her.

'I'll phone you as soon as I find something,' calls Fletcher as the door closes behind them.

I watch as they march down the passage. I hate to see them angry with each other, but thankfully Nat's a bit more open-minded than Elsa about Karlos, and the detective is sure to trace something about the roots of George's psychosis. There must be some record of his psychotic woman hating, especially the 'bitch' he thought he was seeing in the meeting. Then hopefully Elsa's sharp mind will put two and two together and realise it's him, not Karlos.

Nat clicks the car door closed and fastens her seatbelt in silence. Elsa gives her a sideways glance and grips the steering wheel before stabbing the keys into the ignition. The engine purrs into life and they drive out into the busy dual carriageway with the air tense and hot between them.

Nat swallows and grips her hands together. 'I feel so confused,' she says. 'I'm even beginning to doubt Lissa. Why would a drug be listed on her records if...?'

'Liss was not psychotic. We've already established that. What the hell is wrong with you?'

'We can't be certain, can we?'

Elsa turns open-mouthed to Nat and I mirror her shock. How can Nat even think that, let alone say it? Did she really think so little of me that she'd think I'd hide something like that from them?

'I can't believe you just said that.'

Nat reddens and turns to stare out of the window. The air between them bristles while Elsa puts her foot down and squeals in and out of the thundering traffic. They drive in silence until she reaches Nat's house and stops outside with the engine still running.

'I'm sorry. I feel like I'm in some kind of nightmare. I just don't know what's happening anymore.' Nat's eyes fill with tears. 'I just don't think we can assume Liss told us everything about her life, especially when she was drinking.'

Elsa nods curtly but says nothing. Nat sits trembling next to her for a few seconds more before getting out and clicking the car door closed without speaking.

Elsa watches her go into the house with her knuckles clenched around the steering wheel. My spirit is still stinging with shock. I can't believe that Nat of all people would doubt my sanity. How can she betray me like that?

# CHAPTER THIRTY-SIX

Back in Ferret-man's tatty office a few days later, a smug smile slides across his face as Elsa and Nat enter. He pushes back his chair and offers them a limp-fish hand before ushering them to two chairs. He's wearing a crumpled brown suit this time; obviously models himself on Colombo. Let's hope the modelling extends to the quality of his work.

'What have you got?' Elsa's gaze is direct as she leans forward across the desk.

Nat's nose wrinkles slightly from the musty smell of the place. She's pushes herself back into the chair so that she's ramrod straight with a face as serious as a High Court judge. My eyes flick over her. She's obviously lost weight. I'm still so angry with her at thinking I might be psychotic, but at the same time a knot of guilt lodges in my stomach.

Fletcher leans back in his plastic leather chair. He places his hands together in the steeple shape and licks his lips, enjoying the sense of anticipation he's creating. Elsa's expression hardens into a frown.

'I've found nothing more of concern on Beukes, but I've gathered information about Mannering's background. It appears that his mother shot his father dead with his own shotgun when he was ten. She got off with a suspended sentence for culpable homicide. Shot him through the bedroom door, alleging he was in a drunken rage and threatening to stab them both to death. Medical records show Mr Mannering having ongoing psychological problems since that time.' Fletcher pauses dramatically and gives his thin lips another lick.

Nat's shoulders sag. She closes her eyes and lets out a small sigh. I wish I could read her thoughts, but I'm sure she must now realise how wrong she was to doubt my sanity. Elsa frowns and narrows her eyes at Fletcher.

'So he probably hated women.'

Fletcher gives a dry laugh. 'You read my mind. Yes, quite possibly.'

'But that still doesn't mean he's the one who harmed Lissa. There was no sign of a break-in at her house and, as far as I know, she never had anything to do with him outside of rehab.' Elsa twists her finger around a strand of hair before chewing on it, her eyes still narrow with thought. 'No, I'm sorry, we can't just assume it's him. I'm not prepared to just jump at the first possible avenue. I told you I want Karlos Beukes properly investigated. What else have you found?'

Ferret-man's face hardens and he gives a shrug. His fingers tighten around the parker pen he's holding. 'As I said, nothing of concern. The farmer story matches out on paper and so does the dead wife. So far it seems to tie up.'

'Well, until we've fully examined everything I want him to remain high on the list. Is that clear?'

Ferret-man gives Elsa a curt nod.

Nat looks up and leans in towards Fletcher. 'I don't agree,' she says, 'Karlos said he went to the gym early that morning. Maybe George could've broken in when he saw him leave?'

'We've no evidence of a break-in.'

Nat gives a small shrug. 'I know, but what if Karlos forgot to lock up?'

'It's possible,' says Fletcher, flicking his eyes from one to the other. 'Or he could've picked it. A Yale lock's quite easy to pick.'

Elsa slaps her hand on the table. 'We need proper evidence. We can't just have pie-in-the-sky possibilities.'

Nat pulls a face. 'I know, but maybe we should pass this on to the police now. They need to investigate properly? Even Govender can't deny that it demands looking into.'

'I think that's what we're paying Mr Fletcher for because the police are so bloody useless,' says Elsa. She turns back to Fletcher and raises her eyes to the ceiling. 'Okay, let's look into both, but I want you to concentrate on Karlos first.'

Nat pouts and grips her hands together in her lap.

Fletcher purses his lips and looks at Elsa with narrow eyes. 'Will do.' He scrapes back his chair to put an end to the meeting, his stiff back and jaw showing obvious signs of his irritation. 'Later, if you want, I'll also look into the two in the squat; can't trust heroin addicts. They stop at nothing.'

Elsa gives him a slight smile. She pushes back her chair and offers Fletcher her hand. 'Possibly.'

'I still think we need to speak to Inspector Govender and get him to contact Mr Fletcher so that at least they can work together on this,' says Nat, pushing back her chair and getting to her feet.

Fletcher gives a wry laugh. 'I'm sure the inspector will love that.'

Elsa pulls a face at Nat. 'I think Mr Fletcher's right. Govender's not going to want to work with anyone.'

'Well, surely we still need to tell him,' says Nat.

'You could get Govender to check Mannering's whereabouts the night before her fit and her death in the hospital.'

'Good idea,' says Elsa. 'I'll ask him. Thank you and keep us posted.'

'No problem,' says Fletcher, rising to his feet as they leave his office.

Elsa and Nat pace down the corridor in silence, the air tense again between them. My heart aches as I watch them disappear around the corner. I don't want to see them fight over this, but Nat's right; surely the police will find it strange that I've got Trithapon on my record when any investigation into my past shows I've never suffered from psychosis, and as a bonus at least it will also clear up Nat's doubts about my sanity. I think back to George. I never even spoke to him alone; how could he have been so deluded as to think I could threaten him in any way? But then again if he's psychotic, I guess his delusion doesn't need to make sense. But he must be very shrewd to have changed my record. I can't even imagine how he did it. He must've planned things so carefully, so far in advance. He must've stalked us, watched us, and obviously he was much better at doing it than Nic or I'd have seen him. At least if the police look into his whereabouts on those nights and find he's been near me, alarm bells should ring.

# CHAPTER THIRTY-SEVEN

The strong salt scent of sea air tickles my nose and my ears fill with the crashing of breaking waves. I'm on the promenade at South Beach, and Karlos is standing about four feet in front of me. He's wearing faded Levis and a white T-shirt and looks so good. The musky scent of his aftershave wafts over to me, igniting my longing. I want so badly to touch him, to be back in this earthly life as a living, breathing part of it, drinking in every precious second.

Karlos heads towards a row of parked cars basking like a pod of seals in the hot midday sun. He's holds a large brown envelope in one hand as he moves through the rows of cars towards my white Golf. And then I see her, someone sitting in the passenger seat.

Karlos yanks open the driver's door and eases in behind the wheel. He turns to look at the woman, as I stand in front of the bonnet and stare at her through the windscreen. She's no looker; about forty, with lank black hair draped either side of a long, sallow face and a square jawline. Her eyes are lizard-brown and narrow, her lips a thin line, giving her whole face a bitter look. She reminds me of one those rough, poor white types. Her faded yellow shirt is open at the neck and a smoking cigarette burns between two nicotine-stained fingers, with chipped red nail varnish. She's the type I'd pull my nose up at if we met. What on earth is she doing with Karlos, and what the hell is she doing sitting in my car?

'Okay, *Boetie*?'

'Ja, they say it's on track, but will still take about three and a half months. We just had another paper to sign.'

She grimaces. '*Agh*, that's normal, hey? Any problems?'

Karlos shakes his head. 'Just the fucking sisters glaring at me, but fuck them.'

I shake my head and dart my eyes from the woman to Karlos and back to the woman again. She called him *boetie*. Karlos never told me he had a sister.

He leans across her and places the brown envelope in the glove compartment before turning to her with an ugly leer. 'Should be around eight hundred thousand after taxes; not bad for a couple months' fucking, hey?'

His sister throws back her head in an ugly laugh. 'Ja, a lot of people would kill for your job, hey, *boetie*?'

Karlos joins the laughter and pulls out my car keys with the *New South Africa* key ring still attached.

'*Not bad for a few months' fucking?*' Surely he can't be talking about me, but even as I think it, I know it's true. There was no romance. Instead my murder was carefully planned and executed. I close my eyes as the sea swops places with the sky. I thought things felt surreal before but now it's all so much worse. I think back to the lurid tales in magazines of women duped by men with double lives. They'd all sounded too far-fetched to be believable. Things like that didn't really happen in real life, or so I thought.

Karlos' words echo through my mind again and again. '*Not bad for a few months' fucking*' – each syllable is like a disembowelment. I think back to our lovemaking. I thought it was so pure, so full of love, when in reality all he wanted was my money.

I sense a young couple stride through my hunched shell of a body, oblivious to my pain. I look up and see the young woman flinch and rub her upper arm as gooseflesh ripples over it. She looks about nineteen with long golden hair and a tanned, bikini-clad body. I stare after her. The surfer boy at her side looks down and puts his arm around her, drawing her in close to his side. His eyes twinkle and he looks like he loves her, looks like he cares, but does he? I remember Karlos smiling at me, taking my hand, playing the role of the caring lover so well, so incredibly well. We must have looked like that. His eyes twinkled, showed love, showed concern, showed red-eyed pain at my funeral, and in front of Nat and Elsa. He faked things well.

I think back to the last time I saw him at the hospital. He told me he was on his way to the Shaloma meeting so it must've been around seven p.m. I remember him say that he needed the meetings after what had happened, and that he was trying so hard not to turn to alcohol to help him cope. He looked so genuine, so caring when he kissed me goodbye. He could have come back that night and put something in my drip while I was sedated. The nurses knew he was my boyfriend. They wouldn't care and were too busy to watch him. He'd obviously failed with his first attempt to kill me. Had he sedated me and injected me with a mix Trithapon and whiskey to cause my fitting that first time? Is that why Trithapon was on my file? It's feasible. What a shrewd bastard. If they'd done toxicity tests at King Edward's and found it in my bloodstream it wouldn't have looked suspicious because it was on my chart from Shaloma. I hold my head in my hands as the tears prick behind my eyes. Oh Lord. Chance really conspired against me. Going to King Edwards' gave him another fortuitous opportunity; an even better one in fact. Who'd suspect murder if I died in some foul, third-world hospital? Everyone knew if you went to King Edward's the chances were you'd die either of neglect, incompetence or septicaemia. They didn't even bother with post-mortems, so I guess he had to do it before I went to Hillcrest. I retch as I recall his lips on my forehead when he gave me the last kiss goodbye. He knew full well it was a kiss of death.

Oh God. This is worse than I could ever have imagined. I stare out at the breaking waves as they crash onto the sand. How could I have been so stupid, so naïve? I guess it's true that you see what you want. I chose to believe Karlos loved me and was one of the good guys, that we'd have the long 'happy ever after' together.

I guess the only thing I can be grateful for now is that the scales are finally off my eyes. This must be a necessary part of my spiritual journey. I'm being shown the blatant truth. The true Karlos is sitting in front of me, sans his mask and his whole false persona, the one who only his septic sister really knows. The devil isn't called the father of lies for nothing and Karlos is clearly one well versed in them. Maybe this is a truth I had to learn before I could move on? How do you attain spiritual enlightenment and final rest if you're so deluded and ignorant about the real cause of your death?

I close my eyes and try and paint my mind black, but instead all I see is Nat, bent now on a mission of blaming George, and once Fletcher gathers evidence Elsa will no doubt agree with her. I rub a shaky hand across my forehead. What an idiot I've been! There I was thinking he was such a down-to-earth farmer with nothing underhand about him. He's an ace conman.

My Golf's engine coughs and splutters to life and I watch grim-faced as Karlos backs it away from me with a self-satisfied sneer, while his revolting sister blows her dirty smoke in rings towards my car roof. I clench my fists as she stubs out her cigarette in my ashtray. That's my car, mine! What's she even doing in it? I close my eyes and wish I could just reveal myself and scare them both to death, but of course I can't. My helplessness fills me with anger. What's the point of sending me back and showing me this truth if I'm powerless to do anything? What the hell good is that?

A red BMW pulls into the parking space Karlos has just vacated. I laugh in disbelief as Elsa sits behind the wheel with Nat next to her. Karlos is a step in front of them and they've not the faintest idea. The two of them changing places like pieces in a chess game without even knowing it. I have to find a way to let them know the truth. Karlos is much shrewder than I ever imagined; cunning which no doubt comes with experience. I wonder if he's done this before, and who knows how many times? I wonder if he killed his wife? South Africa's a vast country with hundreds of private rehabs, hundreds of vulnerable women, many of them with money. It's a good hunting ground if that's what you're after. You don't go into those type of rehabs unless you can afford it. The pale face of Alison rises back up in my mind. Hattie said Karlos had been friendly with her. Did he dump her because I was better pickings? Of all of us, she was the most vulnerable and her family are very wealthy. He knew Dad was dead and had left me money. He fished for it, listened to the story of my pain and loss like he was catching a prize marlin. How am I going to let Nat and Elsa learn the truth? What a fool I've been. What a ridiculous, gullible fool!

I squint back up at the cloudless sky with its burning African sun and wish it would just consume me. 'Where's my *rest in peace?*' I scream up at the blue heavens. Why can't God just take care of it all? Why do I have to still go on suffering?

But anger eats at the self-pity. No, despite the pain, I do want to play a part. In fact, I want the lead role so I can force my justice down his ugly throat until he gags. I can't change what he's done to me, but I can stop him doing it again. I will make him pay. I stretch and breathe deeply from the salt sea air and, as I do, a thin blanket of peace begins to settle over me. At last my question has been properly answered. I know why I'm here and I will find a way to reveal the truth.

Elsa takes the keys out of the ignition, but instead of getting out they both sit staring out at the living ocean without speaking. Finally Nat clears her throat. 'I was just thinking again about all the weird things that have been happening. It breaks my heart to think Liss is not at rest. It's bad enough her dying so young. The thought that she's not…'

'Shh, Nat. Don't think like that. Don't. We'll just torture ourselves if we do.' Elsa pats Nat's hand. 'I'm sure all these happenings are nothing to do with the supernatural. I think we're just overwhelmed. It's probably post-traumatic stress.'

Nat takes her hand away. 'I don't care how rational your arguments are. When you're dead you don't just rot in your grave. Your spirit lives on. Can't you understand that?'

Elsa pulls a face. 'You're welcome to believe that.'

'You believed in it once. Why don't you now?'

'For goodness' sake, Nat. I was a young and impressionable teenager. It was just emotion Pastor Jorge whipped up in us; it wasn't real.'

Nat pouts and squeezes her eyes shut.

Elsa lets out a long sigh. 'I'm sorry, I can't believe in an afterlife as much as I want too. I can't.'

Nat's voice rises. 'Well, can you at least believe that I can smell her perfume, sense her presence even? I can right now. Right this minute. So strong as if she's sitting in the car with us. For goodness' sake, we had exactly the same hallucination at the same time. Can't you at least admit there's something weird about that? And what about the blank prescription? That's something tangible. How do you explain that?' Nat breaks out into sobs.

Elsa puts her arms around her. 'I don't know, Nat. I don't have all the answers. I'm sorry. Let's not fight,' she says. 'It's just that I don't believe Lissa's spirit is back in any real way. I think we're just wishing she was.' Elsa pats Nat like she's consoling a child. 'I promise, if someone's murdered Lissa, we will nail them. Whoever put that blank script under your wiper knows something. We will look at every possibility and I'll make sure Fletcher and Govender do everything they can to help us. That's all I can do for Lissa. Nothing is going to bring her back.' Elsa's voice breaks.

'I know. I'm sorry,' says Nat. She fishes out a wad of tissues from her bag and hands one to Elsa before wiping her own swollen eyes. 'You're right. At least if we find out who killed her we will have done our best.'

Elsa stares in silence at the crashing waves for a few seconds. 'Actually, Nat, I do believe Lissa's still with us in a way. I guess we're all part of this universe so perhaps our energy just merges back into nature and becomes part of it just like those waves. I guess in a way that's an afterlife.'

She stabs the keys back into the ignition. 'Okay, we're not waiting for these incompetent police arseholes any longer, or even Fletcher for that matter. We're going to Shaloma. We need to find out about this George for ourselves. We'll get to the bottom of it, and then all these weird happenings will stop.' She looks intently at Nat who manages a small nod and smile and swings the BMW into life.

I watch them drive off with a prickle of fear. Karlos is a lot more cunning than they realise. If they take George off the list and only go after Karlos, he won't hesitate to get rid of them. Somehow I need to follow Karlos' every move. King Karlos was what he'd called himself at Shaloma, and now I know why.

# CHAPTER THIRTY-EIGHT

Instead of finding Karlos, I'm back at Shaloma, watching Nat and Elsa march into reception like two soldiers on a mission. Helen looks up with surprise before giving them her habitual welcoming smile. 'Hello, girls. What can I do for you?'

'We need to speak to Dr Brink in private, Helen. Is he in?'

A quizzical look flits across Helen's face. She sets her jaw and nods. 'I'm not sure if he's busy right now. Sit down and I'll go and see.'

Nat and Elsa move towards the black leather couch nestled against the lime-green wall. Elsa taps her red nails on the armrest while Nat stares at the blank wall opposite.

'You're in luck. Please come this way.'

They follow Helen in silence through the courtyard to Dr Brink's office.

Dr Brink ushers them over to chairs in the corner of the office.

'Please, sit. What can I do for you?'

'We need some information on a patient called George Mannering,' says Elsa before sitting down.

Dr Brink gives a small nod and frowns. He clasps his hands

together and looks first at Elsa and then at Nat before clearing his throat. 'I am so sorry about Lissa. I truly am. I know there's an investigation. I've had both the police and Mr Fletcher here and have given them all the information they've asked for. As much as I want to, I can't disclose confidential patient information to you. I can't.'

Elsa's jaw tightens. 'Yes, I realise that,' she says, 'I just want to know how long he was here for.'

'He arrived on the Friday with Wolf and Nic. Lissa came on the Sunday,' says Dr Brink. 'They all started the treatment together on the Monday. He left recently to be admitted to another hospital.'

'Were you aware then that he's psychotic?' Elsa leans forward in her chair and clenches the armrests.

Dr Brink leans back from her anger. 'Yes, but he was controlled by medication.'

'The same medication called Trithapon which somehow became listed on Lissa's file.' Elsa's eyes are fierce.

Dr Brink's mouth drops open. He reddens. 'That shouldn't have been on Lissa's file.'

Nat lets out a small sigh. A tinge of relief trickles through me. At least now she knows the truth.

'Well, it was,' snaps Elsa.

A deep frown etches across Dr Brink's forehead. 'I'm sorry, I never prescribed Trithapon. I have no idea how that happened. The files are locked in the filing cabinet. We've given everything to the police and answered all their questions.'

Elsa stares at him like a threatening cat while Nat shifts uncomfortably on her chair. 'I think you'd better review your security policies, Doctor. If I'd known you were as bad as this we would never have let Lissa come here.'

Dr Brink says nothing.

'Where's George Mannering been admitted to?'

'Fort Napier,' he mumbles.

'Why? Is he dangerous?'

'I'm sorry, ladies. I really can't answer any more questions.' Dr Brink clears his throat and stands. 'If I think of anything else I will contact the police straightaway.'

Elsa shoves back her chair and leaves the office with a curt nod. Nat scurries behind her, eyes fixed on Elsa's back.

'Well, that was a complete waste of time,' says Elsa as soon as they step outside.

'I guess we should've known he wouldn't tell us much,' says Nat, pulling a face. 'But at least we know now that it shouldn't have been on Lissa's file.'

'I think that was pretty obvious already,' snaps Elsa.

Nat reddens.

'We made a right fuck-up bringing her here. I really thought I was helping; thought it would be the turning point she needed. I was so consumed with worry that the thought of the low-lifes she would meet didn't even enter my mind. How could I be so incredibly stupid?' Elsa's head drops and her shoulders slump forward.

Nat places her arm around Elsa's shoulders. 'It was both of us, not just you, and we meant well. If we hadn't forced her here the chances are she'd have drunk herself to death. She was in a bad way, don't forget that.'

Elsa nods as her eyes cloud over.

'Come on, let's go and have a walk around Mitchell Park. I think we both need a bit of time with nature.'

───────

It's hard to remain stressed in a place as beautiful as Mitchell Park and my heart warms as I see Elsa's and Nat's shoulders relax. The air is heavy with the scent from frangipani trees. Smell is one of the strongest triggers for your memory they say, and it's true. I only have to get the slightest whiff of frangipani and happy memories of Dad come flooding back.

The park is pristine and in some strange way its order gives me hope. I know there's a lot of chaos out there, but with God's help they'll get through, and then at least Dad's death won't have been for nothing. I push away the petrol nightmare by focusing on my own death. I can't let it be for nothing. I have to nail Karlos.

Nat and Elsa wander over to the zoo area. They stop briefly in front of the flock of salmon pink flamingos perched comically on one of their pink stick legs, before moving on to the mob of sentry-straight meerkats, peering with sharp, black, fur-framed eyes at the crowd from the soft mounds of brown earth dotting their enclosure. I can't help but smile, with their straight backs and small paws hanging dutifully in front; they're so cute and so loyal to each other. We humans could learn a lot from them.

'Didn't that drug addict from church you were trying to help end up going to Fort Napier years ago?'

Elsa lifts her eyebrows. 'Hmm, I think he did.' She gives a small laugh. 'That feels like a lifetime ago. I'd forgotten all about him. Wonder how he is; probably dead if he went back on drugs.'

'Shit, there's too much of it around, there really is.'

'I could get Fletcher to access George's records there. Shaloma won't help. They're just trying to protect their reputation, but if we can somehow pinpoint George as being able to gain access to Lissa's house early that morning, he could well be our man. I think her death in the hospital might just be down to incompetence. It's quite possible they over-sedated her by mistake – but the fitting that took her there, that came from someone.'

Nat purses her lips and nods. 'That would explain the lack of post-mortem.' She looks earnestly at Elsa. 'Can't we nail them for that, Els? Can't we get them to exhume her body?'

Elsa snorts and shakes her head. 'You've no idea how hard

that would be Nat. I'd never get it through court without the police agreeing, and Govender's unlikely to help.'

'Can't Thabo get him to?'

Elsa shrugs. 'I think what we need to do is get the person who tried to kill her in the first place. At least we'll have a strong attempted murder case if we can find evidence of this George giving her Trithapon.'

'Do you think he's the more likely suspect now? You were so sure it was Karlos before.'

Elsa's eyes follow a meerkat as it jumps from its mound and scurries over to join the rest of its pack. 'I'm keeping Karlos on my list. He got the money, after all, but other than that I guess we don't have much on him. George on the other hand is a dinkum psychotic and the drug he's on is also mysteriously listed on Lissa's file. There's got to be a connection.'

'Karlos did seem genuinely broken, especially at Lissa's funeral. His eyes were raw with pain.'

'I guess,' says Elsa.

Nat draws in a deep breath and turns to Elsa.

'I know this sounds a bit weird, but do you think that's why we found that script at Lissa's funeral? Do you think she was trying to tell us she'd been poisoned?'

Elsa's face stiffens.

'No, I don't.' She turns away from the meerkat compound. 'Come on, let's go and phone Fletcher. I think we'll get either him or Govender to pay Fort Napier a visit.

# CHAPTER THIRTY-NINE

I watch as a young female constable drives up the long hill to the old garrison of Fort Napier. The grey stone walls contrast sharply with the rolling fields of green stretching out in front. The constable parks her yellow police van and stops briefly to look at the panoramic view of Pietermaritzburg nestled below before buzzing on the security button.

'*Wie's daar?*' crackles an Afrikaans voice.

'*Polisie,*' replies the constable and seconds later the heavy iron door creaks open to allow her in.

Her brown police issue shoes pad behind an armed guard. The fort is deceiving from the outside and instead of grey stone, a number of red brick buildings lie within the grounds. The windows are barred and a barbed wire fence surrounds a twenty-metre rectangular swimming pool which squats in the centre of the compound. I follow them towards the largest of the red brick buildings. After a reinforced steel door, we continue down a long corridor and through three more iron security gates. I smile to myself as I pass straight through the high security.

The constable is ushered into an office and told to wait. She perches obediently on one of the wooden chairs and places her knees together like a dutiful schoolgirl waiting to see the headmistress. I study her face. She's quite pretty in a flat face kind of way. Her hair is cut into a short blonde bob and she's got nice pale blue eyes although they're hidden behind black framed glasses. She'd look a lot better with contact lenses and longer hair. I wonder what made her become a policewoman?

The door creaks open and a middle-aged khaki-clad officer with a beer paunch comes in. So far everyone is white. I wonder if they've admitted any black or Indian patients yet or employed any black staff. I guess the new South Africa will take a little time to change.

'I'm Superintendent Coetzee. What can I do you for?'

'Constable Pienaar. Inspector Govender from CR Swart has sent me to collect some information on one of your patients, a Mr George Mannering.'

The superintendent pulls down his mouth. 'Ja, okay. Is it something I should know about?'

'A possible murder case, but as yet we have no proof. Inspector Govender just wants to look into Mannering, and then if there is nothing to go on, to close the case.'

'Okay. Just wait a bit and I will find his file. Viljoen!' he shouts at the door.

The door opens and a young guard stands to attention. '*Kry gou vir my die leer vir* George Mannering.'

Minutes later he's back with a brown cardboard file. The superintendent hands it to the constable. 'Have a look through and if you need copies let me know. Mannering was admitted to us last week after a major psychotic attack.'

'Do you think he is capable of murder?'

The superintendent gives a cynical laugh. '*Agh*, anyone is capable of murder given the right circumstances, don't you think?'

The young constable meets his direct gaze, but says nothing. She pages through the file and then hands two of the pages to the superintendent. 'Can we just have copies of these two pages, *asseblief.'*

'Viljoen!' shouts the superintendent again. The door opens dutifully. *'Maak twee afskripte van hierdie.'* He hands him the pages and they wait in silence. The young police constable remains upright while the superintendent's eyes flicker over her like a lustful St Bernard eyeing a bitch on heat. Another arsehole. Where do they all come from?

I scan my eyes over the page the constable is holding – a list of dates and places with a woman's name and the letters *GBH* after each. My heart sinks. George obviously has a history of attacking woman. *'Highly intelligent and dangerous. Holds a BSc in Pharmaceuticals from Rhodes University.'* I frown at the words. Did Karlos know this? I think back to Shaloma. There were quite a few times when he chatted quietly to George. I thought he was just being kind, but perhaps he was fishing, looking for another marlin, so he could plan his next careful move.

The evidence against George is mounting. I guess in some ways he's the perfect stooge for Karlos. He's psychotic, in a mental hospital, has a history of violence. He's not only a perfect choice, but no public prosecutor is going to take up the case as long as he stays in Fort Napier. I wonder how Karlos got hold of his Trithapon. He must've planned it all so carefully. George is listed as highly intelligent and cunning but he's got nothing on Karlos. The constable reads through the pages again and looks up. 'I think maybe I must speak with him.'

The superintendent purses his lips together for a second. 'He's heavily drugged. He may not make much sense.'

'I think it's best I ask a few questions.'

'Ja, okay. Come with me.'

The superintendent opens the door and leers at the young constable as she passes through. He follows a step behind, his eyes fixed on her arse. They pass through a series of locked steel doors and up two flights of stairs before going down another long corridor which ends with a steel double door. An armed, khaki-clad guard says, '*More*, Superintendent.'

'*Maak oop.*'

The guard gives a salute and unlocks the heavy doors. Two male nurses, clad in white but with truncheons strapped to their belts, jolt up out of their chairs. The ward is dimly lit with four sleeping patients.

'*Goeie more*, Superintendent,' they utter in unison.

'*Bring* Mannering *na die kantoor*,' barks the superintendent, marching past the beds to a wooden door at the end of the dormitory. He ushers the young constable in and I see his hand brush against the small of her back.

The room's obviously an office, with an old wooden desk and three wooden chairs, which look like typically government issue. The young constable seats herself stiffly on the nearest chair. Her face looks like an enraged bullfrog's and it's obvious she's not enjoying the fat superintendent's interest.

The male nurse brings in a sleepy George. He rubs his head while his glazed eyes dart from the constable to the superintendent. He's obviously drugged and even thinner and paler than when I saw him last. His black hair stands up, giving him even more of a rook-like appearance than before. He's dressed in light blue hospital pyjamas and has a plastic hospital label securely fixed around his left wrist.

'This constable would like to ask you a few questions, Mr Mannering. Please have a seat.'

The nurse eases George down onto the remaining spare wooden seat and stands resting his hand on George's shoulder. George's left eye twitches and a small rivulet of saliva dribbles down from his mouth. His tongue peeks in and out as if he's trying to catch a fly. I shiver with distaste. He places his trembling hands in his lap while his eyes continue to flit from the superintendent to the constable and back again as if he's watching a tennis match.

The constable clears her throat and takes out a small notepad. 'Mr Mannering, I believe you were a patient at Shaloma at the time that Miss Melissa Windsor was a patient there also?'

George sits rigidly staring at her.

'Is that correct?'

'You must answer, Mr Mannering,' says the superintendent. He leans in towards George, one hand resting on his fat thigh, and frowns intimidatingly at him.

George's eyes dart back to the constable before giving a curt nod.

'You are aware that she is now deceased?'

George's left eye twitches madly at her words but he nods again.

The constable studies him through narrow eyes for a few seconds. 'Do you have any idea what caused her death?' she asks in a slow, measured tone.

George's eyes widen and his tongue stops halfway out of his mouth. He sits frozen before answering in a voice barely above a whisper, 'She was drinking again.'

The constable continues to stare at him before pulling down her mouth and leaning in towards George. 'Did you have anything to do with her death, Mr Mannering?'

George's head jerks back. 'No. No, no…' he croaks. His mouth drops open and his tongue flops forward as he shakes his head from side to side like he's in a trance. 'No. She died from drinking. She died from drinking. That's what they said. She died from drinking.' He continues to repeat the words, the pitch of his voice rising until he jumps up from the chair and screams, 'Why are you asking me this? Why?'

The superintendent motions with his eyes for the nurse to take George away. George begins to scream and squirm. The second nurse rushes in and they manhandle the writhing body of George to his feet and drag him out of the office with the high pitch of his scream still heard. Both the superintendent's and the constable's faces wrinkle with distaste. The screaming comes to an abrupt halt. The constable and superintendent exchange a look of relief.

'Ja, well, sorry. I don't think that was much help,' says the superintendent pushing back his chair. 'Maybe you must wait a few weeks till we stabilise him. The psychiatrist will be here later and I'll talk to him about this.'

The constable sits for a few seconds with an expression of deep thought across her face. 'Ja, maybe that's best. Thank you for your time, Superintendent.'

'*Agh*, no problem,' says the superintendent, leering down at her again. 'Come, I'll show you out.'

I follow behind as they pace back down the corridor. George certainly doesn't look good and it's obvious he'd never be deemed fit enough to go to court. Karlos certainly chose his pawn well.

# CHAPTER FORTY

I'm on the steps leading down to the Wimpy Bar in Murchies Passage in the centre of Durban. It was a notorious hang-out for drug addicts in my youth. It's where Angie and I used to come on Saturday mornings to score weed. Poor Mom, she would have freaked if she'd known. I look around the crowded eating area and wonder why I'm here. It's packed, and the new South Africa is evident from the mix of race groups, everyone relaxed and happy as if we've always been integrated rather than forced apart. Thank God for Mandela and his new 'rainbow nation'.

The air is thick with the smell of grilled beef and fried onions. The aroma brings back teenage memories of Angie and I, thinking we were so cool and hanging out in a place notorious for addicts trying to score. Heroin didn't seem to be around then. Given the types who used to hang out here, I guess I'm lucky I only tried weed.

Rat slinks back into my mind. He had a peaked nose and thin face, pockmarked and pale just like George's and he was just as repulsive, probably psychotic, too, for all I knew. I was only fifteen and he must've been well into his twenties, but still he was after my body. He used to call out *'Howzit chickies'* to me and

Angie, and call us over to score. As soon as we got close he'd be feeling my arse and breathing his weed stench in my face. If it wasn't for Angie wanting to score weed, I'd never have even gone anywhere near him. Just feeling his hands on me left me feeling so dirty. The memory brings the sickly sweet smell of the weed alive in my nostrils. I really didn't have the best luck in attracting men. The ugly ones who went for me were just as vile as the good-looking ones.

No-one in the Wimpy reacts to my presence and, as I walk between the crowded tables, I see Karlos facing me from a kiosk in the far corner, his bearded face and bulk unmistakable. The woman he's with has her back to me but it's definitely Nat. I'd know my sister anywhere. The two of them are deep in conversation. I stare for a few seconds before striding towards them. I'm tempted to sit down next to Karlos with the hope that somehow he'll sense my presence and realise I'm still here and coming after him. But it's me who baulks as his familiar smell reignites my pain at the whole sorry saga. I clench both my fists and close my eyes for a brief second. Standing here, knowing what I know and thinking back to the whole façade of our relationship, is harder than I thought.

'*Agh*, I don't believe this. You really think she was murdered?'

Nat bites her bottom lip and keeps her eyes down. Her fingers fiddle with the edge of her navy blazer. 'It looks that way.'

'But why didn't you phone and tell me? I thought the hospital said she had heart failure?' Karlos' face is pale and I see him clench his fist against his thigh. I'm not sure whether he's worried that his eight hundred thousand rand inheritance is going to be put on hold, or perhaps it's because there's a small well of fear that he could be seen as a suspect?

'Did they do tests at the hospital after she died?'

Nat shakes her head. 'Not that I know of. Maybe they should've done some before she died.'

Karlos' eyes harden. 'Why?'

Nat shrugs. 'I don't know. Just in case it wasn't alcohol that did it.'

'*Agh*, it could only be. Eunice found the empty whiskey bottle and the doctor said her pyjamas were smelling of booze.'

'I know, but—'

'There's no but. Alcoholics are clever. They hide their drinking.' Karlos leans towards Nat. 'I know that, because I've done it. Lissa did drink again. She just hid it from all of us. You just have to accept that. I don't think there's been any murder, Nat. I think you're wrong.'

Nat bites her bottom lip while Karlos continues to stare directly at her.

'Maybe, but… I don't know. Something just doesn't feel right.' She meets Karlos' stare. 'Elsa thinks so, too.'

Karlos blinks away and pulls down the side of his mouth.

'Well, I think you're both wrong. King Edward's is a dump. It's full of disease and incompetence. She should never have gone there. If she'd gone to Parklands it might have been different.' He utters each word with a deliberate emphasis.

Nat's eyes cloud over. Bastard, he's trying to use guilt now. He really doesn't care how much hurt he inflicts.

Nat's voice breaks. 'It still doesn't explain the Trithapon on her file. Liss wasn't psychotic. She wasn't.'

'Ja, well I agree that's strange,' says Karlos, leaning back against the chair, but keeping his eyes fixed on Nat. 'Have you told the police?'

Nat swallows and nods. 'Yes, they agree it doesn't make sense, but there's not enough evidence to point to George for anything.' She shakes her head and brushes her hair behind her ear with shaky fingers. 'Oh, I don't know. Things just don't seem right. They really don't.'

'That's rubbish,' says Karlos fiercely. 'George is a fucking psychotic and we know now he was taking that Trithapon; of course he could've done something to Lissa.' His fingers rest on his throat for a few seconds before pinching a small wave of its soft flesh between his thumb and forefinger and playing with it. I watch with a mix of revulsion and admiration as he leans back into the red leather bench seat and changes his pose to a Socratic one, his hand resting neatly under his chin, his eyes still fixed on Nat. She must feel the burn of his gaze because she begins to look uncomfortable and I see a pink flush mottle her cheeks. Karlos studies her for a few seconds longer before pursing his lips and leaning in across the table towards her. 'You must tell the police to look properly into George.'

Nat looks up at him and then blinks away. 'The police have said they will.'

'Anyone else they want to look at?' Karlos' tone is clipped, his jaw set and his shoulders stiff.

Nat's chest mottles. He's intimidating her on purpose. Nat gives a small shake of her head and I see Karlos' shoulders relax. He leans back against the seat again and lets out a low whistle.

'Who'd have thought? I'm in shock, Nat. I can't believe that you really think Liss was murdered and it wasn't just the drinking, I really can't. This makes it even worse to lose her. Shaloma should never have let George in. *Agh*, I don't believe this. I really don't.' He gives a dramatic shake of his head and then falls silent, his eyes fixed on Nat's downcast head.

'We've no proof yet that it was definitely him,' whispers Nat, still keeping her head down.

'Ja, well why else would his medicine be on Lissa's file. *Agh*, now I think about it, of course it's him. These psychotics are clever bastards. He must've gone to Brinks' office in the night and changed her file, all the time planning to kill her.' Karlos shifts around on his seat so that the leather squeaks under him. 'Liss always said he reminded her of a rook. I should've seen there was something shifty about him. Maybe he was already putting it in her food or tea at Shaloma, or maybe he somehow got into the house early that morning and injected her with it and then with the booze in her blood it made her fit like that?'

'I still don't understand why he'd want to do it,' says Nat.

'*Agh*, these psychotics don't need a reason. They just take a hate for someone and then want to kill them.' Karlos purses his lips together and shakes his head as if he can't believe it. 'Who would have thought, hey, Nat? You think it was him who tried to come with Hattie and Wolf to the hospital?'

'I don't know. Elsa is looking into things. I just don't know.'

Karlos gives his head a shake and wipes his hand across his eyes. 'I miss her so much, you know, Nat. You have no idea how much.' I watch fascinated as his eyes redden. He really is quite an actor. He suddenly holds his head in his hands and his shoulders shake as he emits a series of low sobs.

Nat instinctively leans towards him. Her hand slides palm down across the table.

'Me too,' she croaks.

I want so much to punch Karlos' supercilious face until it's nothing but a raw and bloody pulp, to claw his eyes out and hurt him as much as he's hurt me and my family. My hands reach out for the heavy ashtray on the table but pass right through it. Karlos continues looking wounded as Nat squeezes his hand. If only I could manifest right here and now and scare the shit right out of him. I throw my head back and give a low laugh. Imagine if he suddenly saw me standing here, looking straight at him with knowing eyes and threatening to haunt him for the rest of his days. He loves playing the bereaved partner and my poor sister is too naïve to notice. Karlos carries the evil gene in his cursed blood line, but we obviously carry the easily duped one.

Karlos takes his hand away and scratches his chin. 'I'm just thinking. Nic was stalking Lissa, you know. She told me. We even saw him when we were waiting in the election queue. I think you must tell Elsa that. Maybe you must look into him as well.'

Nat's eyebrows rise. 'Liss never said anything. When was he stalking her?'

'*Agh*, I think she saw him a few times. He fancied her, you know, was so jealous when we got together. I know he wanted to break us up. I don't think we must rule him out. He could also have had some twisted hatred and want to kill Liss because she rejected him.'

Nat bites down on her bottom lip. 'You're right. I'll tell Elsa. We need to let Govender know about him. Do you know where he is now?'

'Who's Govender?' says Karlos sharply.

'The police inspector. He's a friend of Thabo's, but not very helpful.'

Karlos moves his eyes to the ceiling as if deep in thought. 'I think maybe you must tell this Govender that Nic has some family in Westville or somewhere out there. Helen should be able to help.'

My anger becomes tinged with fear. Karlos is sucking her in. I can see the shade of suspicion fade from her eyes. Nat's looking at him like an obedient spaniel, no doubt beating herself up for unfairly suspecting him. 'Oh Nat, don't let him reel you in by telling you what you need to allay your fears and doubts,' I mouth. 'Please don't.'

Deep inside I know with certainty that whatever shared memories I have still live in the synapses of Nat's mind too, and Elsa's. I think back to the three timeless Karoo hills who remained linked together despite all the external happenings, the storms, the bush fires and the human and animal destruction which stamps on their green shoots or chops down the living trees. God created life, a love energy which nothing can destroy. I move onto the bench seat beside Nat. She flinches and her nostrils twitch as I close my eyes and will us back into the shared forests of our past.

Nat and I sit in silence on my couch. I take a slug of Chardonnay and stare morosely at the television which is blasting out the latest episode of *Baywatch*. 'Maybe if I looked like Pamela Anderson, Mike would've treated me differently,' I say.

'Oh, Liss, don't be silly. He's a fickle bastard who uses and abuses women for a hobby. Don't take it personally. You're much too good for him, you really are.' Nat pats my hand. 'Anyway you're better looking than Pamela Anderson.'

I pull a face. 'No, I'm not.' I fight back the tears which rise up from nowhere, but it's too late; they break through and trickle down my cheeks. Sobs rise and all my sorrow tumbles out. I plonk down my glass and rest my head in my hands.

'I'm so sorry, I really am,' croons Nat. She puts her arm around me and rubs her hand up and down my back before patting it. I lean into her and sob like a child for what seems like ages. Nat takes some tissues out of her bag and hands them to me. I wipe my eyes while my sobs shudder to a stop.

'I'm sorry I didn't mean to let it all hang out. I just can't believe how gullible I've been. I really can't.'

'We can all be gullible at times, Liss. Don't blame yourself.'

'I was such an idiot. He kept telling me how hot I was. Said he loved me; he even bought me Chanel.' I let out a wry laugh. 'I was secretly hoping for a ring next.'

'People are very good at wearing masks and it's hard to tell sometimes. I've done it myself plenty times.'

'Not with guys you haven't.'

'No, but I've had lots of so-called friends in the theatre world who turned out to be back-stabbers. I'm trying to read people better and I'm sure when the next guy comes along you will, too.'

I turn to Nat with a droll smile. 'I hope so. I really do, but I wouldn't count on it.'

The shared memory dissolves. Nat's head jerks back and she rapidly blinks her eyes. At last, I've found a way to communicate. I can will myself back into our shared memories and take my sisters with me. I need Nat to make a connection between Karlos and that memory. I need her to see that he's just putting on a false front.

'Please make the connection,' I urge her silently. 'Please.'

I look back at Karlos. He's leaning across the table, staring intently at Nat.

'You okay? What happened? You looked like you were in some kind of trance.'

Nat swallows. Her nostrils flare as she touches the empty seat next to her and moves her fingers through me onto the warm leather. She swallows again and wipes her sweaty palms against her jeans. She's sensed me. I'm sure she has, and she can obviously feel the warmth of where I'm sitting. I'm sure she can feel my energy. It's clear from her shaken state that the memory's been vivid enough to make her think. I bet she's replaying it frame by frame in her mind right now, I'm sure of it. Please God, let her have understood.

'I... uh... just felt dizzy. I'm okay now.' Nat fumbles at her handbag and clicks it open. She hurriedly takes out a twenty rand note, but Karlos motions it away.

'I'll get this,' he says, his eyes cemented to her face. 'You just look after yourself and let me know what the police say. If they don't get her killer, I will. I promise you that.'

Nat nods, while Karlos narrows his eyes in classic vigilante style. My poor sister's bottom lip trembles as she looks him.

'I need to go...'

Karlos shifts to the end of the bench seat and stands to give Nat a hug. She stands stiffly without returning it, before shoving on her sunglasses and pushing her way out of the Wimpy.

# CHAPTER FORTY-ONE

Elsa sits stony-faced while Nat recounts what happened.

'Do you think I'm just making a false connection?' Nat says. 'It was so real: I really felt like I'd left my body and gone back to that time. Liss was as real to me as you are now and it was almost like she was warning me not to trust him. I mean why would I suddenly have a memory like that at that moment. Why?'

Elsa fixes serious eyes on Nat's face and they sit in silence for a few seconds before she answers. 'Like I've said before, I think it's stress and all the emotional turmoil you've been through, but I also think the fact we don't like him possibly makes us more suspicious of him.' She bites her lip and frowns. 'I wish you hadn't told him we suspect murder.'

'I'm sorry. He bumped into me in town and then, I don't know, it just all came out when we were having coffee. I know I shouldn't have told him anything.' Nat's eyes are wide and filled with confusion.

'It's okay. Maybe we're over-reacting. We've got some psychotic addict on our list who may well be responsible. We don't have definitive proof of anything right now. Don't beat yourself up.'

'There've been too many weird things, Elsa. Please at least agree with me about that.'

Elsa stares pensively ahead before giving a sardonic laugh. 'Okay, have to admit things have been strange. Even my rational mind is beginning to have some doubts.'

Nat looks up at Elsa in surprise. 'Really?'

Elsa pulls a face. 'Not enough to make me believe in an afterlife.'

Nat's body jerks as someone raps loudly on the door. She exchanges a look with Elsa and gets up to peek through the peep hole. She turns open-mouthed to Elsa.

'It's Karlos,' she whispers, pointing at the closed door. She lifts her hands in a gesture of despair.

Elsa frowns and stares at the closed door. She motions Nat out of the way and opens it. Karlos draws back slightly at the sight of her, but is quick to remove the surprise from his face.

'*Agh*, I didn't expect you to also be here. It's good to see you, Elsa.'

'You too.' Elsa's tone is her clipped court-room one. She stands ramrod straight, looking directly at Karlos.

He shuffles his feet and clears his throat. 'Can I come in?'

Elsa stands silently, staring at Karlos for another second before clicking open the security gate. She pushes back the iron trellis to let him in.

'I'm sorry if I'm disturbing you two. I was just shocked at what Nat told me and I had to see her again. Have the police found anything more?'

Nat reddens slightly and gives her head a shake. 'Not yet.'

Karlos looks from one to the other and then clears his throat. 'Ja, well if you could please let me know how it goes. I want to do what I can do to help.' He puts his hand to his forehead and gives his head a shake. 'I still can't believe this,' he says before turning to Nat. 'Did you tell Elsa about Nic?'

Elsa frowns at Nat who gives a small shake of her head.

'What about Nic?'

'*Agh*, I told Nat that Lissa said he was stalking her after we came out. She saw him three times. I think you must tell the police to also look at him.'

Elsa raises her eyebrows at Nat. 'Did Liss say anything about that to you?'

Nat shakes her head. 'No, she said he fancied her and she didn't return the favour, but that's all.'

Elsa looks back at Karlos, her eyes flicking back and forth over his face.

Karlos holds her gaze before rubbing his hand across his cheek. 'Ja, I just think we must also look at him. Okay, well I must go. Please let me know what they say and how I can help. Stay well you two.'

Nat gives a small wave while Elsa nods curtly before clanging the gate closed behind him and clicking the lock.

They wait in silence for a few seconds until they hear the start of my Golf. Then Elsa says, 'Perhaps we should look into this Nic character as well?'

Nat nods. 'Maybe, but I still think I shouldn't have said anything to Karlos.' She twists her hands together. 'He scares me, Els. He really does.'

Elsa says nothing but a flicker of fear passes through her eyes. 'We'll need to watch him. Don't ever be alone with him. Promise me that.'

# CHAPTER FORTY-TWO

My Golf waits, throbbing, on the side of Umgeni Road. The night is blacker than normal with the yellow half-moon hidden behind drifting cloud. It's three in the morning and the wide, dark road is almost deserted except for the occasional taxi filled with drunken passengers. Karlos' hands are clenched around the steering wheel and his eyes are glued to the rear-view mirror. A white Datsun pick-up pulls up alongside him. Loud rap music pulses out into the dark night as the passenger winds down the window. Despite the blackness of the night, he's wearing dark glasses and a blue cap.

Karlos hands him a brown envelope. 'She drives a red BMW. The registration and address is in here and so's your money.'

The passenger rifles through the envelope before giving the driver a nod. The pick-up roars off into the night, and Karlos swings the Golf into a squealing U-turn and speeds back towards the north side of the city.

So much for Fletcher following him. Karlos is so many steps ahead.

I watch Elsa alone in her kitchen. Those men could try and get her now, or it could be this evening, or tomorrow. I need to make her aware of the danger and I need to do it now. I move in beside her. Her eyes glaze over as I take us back in time, pleading silently that she'll be open to my counsel and not let her cynicism cloud her judgement.

---

I'm sitting in Mom's lounge with the *Daily News* spread out in front of me and a glass of Chardonnay in my hand, pointing indignantly at the front-page article.

'They just drove alongside, pulled them out of the car and shot them, right in front of their kids, and then left the kids alone and screaming on the N2 with the bodies of their dead parents,' I slap my hand down on the page. 'It's beyond belief. The kids are only two and six. It's enough to make me want to emigrate.'

'Don't be stupid, Liss. What we need to do is stamp out the criminal element and sort out the poverty, not run away.'

Mom is sitting in her usual armchair, her legs tucked to the side and a large glass of wine in her hand. She takes a slurp before turning to Elsa. 'Ja, Elsa, but how will we do that? Things have got out of control far too quickly. Yvonne says the farmers are being murdered in their hundreds. It's like a bloody genocide. This is not what your Dad died for.' Mom's fingers tighten around the stem of her glass.

'Joburg's rife with it and just now it'll come to us.' I put my head in my hands and give a small sob. 'I just don't want any of us to be shot in our own cars like Dad, Elsa... Please.'

I feel her hand on my back. She gives me a squeeze. 'I know, Liss. It brings back horrible memories, I know.'

'Oh God, I can still smell the blood, Elsa, still see it pouring out of him. It was so awful, so awful.' I hiccup from crying and take a big glug of wine.

'Shh,' Elsa puts her finger to her lips and looks at Mom.

I try and swallow down my tears to stifle the sobs.

'Lissa's right,' slurs Mom. 'I want you girls to get out. Go and look into Australia or New Zealand, even England, anywhere but here. I can't have them shoot you too.' Her voice rises to a crescendo.

'Stop it,' says Elsa with a set face. 'Dad fought for justice and we need to see that justice is maintained. We don't need to flee at the first sign of trouble. What we need to do is tackle it. It'll get better once Mandela's in power.'

'Just be careful, Elsa. Please be careful. I don't want them to hijack you.'

Elsa jerks out of the shared memory. Her eyes flit around the kitchen and she snatches at a flyaway strand of blonde hair. She glances at the clock and then at her car keys which lie on the counter. She pushes back her stool and goes into the bedroom. I hear the click of a key in the bedroom safe. I watch as she takes out Greg's gun. She checks the 9mm Browning Hi-power gun for bullets and clicks down the safety catch. Back in the kitchen, she puts the gun in her bag and picks up the keys. Once in the car she takes out the gun and leaves it resting between her thighs with the barrel facing towards the floor. She locks the car door and checks all her mirrors before pushing the remote for the gates to open. She screeches out of the drive.

Elsa steers the BMW to the end of her road and out into wide expanse of Northway Road. Her eyes flit regularly to her rear-view and side mirrors. My tension eases. She's completely alert. All she needs to do now is stay that way.

A white Datsun pick-up squeals out from a side road just behind Elsa. Her eyes flick again to the rear-view mirror. It's the same two men. They haven't wasted any time. The pick-up veers to the right and accelerates to overtake her, but Elsa pre-empts their move and puts her foot flat, lurching the BMW in one powerful, purring spurt away from them. She hurtles on towards a Ford Focus driving at the speed limit and hesitates for a second before taking a gap in the oncoming traffic and squealing out to pass it. The pick-up blasts its horn at the Ford which pulls to the side to allow it pass. Drivers in the oncoming traffic widen their eyes in fear, aware that something is going down between the two cars which continue screaming down the wide, tarred road like two out-of-control scale electrics.

I watch Elsa approach the traffic lights by Lagoon Service Station. The light has turned red and a snake of cars crosses in front of her; there's no way she can jump the lights without hitting one of them. I see the two men look at each other and laugh. The driver puts his foot down as the pick-up roars forward. My spirit turns numb as I watch the passenger push back his baseball cap and lean out of the window, hands cupped around a firearm with the barrel pointed directly towards Elsa's car.

'No!' I scream. 'No.' Dad's bloodied body rises back into my mind, forcing the iron smell of blood into my nose and throat and making me retch. I shake my head violently to chase away the memory and surge towards the side of the pick-up where the hijacker leans out, his elbows pulled back in a triangle and his hands still cupped around the 9mm in an iron clasp. The driver slows down to let him steady his aim.

My breath freezes in my throat as I see the barrel inch down until it's vertical with the back of Elsa's rear window and directly in line with the back of her blonde head. I lurch forward and spin to face the pointed barrel with its vibrating molecules of steel. 'Please God. No!'

The firearm explodes in a flash of light and noise. A resounding crack thunders through the still morning air. The bullet has whooshed through me so fast I didn't even see it. Cars on the opposite side of the road swerve madly before accelerating away from the violence. Time stands still in the petrol station, the attendants and customers frozen in a tableau of expectant fear.

I turn my head towards Elsa, but she's no longer in front of me. She's already squealed sideways into the service station and is careering down the road in the direction of the vast Indian Ocean in a red blur.

'*Ukudubula wena. Ukudubula*, you fucking stupid—' shouts the driver, punching the passenger on his shoulder. 'How can you miss?' He veers sharply to the side, almost colliding with a Fiat and jolting its young woman driver into white hot shock, before screeching away in the same direction as Elsa.

The hi-jacker removes his sunglasses with a shaking hand. His eyes are wide with terror. He brings the arm holding the dangling firearm back in and sits, shivering, his body a jellied mess. He shakes his head and moves his hand across the barrel of the gun. "*Haibo*, that one is no good, no good. There is *muti* there... bad *muti*,' he croaks, while the driver glares sideways at him.

The wail of a siren shrieks through the air. The driver eyes the rear-view mirror. Two police cars, blue lights flashing, are racing towards them. 'Fucking police now,' he shouts. He squeals the pick-up into a sharp U-turn and races back along the road, forcing his way into the snake of traffic which has suddenly baulked and pulled to the side. The bumper of the pick-up smashes into the front fender of a Mercedes and continues on in the middle of the road while cars on both sides swerve out of his way. The police cars follow fast behind with their sirens screeching. I close my eyes and offer up silent thanks.

When I look back at Elsa she's pulled over to the side of the road and is sitting with her head collapsed forward onto the steering wheel. Her right hand rests trembling on the gun still

233

lodged between her thighs while her chest heaves. 'Fuck,' she whispers to herself. 'Fuck, that was close. Too close.'

Someone knocks on her window and she flinches, her hand flying automatically to the gun. A middle-aged, suited man motions for her to wind down the window. She opens it a fraction and looks up at him with wide eyes.

'Are you okay?' His eyes show concern and his voice is kind. 'I saw what happened. Don't worry, the police are on their tail. I just wanted to check if you're okay.'

Elsa swallows and gives a small nod. 'I'll be fine, thank you. I just need to sit for a bit and breathe.'

The man looks at her a while longer and then gives a half-smile. 'As long as you're sure you'll be alright?'

'I'm fine, thank you.' She winds up her window and lets out a long, shuddering sigh, before leaning her head back against the leather headrest and closing her eyes. I move in next to her. Her nose twitches and she opens her eyes to stare at the empty passenger seat. Her chest is still moving rapidly up and down. My poor sister, she doesn't deserve this. I shake my head to push away the memory of the gun aimed at Elsa's head. I don't know what that killer saw or felt, but thank God something put him off his aim.

# CHAPTER FORTY-THREE

**K**arlos sits in an armchair near the window. We're in a plush hotel room. The septic sister is perched on one of the twin beds, her lank black hair just as greasy as when I saw it last. My eyes rest on a welcome book lying on the counter top, with the name Maharani Hotel in gold lettering. How ironic. The last time I was at the Maharani was with disgusting Chino-man and my turning point for agreeing to go to Shaloma. What a joke, a ridiculous farce.

Karlos bangs the side of the chair with his fist. 'Bloody blacks and their stupid superstition. Fool says *muti* must be protecting her and refuses to try again.'

'So, find some others.'

Karlos throws her an irritated look. 'I paid them a thousand fucking rand. Now I must find some more and if they miss, then they also tell me there's some black magic. Fuck them. Maybe I must just find a way to do it myself.'

'Number one killer hey, *boetie*,' says this sister, giving him a sideways smile.

Karlos ignores her. He gets up and switches on the kettle and deftly tears open a sachet of Nescafé. Every movement is confident and sure. Now that I think back on it, there was never anything nervous or neurotic about him - that should've been a warning sign. What alcoholic is as cool and collected as Karlos? Nic wasn't, nor was Wolf. There was an air about Karlos that unsettled them, but I was too blind to notice. He had the stories of course and put on the act, but now when I think back on it, everything was carefully controlled; his mask fixed firmly in place and never sliding. I wonder if he lay on my bed gloating with his rand-sign eyes at the thought of getting his hands on my money and having my body thrown in as a freebie. The self-satisfaction must have almost smothered him.

I shiver at the memory of his hands on my body; I should've scratched my nails so deep into his flesh that he screamed. Karlos flinches as though he's sensed my anger, but continues making the coffee.

He plonks himself back in the armchair and takes a loud slurp of coffee. He stares with eyes almost dead. For the first time his expression is probably genuine and I wonder again how he got to be like this. Surely people like him can't be born with that level of evil, unless it really does operate as a generational curse, an inherent evil passed down through their genes from a damaged ancestral past?

'Hey, where's my coffee?' Karlos' sister leans back against the padded headboard and puts on a fake little girl face.

Karlos pulls up his top lip. 'Ja, ok, Tania, just relax. I'll make you one.' He gets up and snatches up another sachet.

'Put three of those sugars in. They're too small.' She watches with piggy eyes as he stirs the mug and then plonks it down on the bedside table. She picks up the complementary writing pad and pen and begins to draw a picture of two stick figures outside a large house. As I watch her finger move across the pad, an old physics lesson on two- and three-dimensional objects rises up in my memory. We mocked Mr Sinclair for being a mad scientist when he told us that if a three-dimensional being like us went into a two-dimensional world then all that those people would see would be cross-sections of us as we intersected their universe. He said we'd be able to move things, to take things back into our dimension and make them instantly disappear from their dimension. We were so certain there was no such thing as another dimension, but I guess, like many super-intelligent people, he just saw things that those of us with narrow minds couldn't. Now, the joke is I'm actually living that reality, no longer a three-dimensional being but a spiritual one who can move with ease through walls and doors. But how do I make things disappear to show my presence or scare someone shitless? I think back to the failed hi-jacking. Perhaps the hi-jacker saw some of my hand in front of the barrel and it wasn't just my magnetic field he felt, but if so, what made him see a fraction of me when neither Elsa nor Nat have been able to? What did I do that was different?

Tania sits on the bed staring at Karlos with narrow eyes. 'So?' she says.

'I'll stage a burglary and shoot them both, but I need to have them on their own.'

Tania frowns. '*Agh*, that's too hard. Aren't they married? And anyway, if they both get hit the police will suspect something.'

'Ja, I know that. I need to think. Stop fucking asking me things.'

Tania clucks her tongue and clicks on the television. She stares sullenly at the screen before turning to Karlos again. 'I thought you set it up so that this George and Nic would go to the hospital when she died?'

'Ja, I did. I told them to go visit after the meeting.'

'So, why don't you make sure the police find that out? That will make him look more guilty.'

'Don't you think I've tried that,' spat Karlos, 'These fucking sisters don't believe me. They probably haven't even told the fucking police, and the fucking nurses are so stupid they said they never saw them.'

'Lucky they didn't see you when you went,' Tania snorts.

'You know very well I was fucking careful of that. Now just shut up. I need to concentrate on what to do with these fucking sisters.'

'Get rid of them both,' sneers Tania.

Karlos glares at her. 'Fuck off. You know that's what I'm trying to do.' He gets up and picks up the hotel phone. He dials a nine and seconds later I hear Nat's voice.

'Howzit Nat, it's Karlos. I'm sorry to phone. I just wanted to see if you've heard any more.'

I hear Nat mumble an answer which makes Karlos frown.

'I think maybe we should all go and see George at Fort Napier. Perhaps if the police won't listen, we can find out for ourselves.' Nat doesn't answer. Karlos clears his throat. 'I can fetch you and Elsa tomorrow maybe?'

He scowls as he listens. 'Ja, okay. Well, you let me know when you can. Okay, bye.' He slams down the phone and kicks at the bed. 'Bitch is lying. I can hear in her voice she's scared of me.'

Tania stiffens. 'You think they suspect something?'

Karlos looks down from the hotel window onto the crowded beachfront promenade far below.

'I don't know,' he says after a while. He turns back to look at Tania. 'It's probably that Elsa. She's too shrewd. I don't trust her.'

'Hit her first.'

Karlos sneers. 'I already tried. I have to think of another way.'

'Find some blacks who aren't superstitious. They aren't all like that. Get someone to break in and shoot her in the night. The police won't think anything. If you get rid of that one, the other one will be easier to handle.'

'Ja, maybe that's the way.' Karlos stands deep in thought for a few seconds more and then opens the drawer and fishes around.

He pulls out a folded scrap of paper and picks up the phone again.

A torrent of anger consumes me as I listen to Karlos arrange a meeting to discuss the proposed burglary. He grudgingly settles on two thousand rand. Elsa's price has doubled. I think of Durban North with its high walls, barbed wire and strands of electrified wire aimed at burning any would-be burglar to a crisp. The majority of the homes proudly proclaim their rapid response contracts with the myriad of growing security businesses who are making a nice killing from the growing killing all around.

I shake my head. Surely this wasn't what Dad died for? I'm sure it isn't what Mandela wants, or the majority of South Africans who really care for this country's future. My spirit aches for my family and the country.

Karlos turns to Tania with a smug smile. 'He'll sort something out before the end of the week. They need a good look at the place first. He'll start talking to some of the people who work nearby. I think they must try and hit them in the night and just kill the husband too; the sooner the better. I want to get out of this fucking place now. We need to hit Joeys and enjoy the money up there as soon as it comes through.'

# CHAPTER FORTY-FOUR

Sheet lightning flashes across the heavily blanketed sky, igniting the darkness in a brief show of white light. I gaze up at the fierce night sky as a loud clap of thunder rumbles and is followed by more lightning and a second round of thunder. The headlines of horror I've seen displayed around the streets stream back through my mind: *Husband and wife murdered in their beds; intruder stabs eighty-five-year-old woman thirty-six times; mother and child shot in their own driveway*, a never-ending, blood-dimmed tide of violence and senselessness.

The storm grows stronger. Forked lightning rips its way through the night, followed by a crash of thunder. Heavy raindrops catapult to the earth, splashing hard on Elsa's azaleas and filling the night air with the musty smell of damp vegetation. The wind rises and pummels the lemon tree, ripping into its delicate yellow buds and bruising the young fruit.

Elsa's house sits low and hidden from the neighbouring properties, a burglar's dream once you've managed to get through the gates and down that steep drive, especially when you're hidden in the eye of an African thunder storm. It's probably the best disguise of all. I shudder at the false security of it all. Karlos picked well this time.

A shadow flickers behind the bars of the driveway gates. A heavy clunk, followed by a creak is heard through the noise the thunder of the storm. At least I've picked the right night. I see one of the driveway gates being forced forward. It inches bit by bit through the slanting rain as a crack of sheet lightning flickers across the sky to reveal two figures, dressed in black, their faces covered by sodden balaclavas. They squeeze sideways through the gap in the gates and creep down the driveway like shadows. One points a finger to the front door and takes out a narrow instrument from a side pocket. He wipes the slanting rain from their eyes and inserts the instrument into the lock of the front security gate with careful gloved fingers. Within seconds it clicks open. The gate creeks open in staccatos which blend in with the rumbling thunder of the night. The figure stops with his head to one side while their comrade's eyes scan the wall of the house for any sign of waking.

The comrade gives a curt nod and they begin on the double locks of the wooden door using the same instrument. It is inserted first into the top Yale lock, and then fiddled slowly from side to side. I frown. Why has no alarm sounded; why hasn't Sheba barked? I glance up at the kitchen window as the heavy rain pelts against the glass like a burst of machine-gun bullets. Maybe the storm is fierce enough to hide their sound?

The second lock gives and the front door is opened in starts. The intruder listens intently for any movement, holding this listening pose for a few seconds longer and then signalling with a dripping gloved hand to their comrade to move forward. The eyes of both are cold and dead like a shark's. Waves of fear ripple through me. These men are in a different league from the hi-jackers; they're well-trained, professional killers. They move silently into the house. Why hasn't the alarm sounded?

The killers fall onto their stomachs and inch forward to evade the infra-red sensors which beam out across the entrance. They leopard crawl in the direction of the hall, their firearms clasped out in front. They inch silently, leaving a trail of damp behind them, and head towards the door of Elsa's bedroom like well-trained guerrilla soldiers.

I can't let this happen. I can't let them kill Elsa. Before the words can repeat themselves, I propel myself towards the bedroom door. I move with such speed the air around me hisses. The leading intruder's head jolts back as if he's just been slapped. He stops mid-crawl and cocks his head to the side. The one behind holds his hands up in confusion, unable to work out what's happening. I surge through the door towards the sleeping, humped bodies of Elsa and Greg and bend over Elsa. '*Elsa, wake up! Wake up,*' I shout. Elsa sleeps soundly. Oh God. She can't hear me. My head spins and I throw it back to scream up at the heavens. '*Please God, let her at least sense me... please.*' God must hear me because Elsa opens heavy lids and looks in my direction. She bolts upright and her eyes dart around the room just as a deafening crack of sheet lightning streaks across the night sky. A heavy roll of thunder follows. Elsa turns wide-eyed towards Greg's sleeping body and reaches out to shake him. 'Wake up,' she whispers. 'Greg, wake up.'

Greg blinks up at Elsa's terrified face. He must know instantly why she's woken him, because he whips out the gun from under his pillow and puts his finger to his lips and places a bare foot on the carpet, easing himself off the bed. He creeps towards the closed bedroom door and tilts his ear against it. I watch the other side as the killers inch nearer and nearer, their firearms held taunt, their hands gripped white around the butt. Greg needs to shoot first or he won't stand a chance, but he remains standing behind the door as stiff as a waxwork. I move forward and snatch again and again like a demented madman at the door handle. My hands pass through it but my frantic energy ripples through the atoms of the air and I watch as the handle shivers and moves no more than a millimetre. Greg's eyes widen. He clicks off his safety catch and fires two bullets blindly through the closed door. The crack of the bullets shatters the wood so badly that shards shoot out down the length of the passage.

'Get the fuck out of my house,' he screams, firing a third shot through the door. 'Get the fuck out of my house!'

Both killers croak with fear as more bullets whizz over their prone bodies. The leading killer leaps to his feet and turns like a man possessed, his eyes alive with panic, and the barrel of his gun pointed down at the head of his still-prone comrade. As he lunges forward to leap over him, his firearm explodes in a burst of fiery light and thunder. The resounding crack of his comrade's ruptured skull joins with the violent cacophony of the night.

'Fuck...' screams the intruder as he looks down at his comrade's butchered brain. 'Fuck.'

He scrabbles over the body, slipping and sliding in the mix of thick red blood and grey matter, still shooting up in a dark fountain from the broken, black wool of the dead man's skull. The damaged door swings open and Greg stands frozen, staring down at the bloody carnage, the gun hanging limply from his hand. The air fills with the rank iron smell of hot blood. I gag as Dad's broken skull crashes back into my mind.

Elsa screams and jumps out of bed to come alongside Greg.

'Oh God...' she whispers, as her eyes flit back and forth across the bloody mess sprawled across her white Italian tiles.

'The other one's made a run for it,' shouts Greg, as he jumps over the inert, damaged body and races after the intruder, his gun poised for another shot. He bolts out of the open front door, but the killer is already heading up the driveway like a demon. Greg stops, legs splayed and the gun gripped in both hands as he fires up at him from the bottom of the driveway, but it's no good, the killer is already through the gate, and all he can do is fire at the back of a car as it screeches into the night.

# CHAPTER FORTY-FIVE

Elsa and Greg sit grim-faced opposite Nat and Dave in Elsa's lounge. No-one speaks. The front doorbell chimes. Greg moves to answer it and seconds later he ushers in Thabo and Mannie Govender.

'Thabo's here with the police, Elsa.'

Elsa gives a wan smile and gets up to give Thabo a hug. She takes Govender's offered hand and gestures for them to move to the dining room.

'Thanks for coming, Thabo,' says Nat.

'Least I can do.' Thabo's face is set with anger. He looks grim-faced at Govender who's already seated at the table and sifting through a wad of papers.

'If you could give me all the details, please,' Govender says, looking directly at Elsa.

Elsa's hand trembles and Greg interrupts with details of what they witnessed and of the police who arrived first on the scene and took the body. I look up at the passage. The tiles are white and shinning with no trace of the night.

'You got no look at his face?'

Both Greg and Elsa shake their heads. 'Nothing; they both had balaclavas on,' says Greg.

'The dead one's face is a tad damaged,' says Elsa with a wry smile.

Govender ignores her ironic humour. 'Height, weight?'

Greg gives a shrug of his shoulders. 'Hard to say; six foot at least and well-built – not fat; he got away in a black Ford Cortina.'

'Number plate?'

Greg pulls a face. 'Impossible for me to get in the circumstances.'

Govender nods and jots it all down. Elsa looks at him with irritation. 'We've given all these details to the Durban North police, Inspector; I think what we've got to take on board and investigate is that this is the second attempt on my life in a very short space of time, which makes it obvious to me that someone wants me dead.'

Inspector Govender meets Elsa's eye and turns down the corners of his mouth. 'Possibly, but you must also remember that this is a common occurrence in South Africa. We live in a dangerous country.'

Elsa throws back her head in scorn. 'Don't patronise me, please. I'm quite aware of what goes on, but I'm also quite aware that, given the circumstances of my sister's death, this is not just a coincidence.'

Govender feels Thabo's eyes burning into him from across the table. 'To date, I'm afraid we haven't acquired any more evidence that your sister was murdered. There are some aspects, I grant you, that do not add up, but I'm sorry there is, at the moment, no hard evidence of murder. The same, I'm afraid, applies to this. I can't assume that you are deliberately being targeted until I have evidence.'

Thabo purses his lips at Govender. 'I think we all realise that,

Mannie, but I know you'll agree that sometimes we also need to go with our intuition, and I'm afraid mine agrees with Elsa's. I just don't like what's happening. I need you to put some police protection out for both Elsa and Nat until we get to the bottom of this.'

Govender's jaw tightens. He says nothing for a few seconds and then mumbles, 'We don't have unlimited resources, Thabo.'

'I'm aware of that,' Thabo says. 'But I still need you to do it. If you need help, please fill in an official application and I'll make sure you get it.'

Govender bites back what looks like the beginning of a sneer, but nods at Thabo.

'Okay, will do.' He looks back at Elsa and then at Nat. 'I want you two to stay here until I send some officers to be with you. We'll station them at both your homes and I'll have them follow you for the next two weeks. We'll reassess after that.'

Elsa gives Thabo a smile of thanks.

'Much appreciated, Mannie,' says Thabo, patting Govender on the back.

Govender ignores the pat and hastily draws together his papers.

'Are you still looking into Karlos?' Elsa's gaze is one of challenge. 'You've been given the details of him staying at the Maharani by the private detective we employed so at least you know where he is.'

Govender ignores the barbed tension behind Elsa's comment and pushes back his chair, standing to look down on her.

'As I said, we've not found anything on him yet, but I'll get my officers to look into whether he's made contact with any of the local contract killers we're aware of. Perhaps if we can find this intruder it will help, but unfortunately you haven't given us much to go on.' Sarcasm drips as he utters the final words.

Elsa bites her bottom lip. I'm sure she wants to tell him to go fuck himself.

'I'm sure you'll do your best,' says Thabo in a measured tone.

Govender nods and looks at his watch.

'I'll keep you posted,' he says and without shaking anyone's hand he turns to the front door and leaves.

'He's a hard-arsed bastard, but he's good. Don't worry; I'll make sure he does a thorough investigation.'

'Thanks, Thabo. I don't know what we'd do without you.'

Thabo looks at each of my sisters with a wan smile. 'It's the least I can do given what you've all been through,' he says slowly. 'The very least.'

Elsa sits in silence for a few more seconds. 'If the police don't check the phone records properly from the hotel, I'll get Fletcher to do it. If Karlos has been in touch with any hit man then maybe, just maybe, he's been foolish enough to do it from there.'

'I'll make sure Mannie checks them,' say Thabo.

'Phone Fletcher now,' says Greg, placing a tray of coffee mugs in the centre of the table. 'I'm not having my wife made into some decoy. If the police can't come up with anything then perhaps I'll pay Karlos a visit myself.'

'I'll join you,' says Dave, making Nat raise her eyebrows at him.

'I think both of you should wait for the police,' she says. 'They're going to be protecting Elsa and me from now on; I don't think it'll help things if you two also get involved.'

'Nat's right,' says Thabo. 'Let's see what Mannie comes up with, but I think it's a good idea to have Fletcher watch Karlos' every move.'

Greg scowls and takes a slurp of his coffee. I see his knuckles whiten around the handle. I'm sure he's just as scared as everyone else but trying desperately not to show it.

# CHAPTER FORTY-SIX

K arlos slams down the hotel phone and turns to Tania, his face distorted in an ugly scowl.

'That was a message from the wife. They've caught him. Fuck, I never thought they'd get him. Pack now. We must go.'

Tania's head twitches. 'Who? What wife?'

'The black I phoned to organise the hit,' says Karlos with a snarl. 'His wife said the fucking police have just arrested him. They think he's behind the break-in at Elsa's.'

'Shit. How did they find him? You think they'll find out about you?'

Karlos clenches his jaw.

'I'm not taking any chances. He'll squeal like a pig. Get your things, I told you. We need to go.'

His voice reverberates through the room and Tania angrily puts her finger to her lips to quieten him and points at the walls. She starts throwing the contents of the drawers onto the bed while Karlos whips out the suitcases from the wardrobes and pushes everything inside.

Minutes later, they're heading down in the lift and wheeling their cases into the hotel parking garage without even a thought of paying their bill. I shake my head at the never-ending audacity of the man. Karlos stuffs the cases into the boot of my Golf and then squeals out from the garage into the hot Durban sun. He heads towards the west side of the city, heading no doubt for Joburg where it'll be easier for them to get lost. I wonder if that's where he's really from and if all the Greytown story is just some very well-planned front?

A white Mazda 323 pulls out from a side lane and follows him. Fletcher is at the wheel. I have to give it to the detective. He might look like a scruffy and arrogant sod, but he's good at his job. Karlos heads down the N2 in the direction of Maritzburg. He must be unnerved, because I see him glance frequently into the rear-view mirror. Fletcher thankfully is no fool; he keeps his distance at least two cars behind, which surely shouldn't make Karlos suspect he's being followed.

The wail of a police siren suddenly cuts through the air.

'Fuck, I knew it,' says Karlos, as the blue flashing light darts in his rear-view mirror. His knuckles tighten on the steering wheel. Tania cranes her neck to stare with narrowed eyes at the row of cars behind.

'They're chasing someone.'

'Of course, they're fucking chasing someone,' says Karlos with a snarl. 'I just hope to fuck it's not us.'

Tania falls silent. She sits back in the seat, her eyes fixed on the side mirror. The blue flashing lights grow closer and the suddenly the wail of the siren is on them. Both Karlos and Tania stiffen as the police car swerves out to the side of them and then sails past.

'Not us hey, *boetie*,' says Tania. She breaks into ugly laughter and takes out a cigarette, but her fingers tremble as she lights it.

Karlos lets out a long sigh of relief. His knuckles are still white around the steering wheel. 'The sooner we get to Joey's, the better.'

'I don't know why you thought it was us; stop being so paranoid.'

'Fuck off,' says Karlos.

They carry on driving in silence along the N2 with Fletcher three cars behind. Karlos continues to glance in the rear-view mirror and I see his eyes linger for a few seconds on the white Mazda.

Tania settles back down in the seat and turns up the radio. She closes her eyes but then opens them quickly as Karlos suddenly squeals the Golf down an exit. He races under the bridge and heads back onto the up ramp towards Durban.

Tania turns to him with her mouth open. 'And now?'

'Shut the fuck up. There's someone following us.' Karlos speeds back down the freeway, his eyes flicking constantly to both his mirrors.

Fletcher hits his steering wheel in frustration. He's missed the off ramp Karlos has taken and it's a good ten miles to the next one. Colombo is obviously not as good as I thought he was. He pulls over to the emergency lane and takes out a cell phone, no doubt to give Elsa the bad news of his incompetence.

I keep my eyes on Karlos as he continues down the freeway towards the Pinetown turn-off. He takes it and then swings my Golf under the bridge and heads back up towards Maritzburg.

'*Round and round the mulberry bush, the mulberry bush, the mulberry bush ...*' sings Tania until Karlos turns to her and tells her, 'Fucking shut up!'

'*Agh*, well maybe this time we'll make it.'

Karlos turns to her and sneers. 'This isn't some joke. You're lucky I'm driving. If it was you we'd be caught long ago.'

'You really think someone was following?' she says with a frown.

'Of course someone was fucking following. I'm not stupid.'

Tania swivels her head and looks down the snake of traffic behind them.

'Ja, I know. I'm sorry. *Agh*, the sooner we get to Joey's the better hey?'

'I'm not stopping now until we're there,' says Karlos, putting his foot flat and screaming my Golf down the fast lane of the freeway.

Karlos changes into the middle lane and travels on for about twenty minutes before another siren breaks through the air. Blue flashing lights dart in and out of the line of traffic behind them. Karlos glares into the rear-view mirror as a white police BMW draws closer and closer.

'*Agh*, stop being so paranoid. They're not after us,' says Tania, punching Karlos playfully on the shoulder.

'Fuck off,' says Karlos. He looks back into the rear mirror and then turns pale as the police car pulls astride them but this time keeps pace. The policeman in the passenger seat dangles his arm out of the window and motions for them to pull over.

Karlos keeps his eyes to the front and continues on for a few seconds more with the policeman shouting and gesturing angrily for him to pull over. The traffic behind slows to allow Karlos and the police to pull over to the hard shoulder. He stops but leaves the engine running. The police car halts in front of him. The siren wanes but the blue flashing light remains.

'Let me talk,' Karlos hisses to Tania.

The two officers pace over to the Golf with wide steps, looking like two cowboys with their hands resting just above their weapons. Karlos lifts his eyebrows in feigned surprise as one of the officers points for him to wind down the window. 'What can I do for you, officer?'

'Mr Karlos Beukes?' The officer has a thick Afrikaans accent.

Karlos' eyes widen. He swallows before replying, 'Ja?'

'Have you been staying in room 501 of the Maharani Hotel?'

Tania's eyes dart to Karlos and I see her hands tremble. Karlos looks stonily at the officer.

'Ja, we're staying there. What's the problem?'

The police officer smirks. 'The problem is payment.'

Karlos snorts. 'We're still staying there. What must I pay for?' He touches his throat with his thick fingers and keeps his eyes fixed on the officer's face before giving him a wide smile.

'*Agh*, officer, I think this is all a big misunderstanding. We're not leaving anywhere. We're just having a drive.'

Tania leans over towards the officer. 'Ja, I just wanted to go to the Rob Roy Hotel for afternoon tea, officer. I asked my brother to take me.'

The officer ignores her. 'Please open the boot.'

Karlos clenches his jaw and throws open the driver's door. He stomps over to the boot and clicks it open. The officer eyes the suitcases. He takes out a notebook and pulls a pen from his shirt pocket. 'Can I have your licence?'

Karlos rummages in the cubbyhole for his licence, his face set in an angry sneer. 'This is bloody ridiculous,' he says. 'I told you we're only having an afternoon drive. There is no evidence that we're running away and anyway they've got my credit card. This is just a frame-up. I want to phone my lawyer now.'

The policeman scowls at Karlos, but ignores his protestation as he hands the licence to his colleague. He looks down at it and scribbles something onto his pad. He turns to Tania. 'Name please.'

Tania's voice is shaky. 'Tania Beukes.'

'Address?'

'Maharani Hotel, room 501,' says Karlos, sarcastically. 'My house is sold, which is why we're staying at the Maharani. I've got plenty money coming. I don't need to run away from any hotel.'

I tense at his use of possession for my house.

'The credit card you've used is not yours,' says the officer. He smirks at Karlos for a few seconds and then intones, 'Karlos Beukes, I'm arresting you for alleged fraud against the Maharani Hotel. You have the right to remain silent but anything you say can and will be used in a court of law against you. You have the right to legal representation and if you cannot afford this the court will appoint this for you. Do you understand?'

The second policeman takes out a pair of handcuffs.

'This is ridiculous,' shouts Karlos. 'You have no grounds for this, none at all...'

But the policeman click the cuffs onto him.

Karlos falls silent, his eyes fixed in shock. The second officer pushes him towards the police car and shoves him onto the back seat. He eases himself into the front passenger seat and turns around, his eyes trained on Karlos like a German Shepherd just waiting for him to make a move. His hand rests on the holster at his side.

The first officer reads Tania the same caution. She stands ashen-faced in front and says nothing in reply. She whimpers as the cuffs click tight around her wrists and almost stumbles as the officer guides her into the back of the police car.

Relief floods through me as I watch the blue light of the police car head back towards Durban.

'I take back what I said about you, Mr Fletcher,' I mouth silently. If and how the charge will hold I have no idea, but at least for now Elsa and Nat are safe.

# CHAPTER FORTY-SEVEN

Elsa, Nat and Thabo sit silently in front of Mannie Govender. 'We've traced one of the phone calls Beukes made from the hotel to someone in Kwa Mashu we suspect could be a middle man for contract killings. We arrested him yesterday and are working on him at the moment, but we don't have enough to go on yet. Beukes maintains it was just a deal about buying a truck.' Mannie Govender clears his throat. 'Our suspicions are that he's possibly behind this but we just don't have enough proof yet.'

'Have you confronted Karlos about Lissa's murder?' Elsa's voice is tight.

Inspector Govender frowns. 'Alleged murder. Of course, but as I said before, we don't have enough evidence against him for anything at the moment other than the hotel fraud.'

'And he knows that of course.'

'He does, but he also knows we're watching him. We've warned him that if anything happens to you two, he'll be first on our list. I think he's got the message. It's the best we can do at the moment.'

'Checkmate,' says Thabo with a smirk.

Inspector Govender looks up at the wall clock and closes the brown paper file. Thabo scrapes back his chair.

'Much appreciated, Mannie. I'll wait to hear from you later.'

'No problem. We'll hopefully get a conviction for the fraud charge at least. We had to let him out on bail, but the case is fast-tracked for next Monday.'

'Good man.'

'No problem,' says Govender.

Thabo shakes his hand while Nat and Elsa leave the office in silence.

Thabo catches up as they step out of the building into the hot midday sun. 'I'll be in the court on the Monday,' says Thabo.

Elsa giving him a hug. 'That would be good, Thabo.'

I let out a long sigh as I watch my sisters walk hand in hand to Elsa's BMW. Their energy is tangibly different. The awful tension and ravaged grief has been smoothed at the edges and their shoulders are no longer hunched, nor are their eyes as shadowed by sadness.

'We'll go and tell Mom the good news, and then there's just one more thing I want to look into,' says Elsa.

———

Later that afternoon Elsa sits at her dining-room table, a pile of bank statements strewn in front of her. She turns her head towards the passage.

'Nat,' she calls.

'What?'

'Major withdrawals from Lissa's account were made at the Wild Coast Sun Casino both before and when Liss was in King Edward's.' Elsa stabs her forefinger down at the statements in a triumphant manner.

Nat comes back into the dining room, 'Before she went in?'

Elsa nods. 'He must've got access to her card somehow. The

bastard was gambling away what money he could until he got his hands on the whole lot. We'd have to try and prove she knew nothing about it, but given that it includes the time she was in a coma, we could have a case.'

I shake my head in disbelief at how naïve and trusting I was.

'Phone Govender,' says Nat, her voice raw with anger, 'and the prosecutor.'

'I will, but first I think I'm going to phone the Wild Coast Sun and ask who the hotel doctor is?'

'Doctor?'

Elsa narrows her blue eyes at Nat. 'I just think that maybe, just maybe, Karlos paid him a visit.'

Nat sits silently, clenched fists perched in front of her while Elsa gets the doctor's name from the hotel. She scribbles it down and turns to Nat with wide eyes. 'The doctor's name is... Clark.' She stumbles on the name.

Nat's mouth drops slightly open and mirrors mine.

'Phone him quick,' she says.

Elsa asks to be put through and recounts the story to the doctor and then listens silently.

'Yes, I'm a practising advocate. I'm investigating Mr Karlos Beukes,' she says, turning to Nat and pulling an impatient face at his insistent questioning. She turns back to the phone and listens carefully, her face etched in a serious frown. 'I see,' she says after a while. 'Could you please let me know the date of his visit and what you prescribed for him?' She glances over to Nat and gives a small nod. 'I see. Was that at his request?' She nods again. 'Well, thank you very much, doctor.'

She clunks down the receiver and turns to Nat with a victorious smile. 'Karlos saw him and asked for a script for Trithapon; he told the doctor he was a registered psychotic and had left his medication at home. The doctor said he was in quite a state and it all appeared genuine as Karlos could provide him with all the details he asked for so he gave it to him.'

'When?'

'A week before Lissa's fit.'

Nat's bottom lip trembles, 'Oh Elsa, that means it was definitely him. Have we got enough to nail him now?'

'I hope so. Govender can't argue that it's only circumstantial evidence now. I'll demand he exhumes her body. I don't care what it takes. I will see that fucking bastard rot in jail for what he's done.' Elsa clenches her jaw and snatches up the phone. 'Inspector Govender, please, tell him it's important,' she says turning to Nat and giving her a thumbs-up.

She speaks quickly to Govender but seconds later her smile fades. 'Keep us up to date,' she says before slamming down the receiver. 'Karlos has skipped bail and done a runner. They think he's in Joburg. They've alerted the police up there.' Elsa stamps her foot. 'Idiots – so much for them watching him.'

'Damn them,' says Nat. She pushes back her hair behind her ears as if she's chasing away an irritating fly and asks angrily, 'Why didn't Govender tell us? When did he go?'

'Yesterday apparently. I knew I should've kept Fletcher on his tail instead of relying on Govender.' Elsa frowns and bites on her bottom lip.

'I don't believe this,' says Nat with a shake of her head. 'How useless can they be? How can they not be watching him?'

Elsa gives a sardonic laugh. 'It's not a priority for them.' She rubs her hand across her forehead. 'Fuck it. I should have kept with my gut feel.' She clenches her fist and pumps it through the air. 'Damn, why didn't I?'

'Joburg's an easy place to hide. Do you think they'll find him up there? How do they even know he's there?' Nat's voice rises in pitch with each frenzied question.

'I'll ask Fletcher to hunt him down and I want some answers from Govender. This is not good enough!'

'Thabo will be furious,' says Nat. 'I really thought it was over at last.'

'How could I be so fucking stupid.' Elsa places a strand of blonde hair in her mouth and chews angrily.

'Don't berate yourself Els. You couldn't have known he'd run.'

'Of course I should have,' snaps Elsa, spitting away the piece of hair. 'The only thing we can hope for now is that maybe some Joburg hi-jackers will do our work for us and blow his fucking brains out.'

The police guard patrolling outside Elsa's front window pauses and looks through at them. Elsa glares at him and turns away.

A long sigh shudders out of Nat. 'I just want so badly to see him rot in jail.'

Elsa looks at Nat in silence for a few minutes. 'I'd prefer dead. Damn, I can't believe they lost him. How much more incompetent can they get?'

'Maybe they'll get him if he tries something else up there.'

'Maybe,' says Elsa. 'At least we know now it was him. What a cunning bastard. Must've tried to frame the psychotic patient all along. Probably preyed on vulnerable women in rehab. Wouldn't surprise me if Liss isn't the first one he's killed for money.'

'Me neither,' says Nat. Her eyes fill with tears. 'I wish we'd never talked her into going there.'

Elsa nods.

'Me too,' she whispers. 'But what's done is done. I don't think Liss would want us to be eaten up with guilt.'

'I guess not,' says Nat. 'Why don't you phone Mom and Yvonne and tell them? In some strange way, even though we haven't caught him, it helps to know it was him.'

'Yes, it does. I guess it gives a sense of closure.' Elsa picks up her car keys. 'Come, let's go and tell them in person. I'm sure Mom needs a hug.'

# CHAPTER FORTY-EIGHT

The next morning Nat and Elsa sit silently in Elsa's lounge staring out through the open French doors at the green manicured garden. The air outside is still and already its humidity is making its presence felt inside.

'I had such a vivid experience of Liss speaking to me early this morning,' says Nat, her tone wistful. 'It was like she was right there with me.'

Elsa stares at Nat without blinking as Nat continues, 'I felt an electric shock paralyse me, and then clear as a bell I heard her say, *Don't worry Nat. I'm alright... I'm alright.*'

I smile to myself. I'm thankful that this time she could hear my voice.

'Maybe it was her,' says Elsa, her voice barely above a whisper.

Nat's eyes widen. 'You mean that?'

Elsa gives a sardonic laugh and shrugs her shoulders. 'My rational mind can't cope with it all anymore. I've decided it's easier to just go with the irrational.'

'To me the irrational version is really the rational one,' says Nat. She looks intently at Elsa. 'I'm sure she really spoke to me. I'm sure of it. Mom phoned me this morning and said she had a dream last night where Liss spoke to her. I'm sure she's visited us to say goodbye.'

Elsa clears her throat before looking at Nat with a sheepish expression. 'Actually, so did I.'

Nat looks triumphant. 'You see. I know it's her, Els, I know it is. It's got to be if we all had the same dream and heard her speak to us.'

'I hope so,' says Elsa. 'It would be really good if she did.'

Nat looks back out at the garden for a while before asking, 'Do you think they'll catch him?'

Elsa shrugs. 'I don't know, but whatever, he'll have to keep running, and I'm not going to stop looking.'

'I guess, in a sense, a prison of the mind is probably worse,' says Nat with an ironic smile.

Elsa laughs. 'Maybe. Anyway our formal contest of her will has a strong case. I'll make sure he doesn't get one cent from her estate.'

'That would be good. I'm sure Liss would be happy if she knew.' She falls silent for a few seconds and blinks rapidly before whispering, 'She'll always be with us, you know. I think about her every day, talk to her in my mind, tell her I love her and miss her and that'll never change. No-one can take our memories away.'

'No, you're right. They can't.'

'Do you remember that time we went to Antonia's and Liss fell face-down into her spaghetti? I laughed about it for days.'

Elsa smiles. 'So did I.'

Nat leans forward, her elbows perched on her knees and her chin resting between cupped hands. She blinks rapidly. 'She was one of the most caring people I ever met. I'll never forget her stopping the entire school bus when she about seven because I wasn't on it. She thought I'd missed it and apparently kicked up such a fuss the driver just had to stop and wait for her to come and fetch me. I had to leave my gym class and get on still wearing my leotard. I remember being so angry and embarrassed, but afterwards it touched me.' She blinks rapidly for a few seconds before walking over to the open French doors. She looks out at the distant ocean with pensive eyes. A gentle breeze breaks through the humidity and flutters a few strands of hair across her cheek. She shudders out a long sigh and turns back to Elsa with a sardonic expression stamped across her face. 'Funny old thing, this life.' Her voice breaks. 'I never expected our baby sister to go before us.'

'Me neither.'

'I guess she'd want us to keep going,' says Nat.

Elsa nods and a warm glow tinged with sadness fills my spirit. Nat's right; that's exactly what I wish for them: long and happy lives. Karlos will pay because it's part of the very design of life itself. An image of Karlos always looking over his shoulder rises and I shake my head in pity. I wouldn't want to be him for all the sardines in the sea, not that I even really like sardines.

A soft mist filled with light surrounds me and deep in my spirit I know that the time has come to say goodbye. 'Stay well, you two,' I whisper. 'No-one will ever separate us, just like those three Karoo hills.'

# EPILOGUE

*And so now it all makes sense*
*this time of mine called life;*
*and with all its hills and valleys, smiles and sorrows,*
*it was still mine!*
*Cast a calm eye on life, on death, not cold,*
*for its truth lies deep with our Creator*
*and the ties we share with our own precious web of close*
    *humanity.*
*Guard it while you can,*
*and if Time whisks it from your grasp,*
*don't despair;*
*That end is nothing but a new beginning.*
Sale Kahle!

*He will wipe away every tear from their eyes, and death shall be no*
*more, neither shall there be mourning, nor crying, nor pain any more,*
*for the former things have passed away.*
*—Revelation 21:4*

# ACKNOWLEDGEMENTS

Grateful thanks to my editor Yvonne Barlow for her superb editing and her readers for believing in this story. Much thanks also to my fellow writers for their valuable feedback and their time: Nina Milton, Timothy Bertram, Anne Jenson, Dave Key, Anthony Lansing, Emma Marshall, Kathleen Marshall, Dilys Rose, Tracey Rosenberg, Cynthia Rogerson, Stephen Thompson, and of course my wonderful daughter Simone.

# ABOUT THE AUTHOR

Julia North is a dedicated and passionate writer who writes about gritty reality and the human condition. She has previously published two books and is a member of the Salisbury Writer's Circle. She lives in Salisbury Wiltshire.

# A NOTE FROM THE PUBLISHER

**Thank you for reading this book**. If you enjoyed it please do consider leaving a review on Amazon to help others find it too.

**We hate typos.** All of our books have been rigorously edited and proofread, but sometimes mistakes do slip through. If you have spotted a typo, please do let us know and we can get it amended within hours.

**info@bloodhoundbooks.com**